Darkside:
Damned If You Do

S.K.S. Perry

To Lisa and Damian,

Copyright © 2012 S.K.S. Perry

All rights reserved.

ISBN: 151474757X
ISBN-13: 978-1514747575

DEDICATION

To my loving wife, Penelope, who is awesome, as always. Seriously, have you met her?

CONTENTS

Acknowledgments   *i*

Chapter One	Pg 1	Chapter Thirteen	Pg 106
Chapter Two	Pg 12	Chapter Fourteen	Pg 114
Chapter Three	Pg 21	Chapter Fifteen	Pg 123
Chapter Four	Pg 31	Chapter Sixteen	Pg 133
Chapter Five	Pg 39	Chapter Seventeen	Pg 140
Chapter Six	Pg 47	Chapter Eighteen	Pg 148
Chapter Seven	Pg 57	Chapter Nineteen	Pg 155
Chapter Eight	Pg 65	Chapter Twenty	Pg 163
Chapter Nine	Pg 74	Chapter Twenty-One	Pg 172
Chapter Ten	Pg 82	Chapter Twenty-Two	Pg 181
Chapter Eleven	Pg 91	Chapter Twenty-Three	Pg 189
Chapter Twelve	Pg 98		

ACKNOWLEDGMENTS

For all those fans, friends and family who ~~nagged~~ encouraged me to hurry up and "write the next one": Ryan Perry, Jennifer Cox, Chantel MacIntyre, Kat Willette, Joey Pagiliaro, Sumedh Sinha, Tony Hall, Mark Sheppard, Nicholas Knezevic, Ivo Jemin, and Cristi Muresan, to name a few.

For the usual gang, because you're always there for me, even when you're not: Kelly Morisseau, Jenni Smith-Gaynor, Charles Coleman Finlay, Elizabeth Glover, Jaime Lee Moyer, Marsha Sisolak, Jason Venter, and Deanna Hoak.

For Sgt Hagop Vanayan, who helped with the cover art (and keeps me from climbing the clock tower at work—so what if we don't have one?)

For the 1st Terran Rangers, for letting an old man play Planetside 2 with them, an outlet which helps me to preserve a modicum of sanity.

For Phyllis "Winky" Zanoria. For nagging, beta reading, and not complaining when I turned you into a gremlin.

And finally, for Day Venereo, my No. 1 Fan, best friend, and a most awesome troll!

CHAPTER ONE

If you've never been to a troll wedding, I highly recommend it. Just be sure you have a ride home afterwards because you certainly won't be in any condition to drive...or walk...or perform any of the mid-level brain functions.

Drat and Tirade were married at Butchart Gardens on a clear winter's night in December, under the Tree of Serenity that sat atop the ivy-shrouded rock mound in the Sunken Garden. I know what you're thinking—that arbutus tree came down with fungus in '09 and was removed—but the Tree of Serenity is still there. You just have to have the Sight to see it.

The gardens were in full bloom and everything smelled green and fresh. No magic required—that's just Vancouver Island for you. It was still chilly though, and tall, copper deco patio heaters had been scattered throughout the basin of the garden that had once upon a time been a rock quarry. Crystal-white path-lighting illuminated the stone walkways, and twinkling pin lights decorated the trees so that it became hard to discern where the myriad stars of the night sky ended and the gardens began. At least I thought they were pin lights; turns out they were sprites.

Charlie had worried that the Sunken Garden wouldn't hold all of the wedding guests. After all, Drat was the new Chieftain of the Tor Clan. Everyone who was anyone—or anything—would be attending. Charlie needn't have worried. Butchart Gardens is one of those places where Summerland and Darkside overlap, but trust me, it's much bigger when you see it from the Summerland side. There was plenty of room for the Light and Dark Sidhe, the vampires and shapeshifters, the heads of the various troll clans, the ogres, gremlins, bogies, dwarves, sprites, brownies, centaurs and...well, you get the picture. There were even a couple of dragons in attendance.

Tirade looked stunning—a diminutive Jessica Rabbit in her strapless, red silk wedding gown, her little feet kicking and her hands pounding against Drat's back as he carried her slung over his left shoulder through the crowd toward the stone steps that led to the top of the mound. Even Drat looked dapper. His battle armour had been polished so that it gleamed under the light of the full moon, and I'd had the two-headed axe he carried in his right…claw…electroplated and inlaid with gold scrollwork so that it matched his black and gold armour.

I did my part as best man, rapier drawn and covering Drat's back, dressed to the nines in the formal fighting leathers Skatha had gifted me with. Leanne said I was the best looking dead guy at the wedding. Normally that wouldn't be saying much, but the place was crawling with vamps and we all know what pretty boys they can be.

Charlie cleared a path for us through the onlookers. Let me tell you, nothing moves a crowd like an eight-foot tall ogre waving a war hammer the size of a small tree about, especially an eight-foot tall ogre wearing a tux. Charlie led and I covered the rear as Drat carried his bride to be up the stone steps. Drat's Boyz—his own personal troops—lined both sides of the stairs. They held their axes aloft in salute as we passed beneath them, each troll resplendent in highly burnished armour. Of course the tallest troll was only a little over four feet in height, so Charlie and I had to duck or risk beheading.

The ceremony itself was short and to the point:

"I promise ta loves ya and cares for ya until da sun turns da last troll ta stone, and den some," Drat vowed.

If I didn't know better I'd swear those giant, forest-green eyes of his misted up some. Drat tried to wipe at his nose with the back of his hand but it was still tied to his bride's so that he only succeeded in having Tirade punch him in the face.

"And I promise ta never tries ta escape," Tirade vowed.

Charlie blubbered like an idiot at that, and I had to lend him my hanky—which I hope he never returns after watching him blow his nose into it. I mean, ogre boogers. Eww.

Anyway, that seemed good enough for the druid that officiated. Um…the vows, not Charlie blowing his nose. The druid tapped the long twisted staff he carried against the ground to the resounding crack of thunder. A lightning bolt struck the Tree of Serenity and the tree blazed into brilliant white light as if it were made of the stuff. There was a jubilant cheer from the gathered crowd as Tirade drew a dagger from the hilt at her thigh and cut the bonds holding her and Drat captive, and threw herself into the troll's arms.

"Commence wit da partying!" Drat commanded as he hugged his new bride before the luminescent Tree of Serenity.

"KILL DA BASTARDS!" Drat's Boyz' war cry drowned out the rest of the revellers.

After a lot more cheering and hip-hip-hooraying and whatnot, the guests made a beeline for the white, high-peaked pole tent that had been set up for the reception, because—let's face it—that's where the food and alcohol was. At least we didn't have to wait for hours while everyone posed for wedding photos. After all, most of them couldn't be photographed anyway. Charlie and I followed the bride and groom into the reception tent and across the dance floor to the head table where Leanne was already waiting for me.

Leanne looked otherworldly beautiful as always. Her long, luxurious black hair was pushed back over her slender shoulders to the small of her back. Delicate braids at her temples tied at the nape of her neck, and were entwined with gold-leaf wire and tiny blue flowers that set off her cobalt eyes. She wore a strapless azure evening gown that hugged the lissom contours of her body, and three-inch heels that made her legs look impossibility longer than they already were. Leanne had always been stunning, but ever since Bran's Cauldron had burned the demon out of her the Fae heritage had gone into overdrive. I suppose it only made sense that with the vampire gone she should seem more…alive. Or maybe it was that she still held that small piece of Allison's soul—something none of the other Fallen had. It just may possibly have been that I was completely and madly in love with her. Whatever it was, Leanne was simply breathtaking.

Leanne kissed me lightly on the cheek, then took my hand and entwined her fingers with mine. "Good job."

"Yeah, I didn't trip or accidentally stab anyone or anything," I answered proudly.

"The evening's not over yet," she said, and squeezed my hand.

Day, Drat's new War Chief and head of security, gave me the evil eye as I took my place beside the Clan Chieftain. Apparently Day felt that it was her rightful place as Drat's right hand, and saw me as an usurper. That's right, I said, *her*.

Like all troll women, Day was hot. She was blonde, green-eyed, and curvaceous under all that armour, and all of three and a half feet tall, and while all the other trolls talked like rejects from Goodfellas, Day sounded more like a reject from…well…Scarface. Apparently she was an import from another clan—a sort of Foreign Exchange Troll.

"I've been meaning to ask you," I said to her, trying to make small talk as I leaned forward of Leanne for a face to face with the new War Chief, "what kind of name is Day for a troll?"

I know. Leanne kicked me under the table, but it was already too late. Seriously though, every other troll I'd met had names like Rant and Drat and Snit and Hassle.

Day's green eyes narrowed and she smiled at me. "Ju wanna go? I'll get your girlfrien' here to hold my earrings and we'll take dis outside."

Sure, like that wouldn't tarnish my image a tad. While I was at it I could maybe strangle a puppy, or molest a Hello Kitty doll on YouTube.

"Sorry," I said. "I didn't mean to offend you."

Day looked disgusted, although I wasn't sure if it was because of my faux pas or that I'd cheated her out of a good rumble. She said something in Cuban that sounded like she'd just hocked up a good one. I have no idea what it meant, but I'm guessing it wasn't, "think nothing of it."

"Day is short for *Daylight*," Leanne whispered to me. "It's about a strong a curse-word as you can find in Troll-eese, for obvious reasons. About the only one more reprehensible to them is Sunshine."

I stole a glance to my right at this tiny blonde bombshell of a troll who had worked her way up the ranks to War Chief. "No wonder she's so tough."

I was just wondering what kind of parent would name their kid something like that when I noticed Alex slow dancing with some tall, lanky kid out on the hardwood dance floor. I'm giving them the benefit of the doubt by calling it dancing, since the band hadn't actually started playing yet.

Alex was still only sixteen years old. I'd mistaken her for twenty when I'd first met her. If anything she had matured since. She was tall and…er…well-endowed, yet willowy, with long legs, narrow hips and a tiny waist. Her chocolate skin and long, dark hair in tight ringlets set off a face that would have made Paris ditch that Helen of Troy pig-dog in a hurry.

She wore a Champagne-coloured silk chemise that only came down to about the bottom of her ribcage. A thin strip of the same colour and material passed for a skirt.

Did I mention she was the Innocent? The Powers That Be must have pissed themselves laughing over that.

"Why is it that all women's fashion lately looks like it's the result of some freak dryer accident?" I asked.

"They make a nice looking couple, don't they," Leanne said, ignoring me.

She'd probably helped Alex pick out her outfit, come to think of it.

"They do," I agreed. "It's too bad he won't live."

Josh, Alex's dad, stood to the side. He didn't look happy. If it weren't for the rented Armani tux Josh wore I swear he would have morphed right there and then and tore the boy's throat out. Well, that and Sabrina's hand on his arm restraining him. Either the boy didn't know who Alex's dad was, or he severely lacked a sense of self-preservation. Josh was a shapeshifter, and a big one at that. At least six foot six and three or four hundred pounds of man-wolf-bear-whatever when he changed.

"Maybe I should go say something?"

Leanne smiled at me sweetly to let me know how ludicrous the idea was. "Because you have such a way with words?"

Okay, she had a point. I seem to have a penchant for saying the wrong thing at the right time. Besides, Sabrina was handling her husband just fine without me.

I loved Alex like my own daughter—I was her protector, after all—but I wouldn't have wanted to be Josh for all the mocha frappe lattes in Starbucks. Not that I'd ever have to worry on that account.

Eternals couldn't have children. Maybe it was because we weren't really alive in the traditional sense of the word, or maybe it was just another of the Stupid Rules, but I would never have a son or daughter of my own. And before you go getting all choked up about it, I'm okay with that. I had already lost one child. I know, Sarah wasn't exactly mine—I was just her step-dad for a couple of years—but I had raised her and loved her as my own. When Alison died and I was cut out of Sarah's life…well, let's just say I never wanted to go through anything like that again.

"Who is that kid, anyway?" I asked Leanne as Sabrina walked Josh to their table and practically forced him into a chair.

"Cael Moon Hunter."

I gave Leanne the look, certain she was pulling my leg.

"For true!" she said. "He's a shapeshifter, like Josh."

Josh's full name was Joshua Ezekiel Shadow's Paw Faye. Maybe it wasn't that far-fetched after all. Faye was actually Sabrina's maiden name. Josh had confessed that once they had decided to live in Darkside he hadn't had the heart to saddle his little girl with a last name like Shadow's Paw and so had taken his wife's name, which I thought was awfully progressive of him. And no, the irony that Josh had married a mortal woman named Faye wasn't lost on him, either.

The band—or more correctly, orchestra—started up with some big band number I couldn't remember the name of. At least Alex and Cael had an excuse to grope each other now.

Charlie had managed to book Cab Calloway and his band for the wedding, although Dizzy Gillespie had refused to show. I guess some feuds carried over even after death. Originally they'd tried for the Rat Pack, but Frank and Sammy were already booked. Dean Martin agreed to do a few tunes with Cab's band though, so it wasn't a total loss. Trust me, you haven't heard anything until you've heard the ghost's of Cab Calloway and Dean Martin riffing to *Arrowsmith's* "Walk this Way."

In case you hadn't noticed, Troll weddings aren't exactly conventional. There's no speechifying, and the meal and dancing all happen at the same time. Trolls believe in getting right to the celebrating part as soon as possible. Apparently their guests felt the same way. Already there were a group of dwarves near the dessert table engaged in an impromptu human-tossing contest.

Oh, and there's none of that First Dance stuff either. As soon as the band started everyone was up. You'd never know it to look at him, but that Drat can do a mean Electric Slide.

I myself was doing a passable imitation of the Hustle with Leanne when I caught a glimpse of a commotion out of the corner of my eye. A small crowd had gathered to my left. Josh faced off against no less then seven men, all dressed in Armani, Hugo Boss, and Ralph Lauren. Alex and Cael stood just behind Josh, as if he were the only thing keeping the mob from them, and while it hadn't come to fisticuffs yet it was only a matter of time.

Their leader was a big man, and hairy. Dark curly hair covered his head and face—and neck, and knuckles, and—well, at least he wasn't sweaty. He was muscular, not in that Arnold Schwarzenegger kind of way, but more in that pull-a-train-with-your teeth way, with a massive chest and arms, and a belly that strained the limits of his cummerbund. He stood face to face with Josh, literally, and his shouting could be heard even over the orchestra.

"You keep that trollop of a daughter away from me son," he said. "I'll nae have your traitorous blood-line mixing with mine."

Josh said something in return, his face calm at least, although I could see the knuckles of his fists whiten. I couldn't make out what he said, but whatever it was it made the hairy guy either really mad or really embarrassed, because his face turned beet-red. I'm guessing mad.

I moved to go give Josh a hand—you know, debating—when Leanne grabbed hold of my arm and gave me that warning look of hers.

Who was she kidding? "But Honey, them's fight'n words!"

Leanne shook her head and sighed, surrendering to the inevitable. "Do you even know who that is?"

"Uh huh," I said. "That's the dead guy who just called Alex a trollop." I should clarify, considering where we were and all, that he wasn't dead yet.

"That is Liam Moon Hunter, Cael's father. He's the Therian King. Therian--as in *shape shifter*."

I'm guessing she broke that last word into two and enunciated it clearly like she did to make sure I could keep up.

"Once upon a time our friend Josh there was a berserker—a member of the King's Guard. The Captain of the Guard, as a matter of fact. When Josh left to marry Sabrina—a mortal woman—the King apparently took it personally and banished him. As you might imagine, they don't get along too well now. And you want to step in the middle of that?"

I gave Leanne a light kiss on the cheek. "Well, since you put it that way—hell yes!"

"Okay, just checking," Leanne said, and took my hand.

I squinted my eyes at her in mock consternation. "And just where do you think you're going?"

Leanne smiled. "I'm coming with, of course."

I entwined my fingers with hers. "That's my girl."

Leanne wasn't quite as fast or as strong as she'd been when she was part vampire, but she was still Fae, and with a gazillion years experience. Not that I really needed her for backup. Just knowing she was with me, that she was there for me, was enough. She'd done her bit to try and talk me out of it, but really, she hadn't tried all *that* hard. Leanne was the worst Jiminy Cricket ever.

"Is this a private party or can anybody join?" I announced as we approached Josh and his fan club.

"Why don't you just p—," one of the shifter's began. He cut the last word short and his eyes widened as he realised who he was talking to.

"—ull up a chair?" I finished for him. I guess I'm somewhat of a celebrity. Not one of those pretty-boy celebrities either, but a badass celebrity like Arn...er, Syl...Martha Stewart. Anyway, you get the point. After all, I am the only one in known history ever to kill another Eternal. Well, okay, I didn't exactly kill him, it was more like assisted suicide, but it still counts.

"This is none of your affair, Eternal," Liam growled. He was even hairier close up, and apparently not impressed by my celebrity.

"Yeah, I got this, James," Josh said. He must have been really pissed. I mean, no jokes or smart-assed comments? Just "I got this."

I cocked an eyebrow. Well, both eyebrows. I still can't do the single eyebrow raise, damn it. "Hey, I'm just here for the VIP seating," I said. Leanne and I took a chair at a table just off the dance floor. "Why don't the rest of you fellas join us, seeing as this is just between Josh and Liam? Come on, you can help us keep score."

Liam's posse fidgeted about and looked rather uncomfortable at that until Liam agreed with a low, guttural growl and a nod towards the tables.

I waved one of the waiters down as the shifters pulled up chairs. "Gherkin, a round for the table." Hey, it was free, so why not? And yeah, my French sucks.

Josh stepped even closer to the Therian King, almost toe to toe if not for the fact that Liam's enormous belly stuck out further than his feet did, preventing it. "Now that that's settled," Josh said, "Go ahead; call my daughter a trollop again. I dare you."

Liam jutted out his jaw. For a minute there I thought he was going to belly-bump Josh. "I apologise," he muttered, his thick Scottish brogue evident now that I could hear him clearly over the sound of the orchestra. "I shouldnae said that. Tis nae the bairn's fault her da is a chanty wrassler."

I leaned in closer to Leanne. "That didn't sound like an apology to me?"

"It wasn't. Trust me."

"That's one point for Liam," I said, sitting up straight once again. The Shifters seated at our table nodded in general agreement.

Josh smiled, and his eyes narrowed. "You know, I'd be insulted had I any respect for you or your opinion in the first place."

"Or understood what he said," I added in aside to Leanne.

Sabrina pulled up a chair beside us just as the waiter arrived with our drinks. "Weddings," she mumbled, not looking the least bit concerned over the predicament her husband and daughter was in.

And why should she? Josh could take care of himself, and no one here was about to let anything happen to Alex. It's not like there were demons after us, or a mad, half-crazed Eternal. Been there, done that. This little difference of opinion didn't even rate in the top ten of things to worry about.

Cael tried to step around Josh, but Alex still clung tightly to his hand. "Da, that's enough."

Liam growled, and rocked his head from side to side, cracking his neck. "I'll tell ye when it's enough, boy. You've caused enough trouble already.

Alex reached out her other hand to Josh. "Dad, stop. This isn't what we're about."

"Oh, not fair," I said, and Leanne nodded in agreement. Alex was the Innocent, and the embodiment of Hope. I guess that didn't stop the kid from fighting dirty. "She's even using the sad face."

Josh glanced at his daughter. Even from our seat at the table I could see his resolve melt. Jaw clenched and eyes steely, he slowly stepped back, distancing himself from the Therian King.

"Ha!" Liam barked, and puffed out his chest even more. Alex reluctantly let go of Cael's hand as the boy joined his father. Liam cuffed the boy in the back of the head. "Git over there, with yer own kind."

"I hate to see a hairy man gloat like that," I said.

"Especially when Josh so would have kicked his ass," Leanne added.

Josh and Alex slowly made their way to our table. The rest of the shifters had left with Liam and Cael. I could see Josh was still seething inside, but it was Alex that had me worried. She looked so despondent. Not a good look for the embodiment of hope.

"I guess you two will just have to sneak around behind your parents' backs like normal teenagers," I suggested.

Josh gave me the look which told me just what he thought of that idea.

"Yes, just like your father and I did back in the day," Sabrina added, smiling at her daughter.

Oddly enough, that seemed to actually cheer Alex up a bit.

"Remember that old Dodge Charger you used to have?"

Even Josh looked down at the table, trying to hide a smile. He looked up at his daughter and shook his head. "Why'd it have to be him? Couldn't you have dated a nice normal boy? Even a...a...vampire?"

Sabrina snorted Champagne through her nose at that, and everyone laughed, which lightened the mood somewhat. It did highlight just how much of a problem Cael presented for Josh, though. Even in jest, to suggest that a vampire might be preferable to the Therian King's son?

"I told you sending her to Hogwarts was a bad idea," I told Josh, who for once seemed inclined to agree with me. And no, the school's name wasn't really Hogwarts, but it's what I'd taken to calling it for obvious reasons.

Our Lady of Charity, while located in Darkside, or Victoria to be exact, catered to the offspring of the Summerland folk that abided here. Josh and Sabrina had hoped for a more normal life for Alex, and so had sent her to school in Kingston. Everything had worked out fine until I came along. Next thing you know she's being kidnapped by demons and getting mixed up with zombies and vampires and even the odd Eternal or two. Heck, she was even almost married off to a troll.

Anyway, after our last little...mishap, it was decided that it might be best for all concerned that Alex attend Our Lady of Charity, which meant we'd all loaded up our truck and moved to Beverly...or Victoria. We'd even wrangled scholarships for Alex's best friends—Julie, Olie, and Michelle—who, as luck would have it, turned out to be three very powerful witches. And we'd done it all with the hope of keeping the Innocent safe.

And now she'd gone and gotten mixed up in *this*.

Leanne keeps telling me there are no coincidences—at least not where Alex and I are concerned. I suppose, given that, I should have been more worried. But I wasn't. It was Drat's wedding—a celebration—and after all we'd recently been through, a sorely needed one.

I spied that little red-haired gremlin that seemed to follow me around; the one that had helped me out of that pentagram when I'd been trapped in the alley. I'd taken to calling him Grin, because he did, a lot. It seemed he'd brought along a plus one to the wedding. Another gremlin, a little smaller than Grin, and with long, straight, dark hair—I'm pretty sure it was a wig—smiled, and winked at me. Anyway, they both had bottles of olive oil in their little hands, and I couldn't help but wonder what they'd been up to. That's when I saw Liam, over by the dessert table, seemingly slip on the hardwood floor. His feet flew up in the air so that he landed with a resounding thud on his back. Winky gave me the thumbs up.

I heard Josh chuckle beside me. "Instant karma."

"Actually, gremlins," I said.

"Same thing."

I hate it when he does that, because I never know when he's serious or just having me on, and I don't want to feel like a rube for asking. Made sense, though.

"Well, now that the universe has sorted itself out, I say we get back to partying!"

I thought about asking Day to dance, but when she saw me looking her way she drew a dagger, spun it about in her dainty hand several times, then made a throat slitting gesture with it. I figured a fox trot was out of the question after that.

I saw Charlie off in the corner with several other ogres, probably talking about books or politics or…Star Wars. Ogres really are the nerds of the supernatural world, and you gotta love 'em for it.

I decided to head for the chocolate fountain because, hey, chocolate fountain. When I got there I have to say I wasn't exactly impressed. Chocolate should fountain, not flow, like lava. I looked about and noticed there was a kink in the hose leading to the device, so I reached down and straightened it out. That's when I saw Grin. I was just thinking, *"This can't be good,"* when the fountain began to shake and make this odd grinding noise. There was this loud pop as the pressure suddenly released, and fruit that had been stuffed into the summit shot ceiling-ward in a blast of compressed air, covering me from head to toe in milk chocolate—so it wasn't all bad.

I saw a peach careen off an overhead chandelier which set it to swinging, and watched fascinated as the swinging chandelier knocked over a faux pillar. The pillar crashed down on the end of a table filled with—no word of a lie—custard pies, vaulting them into the air. I traced the pies' trajectory as they made a beeline for the very spot where the new War Chief of the Tor Clan, Day, stood. Still, it looked like the pies were going to miss her by a good foot, when suddenly Winky appeared behind the troll and gave her a good shove. No less than six pies struck Day; two of them directly in the face.

Winky bowed.

Day slowly scooped the custard from her eyes. When she finally opened them, the first thing she saw was me, standing by the fountain and covered in chocolate. I don't know how she knew, but she knew. Somehow, *I* had done this.

Even from across the room I could hear her cursing in rapid fire Spanish. I couldn't understand her, but I could hear her.

Day drew her dagger and aimed it at my head, so I caught it. Hey, I'm an Eternal; I can do that.

Leanne, who was snorting rather unladylike as she laughed uncontrollably at the sight of me covered in chocolate, could barely catch her breath. She threw up her hands in surrender and leaned into a pillar for support when she saw Day, and only laughed harder as I held up the black gun-metal throwing knife for her to see. Seriously, who throws knives at a wedding? A Bar Mitzvah, maybe, but a wedding?

A vamp stepped in Day's way as she made a beeline for me, and she shoved it into a couple of Fae who were busy doing the jitterbug, who careened into a couple of shifters, and before I knew it there was a free for all with fur flying and vamps making hissy faces and everybody on the dance floor was kung-fu fighting.

I think that's about the same time someone yelled "food fight."

Day never did actually make it to me. She got caught up in a wave of shifters and bogies, but I'm pretty sure I saw her blonde hair in the crowd when she head-butted that dragon.

I spent most of the time ducking or stepping out of the way. Okay, so I shoved a Fae into the chocolate fountain, and maybe a vampire or two. Three tops.

I had just spied Drat, dragging a hobgoblin along the length of the wedding table—one hand on its collar and the other by the seat of its pants—when the crowd broke in front of me to make room for the bride.

Tirade rounded on me, her hair in disarray, her wedding dress torn, and her left eye already swollen and purple.

"Decker!"

This is going to get ugly—er, I thought.

I don't know why everyone had jumped to the conclusion that this was all my fault, but obviously they had. I raised my hands in front of my face to protect myself, which was pretty dumb now that I think about it. Tirade was little over three feet tall, and a woman. Odds are she wouldn't be aiming to kick me in the face. Women tend to go for a somewhat lower, more sensitive target.

Instead she jumped up and threw her arms around my neck, practically shoving my face into her ample bosom, then kissed me lightly on the cheek as she slid to the ground.

I looked down at her, somewhat confused as she grinned ear to ear—which only served to show off the tooth she had apparently lost in the tussle—and gave me the thumbs up.

"Best. Wedding. Ever!"

CHAPTER TWO

We made it home just after seven in the morning. The thing you have to remember about troll weddings is that if the festivities aren't over before sunrise, half the wedding party turns to stone. A lot of the other guests weren't all that fond of daylight either.

Regardless, the wedding was a smashing success. Charlie had done a masterful job with the planning and preparation. The reception-rumble-food fight had just been the icing on the cake—or the custard in the face, depending on whom you asked. I *still* had chocolate in my ear. Anyway, Leanne and I pretty much closed down the party. We stayed around just long enough to see everyone safely away before heading home ourselves.

I'd once described Leanne's home in Kingston as a Herman Munster-looking affair. Her home in Victoria couldn't have been more the opposite. When I'd first seen it I thought it was a resort. Her *estate* in Oak Bay—the hoity toity section of the city—was open, bright and airy, and done up in white marble and pastel colours. A cross between Spanish and Greek architecture and set against the backdrop of the ocean, it reminded me of those homes I'd seen in pictures of Bermuda or the Greek Islands. And it's, well, palatial—some 17,000 square feet, with eight bedrooms and nine baths so there's plenty of room for those guests who drop by on a regular basis. I swear every bedroom has a walk-in closet that I invariably mistake for another room, and even though I've seen the blueprints I still get lost in the house on a daily basis. I don't feel so bad though; even Drat got lost in it once, and he's a troll who can navigate the Ways.

At least this place has furniture I can relate to. None of that stuffy old Victorian antique crap, but big, comfy leather sofas and plush chairs, and flat panel TVs everywhere. There's even an Xbox *and* a PS4. As a matter of fact, the décor would do any article of *House and Home* or *Canadian Living* proud.

I suspect that Leanne had had the library transported straight from the old place, right down to the vaulted, stained-glass dome, antique cherry wood desk, and the wrought-iron stairs that traversed the stacks and stacks of bookshelves. Or more likely it just exists in both homes simultaneously.

There's a boathouse out back bigger than the house I used to live in, and a pool house bigger than that, right next to an Infinity pool surrounded by manmade cliffs and waterfalls that make it seem as if the ocean comes right up to the back door.

Leanne had told me she was a Trooping Faerie, which I think is just a Fae excuse for moving to wherever it's warmer twice a year. As much as I had come to love her manor in Kingston, this place was *home*.

Of course it really isn't my home; it's Leanne's. I'd finally received the insurance money for my place in Kingston—the one that Azrael had burned to the ground—and a check for the car he'd blown up, but it still didn't add up to enough to buy a place in Victoria. Especially not in Oak Bay.

Leanne insisted that I move in with her. Even had we not been involved, the house was big enough that I could have taken up residence in one of the guest rooms—or the boathouse or pool house—and the two of us would rarely have caught sight of one another. That I get to share the master bedroom with Leanne, a woman who near takes my breath away every time I see her, is a dream come true. Honestly, dying is the best thing that ever happened to me, even if I do feel like a gigolo every now and again.

I lay with Leanne curled up beside me and watched her sleep for a while—but not in that sparkly-vampire-stalker kind of way. Honest. Eventually my ADHD kicked in, so I pulled the covers up and kissed her on the forehead before heading out by the pool. I like to sit on the deck chair and look out over the ocean and watch the sun come up. Leanne often accompanied me—having been a vampire for so long she couldn't get enough of the sunrise—but the wedding had tuckered her out and I thought it best to let her sleep.

Bear, my ghost dog, appeared at my side, spectral tongue lolling as I scratched him behind the ears. I find I can pet him as long as I don't look directly at him. His shifting in and out of existence and from one plane of reality to the next makes it near impossible for me to focus on him.

"Sorry you couldn't come to the wedding, buddy, but I brought you a treat," I said, and materialised the chocolate cake I'd brought for him. And yeah, I know; chocolate is poisonous to dogs, but ghost dogs love it.

Bear wolfed the cake down leaving behind only a minimum of ecto-slobber, which I appreciated, and the two of us watched the sun slowly rise on the horizon.

"Enjoy the peace and quite while you can, because it never lasts."

I turned my head to see my dad, done up in the dress blues they'd buried him in.

"Hey, Dad."

Dad smiled, and I saw myself mirrored in the way he did so. Mom always said I took after dad, especially when I smiled.

Just as suddenly he was gone, and I couldn't help but wonder whether he was being prophetic when he'd said the peace wouldn't last, or just speaking from experience. As a ghost, he's not tied to the space-time continuum the way the rest of us are, so it isn't out of the question that he'd been to the future, or at least a future, and knew what was coming. It's also just as likely he'd been to the past, and was talking about something that had already happened—my run in with Ashema, or Azrael. The past and present are one and the same to a ghost.

"Just as long as it doesn't involve zombies this time, right buddy?"

Bear barked in agreement, that spectral hell-hound bark of his, and I winced at the discordant harmonies.

I scratched him behind the ears some more. "Next time just nod your head."

Today was Sunday, and as we had nothing pressing to do I figured I'd let Leanne sleep until at least noon, and then maybe take her down to Chinatown for some Noodle Box.

By the way, calling it Chinatown is rather a misnomer—more like China square. Historically it had once occupied an area of about six city blocks—now, not so much. Still, it's the oldest Chinatown in Canada, the second oldest in all of North America, and a pretty darn cool place to visit, especially if you have the Sight.

I'd pretty much decided on my plan of action when I caught a shape out of the corner of my eye, flitting across the face of the sun still low on the horizon. Sure enough, there it was again. Was that—a dragon?

It was a clear morning, and I could see across the Strait of Juan de Fuca to the craggy, snow-capped peaks of Mt Baker. There it was again, silhouetted against the backdrop of the mountains as the sun crested the peak. Maybe it was a wyvern. I'm not sure what the difference is, other than I think maybe a wyvern only has two legs instead of four. I know dragons get mighty huffy when you confuse them. Anyway, whatever it was—dragon or wyvern—why the hell was it doing barrel rolls over the Strait of Juan de Fuca, in Darkside, and in broad daylight? Or more accurately, how?

It takes a lot of power to cross over from Summerland into Darkside, and vice versa. I'm not up on the physics—or magic—behind it, but from what I can gather, there's this Veil that separates the two. The Veil keeps most of the really nasty stuff on the other side, or at least the stuff that can't pass for human—glamour or no. You can still cross at the various portals where the intersecting ley lines have weakened the boundaries, like the one in that dumpster behind the MacDonald's in Kingston for instance. And trolls can use the Ways to cross back and forth almost at will.

Apparently the Veil weakens at night, which is why so many of the creepy crawlies slither over here in the dark, and back to Summerland during the day. It's also why most hauntings happen at night. Anyway, as the sun comes up, the Veil strengthens. Most of what's not supposed to be here automatically transitions back. They sort of fade from reality here and reappear over *there*.

As for the things that can pass as human—like vampires and shapeshifters—well, they can stay, but generally anything that preys on humans can't abide the daylight.

But something like a dragon? They hold so much inherent magic it's as if our world instinctively knows they don't belong here. Drat had to bring the two that attended his wedding through the Ways, and even then it had to be done at night.

And they're huge! I mean, even if they could stay, what kind of glamour is going to hide a dragon? I suppose it could pass as a fighter jet—an F-18 or something, but I'm pretty sure the Canadian military keeps a pretty good track of where theirs are at all times. To just suddenly have one show up on radar over Mt Baker, and on the American side no less? I'm surprised the Americans hadn't already scrambled fighters to shoot the dragon down no matter what it looked like to them. They generally treat anything unknown that invades their airspace like a giant game of Duck Hunt.

The phone rang, and I picked up the outside line before Bear started barking and woke up Leanne. Ghost dogs hate phones, although I'm not sure whether it's the ringing or the wireless signal messing with the electromagnetic spectrum. I've noticed Bear often starts barking before the phone actually rings.

It was Josh. "Are you watching the news right now?"

"Hello to you, too. And no. Should I be?"

"Well, I suppose not, unless you're interested in seeing news footage of a dragon being shot down by the Americans over Mt Baker."

"Again?"

There was silence on the other end of the line.

"Actually, I can see it from my back door," I said when I realised Josh wasn't going to take the bait. "What channel is it on?"

"Pick one."

"Just a sec," I said. "I think there's a TV out here somewhere." I didn't want to risk going into the house to find one. I'd probably just get lost anyway, although even if I ended up in the broom closet odds are there'd be a TV in there. "Ha, got one!" I said, spying a monitor over by the poolside kitchen. And yes, we have an outdoor kitchen for serving food by the pool. Doesn't everyone?

I found the remote on the side of the TV and turned the set on. Sure enough, I didn't even have to channel surf. "BREAKING NEWS. MILITARY SCRAMBLES FIGHTERS AS UFO SPOTTED OVER MT BAKER."

So they were calling it a UFO. I suppose the thought of little green men was more palatable to them then the idea that it was a dragon, which, even from the grainy, far away footage, it clearly was. Or maybe by calling it a UFO they figured they could claim it was a weather balloon later.

I pressed the record button. Every TV set in the house was hooked up to a PVR somewhere. And you thought dragons were magic.

"Isn't it like the Prime Directive or something that Darksiders aren't supposed to know all this supernatural gobbly gook is real?" I asked Josh.

"Uh huh."

"So then news footage would be bad?"

"Uh huh."

"Just checking," I said. "And you must be tired. You're usually way more articulate than this."

Josh blew me a raspberry over the phone.

"That's better. Oh, look, there's an F-15!" I said as the first of two appeared on the scene. "I'd have thought they would have shot it down from like a mile away using one of those Hindgrinder missiles."

I could almost hear Josh facepalm over the phone. "And exactly what would they lock on to?"

"I don't know—heat signature, optical recognition." Suffice it to say everything I knew about fighters and missiles I learned from repeated viewings of Top Gun. Probably not the most technically accurate of sources.

"Uh huh, I'm sure they have 'dragon' somewhere on file in their pre-programmed threat analysis doohickey."

Two could play that game. "Is that the technical term for it, or did you just make that up."

"Shaddup, you!"

Ha, got him.

"Maybe they just want a better look," Josh said. "I mean, wouldn't you?"

"Yeah, or maybe they'll try to force it to land."

Whatever they planned on doing, they were in for a big disappointment. The fighters were closing in on the dragon fast, when suddenly, it was gone.

"The Veil must have reasserted itself," I guessed out loud.

"Sure, why not," Josh said.

"You mean I'm right?" More silence. Even he didn't sound too sure. "So, weather balloon?"

"Swamp gas," Josh said. "A weather balloon would have left wreckage."

"How about lights off a low lying fog patch?"

"That would do it," Josh said. "Anything but dragon. Goodnight."

"Night, Josh," I said, and hung up. Sure enough, not twenty minutes later the news was reporting the sighting as a prank, some tech geek from the university bouncing a holographic laser image off the fog bank over the strait. The fact that there wasn't any fog didn't seem to matter, or that short of Star Trek, I didn't know we had holographic laser images you could bounce of clouds. I won't even bring up the fact that all the university students had already gone home for Christmas break. But hey, maybe I was wrong. Maybe it wasn't a real dragon. That hobbit movie had come out a little while ago; maybe this was just a publicity stunt.

And if you believe that, I've got a bridge for sale—complete with real trolls.

So let's assume it's a real dragon. What was I supposed to do about it?

Wake Leanne up and go get some Noodle Box, that's what. It's not like it had bothered anyone. It didn't gobble up any virgins or flame-broil a herd of sheep. It just went for a quick fly by over the mountains and got caught on camera. As Leanne is fond of telling me, I'm an Eternal, not the Supernatural Police. What was I going to do, give it a ticket for joy riding?

I let Leanne sleep a few hours more while I researched dragons and wyverns in the library, just in case. And I was right; wyverns only have two legs, so I'm pretty sure this one was a dragon. Probably one of the two that were at Drat's wedding. I'd only chatted with them briefly, but found them both to be...well...kind of immature. Take their names, for instance. I'd expected something majestic, or at least...dragon-y. But no, they went on an on about how they'd changed their names a decade or so ago to keep with the times. They called themselves Heckler and Koch, like the gun, so I'm guessing they hung out together a lot. I wondered which one got caught on camera? Probably Koch; Heckler would've mooned the F-15. Well, if he wore pants, that is.

Leanne walked into the library just as I was finishing my research, looking like some diva actress who'd just spent an hour on the movie set in hair and makeup. Not that she wore makeup, or needed it. No one should wake up looking that good, even in yoga pants and a hoodie. She even had a mild wind machine effect going for her. It must be a Fae thing.

She seemed unconcerned as I told her about the dragon sighting on the car ride into Chinatown, so I let it pass. If she wasn't worried about it, why should I? Besides, she let me drive the Bentley convertible, which was trusting considering what had happened to my last car. I probably could have bought a house for what this car was worth.

I grabbed a handful of toonies out of the change box by the door before we left to give to the homeless folk that hung about downtown. It helps to assuage my guilt over spending five dollars for a hotdog.

Victoria is pretty much the Florida of Canada—except colder and rainier, and with less guns—and the homeless population tends to climb in the winter. And I know, some of them are probably just scamming me. But what if they aren't? I'd rather waste two bucks here or there on someone who didn't really need it, than deprive someone that did.

There's this one guy, for instance, an older guy, probably late fifties. He's got one of those deep-lined, weathered faces, like he's lived his whole life outside. His hair is long and tangled, and might have been black at one time, but now was streaked with grey. His eyes are a pale green that look like they've seen everything. Someone had given him an old olive green army combat jacket—or maybe he'd actually been in the army at one time—that he wore over a food-stained, navy blue hoodie and track pants. A black wool toque covered his head, and a pair of old Mark IV combat boots kept his feet dry, if not warm.

He never asked me for money. The first time I'd seen him, he'd asked me for gum. I figured what the heck, and bought him a pack. He thanked me, took a stick for himself, then shared the rest with the other folks huddled in the doorway where I'd found him. Once he asked if I'd buy him a hotdog, so I did. I ended up buying him two, seeing as how he gave the first one away to a kid who looked so strung out that I doubted he even knew where he was. The kid couldn't have been more than twelve.

Leanne says I just feel guilty about suddenly having all this money. Maybe she's right, but I've seen her dropping money into the change box when she sees it getting low, and she's the one who routinely drops off the food and clothes at the homeless shelter.

I parked outside the restaurant while Leanne ran in and picked up our order. We'd called ahead so it was ready when we got there. The staff knew us pretty well by now; we were regulars and always got the same thing—the Thai-style chow mein for me, and the teriyaki box for Leanne.

If you had asked me a few months ago what I'd be doing now, sitting in a Bentley with the top down, in December, eating takeout with a smoking hot faerie woman who for some inexplicable reason was crazy about me wouldn't have even been in the top ten…thousand.

Of course, I'd have bet seeing Bigfoot shopping for fruits and vegetables in Chinatown wouldn't have made the list either.

"Do you see that?" I asked Leanne around a mouthful of noodles. I used the chopsticks to spear a piece of chicken at the bottom of the carton. And yeah, I know it's cheating. So sue me.

"You mean Mike?" she asked, and nodded towards the Bigfoot thumping on a melon, apparently checking for freshness. "Yeah, he's here every Sunday. Takes the ferry over from the mainland so he can go to the Butterfly Gardens."

"Mike?" I said, sceptical of the name. Then again, I guess it's no worse than an ogre named Charlie."

Leanne shrugged. "What can I say, he likes butterflies."

Mike looked exactly like he did in all the footage you've ever seen of Bigfoot, just less blurry. Big and hairy, he stood a good seven feet tall from the tip of his slightly conical shaped head to the gnarly toes on his big honking feet. A pronounced browridge cast a shadow over a pair of big, emerald-green eyes, and thick lips covered a mouthful of dull, rounded teeth. And the smell! The glamour must have hidden that too, because even from where we sat at a good fifty feet away, the fragrance of O *de Compost* was unmistakeable.

His reflection in the window opposite the booth where he shopped showed me the glamour he presented to the world at large. To anyone without the Sight, Mike looked like a stereotypical hippy. A tall hippy—maybe six foot six—but a hippy: long brown hair tied back in a ponytail, a hemp surf pullover baja hoodie, a pair of cotton beige cargo pants with Grateful Dead logos on the pockets, and a brown leather cross-body fringed shoulder bag. Well, okay, the shoulder bag was real.

I was just admiring the detail in the glamour when the image flickered.

"Um...Leanne?"

Leanne grunted acknowledgement as she chased a peanut around the bottom of her noodle box with her chopsticks.

I nodded to Mike's reflection. "Is it supposed to do that?"

Leanne looked up just as the image flickered out entirely. "Do wha—?"

With no glamour to camouflage him, Mike stood revealed in all his Bigfoot glory. The vendor screamed, so of course now everyone looked. Mike did what any self-respecting Sasquatch would do; he called for help. Unfortunately, a Bigfoot's call for help sounds a lot like a huge, hairy monster growling and threatening to tear your head off. As you might imagine, a lot of running and screaming and general panic ensued, except for poor Mike who stood there stunned like a deer caught in the headlights.

Leanne gave me the look, which in this case meant "do something."

I started the car. "Okay, but he won't fit in the trunk." I gunned the car in Mike's direction and pulled up beside the Sasquatch with the passenger side and Leanne facing him. Mike blinked, still holding a melon in one hand and cash in the other.

"Come with me if you want to live," I said in my best Schwarzenegger.

"Hey, Leanne," Mike said as he climbed into the back seat. The Bentley was a two-door, so when I say climbed, I mean climbed.

Even with his legs stretched out across to the driver's side of the car and with his knees up around his chest, Mike barely fit in the back. There was no way we were going to get the top up. Somehow I didn't think driving around Victoria with Bigfoot in the back seat of a Bentley was all that much of an improvement to finding one standing in the middle of Chinatown, but hey, I'll try anything once.

I grinned at Leanne. "Maybe we should have just strapped him to the hood."

Leanne shook her head, then in her best southern drawl said, "Sure, we could just tell everyone we bagged us a bigfoot."

Mike kept his opinion to himself, but I'm guessing he would have voted no.

I made a beeline for Pandora Street. I figured we take Hwy 17 south to Douglas, then skirt Beacon Hill Park and take Dallas Road along the coast back to up to Leanne's place—our place—in Oak Bay. It would have been faster to take Douglas north to Hillside and follow it to where it turned into Landsdowne Road and home, but that way just travelled through too much of the city and with too many stops.

We hadn't even made it to Pandora though, when the Veil reasserted itself again. The skin on my face crawled, as if I'd just walked through a spider's web, and then the sensation was gone. I looked in the review mirror. Sure enough, Mike looked like a hippy again.

"Maybe you should just go back home until we find out what's going on, Mike," Leanne suggested. "We could give you a lift back to the ferry?"

"Awesome," Mike said.

"What if things—slip—again?" I asked. "It would suck if the glamour failed on the ferry, in broad daylight, with no place to hide."

"I could just stay in my van?" Mike suggested.

A van. No kidding. I should have seen that coming. "Yeah, that'll work."

We drove on in silence after that. Mike seemed to like the wind in his face, kind of like Bear did. We dropped him off at his van, and yes, it was a 1967 Volkswagen Kombi, all painted up with flowers, rainbows and dragonflies.

"I think we should get the gang together," Leanne said out of the blue on the way home. "I think the Veil is failing."

I reached over and held her hand. "Not good?"

"Definitely not good."

CHAPTER THREE

Charlie looked worried. Well, tired and worried. He was the last to leave the wedding, staying around to do a final sweep of the gardens even after Leanne and I had left. It wouldn't do to have someone leave—say—an enchanted ring or an open portal laying about. There were a lot of important personages who had attended Drat's wedding. Who knew what artefacts they might have brought along with them for bragging rights? The last thing anyone needed was for some poor gardener out to get an early morning start at trimming the begonias stumbling across the Necklace of Harmonia, or the Horn of Gabriel, and accidentally triggering the apocalypse.

It was only two in the afternoon now, so I doubt the big guy had seen much in the way of sleep. That still didn't stop him from pacing. Like I said, tired *and* worried. At least he'd had time to change out of his tux. Charlie swore it was a rental, though where you find a tux for an eight foot tall, seven hundred and something pound ogre is beyond me. He was comfortably attired in his patchwork coat and trousers once again, although if I didn't know better I'd swear they hung on him a little more loosely than they had previously. I think the poor guy had lost weight, what with all the stress of planning Drat's wedding. And here I was, adding to it. Um, the stress, not his weight.

Josh lifted his head from where it rested on the patio table and looked out over the ocean through bleary eyes. Obviously he hadn't gotten much sleep either. "Charlie, would you sit down please? You're making me tired just watching you."

Sabrina stood behind her husband and ruffled his hair. She, of course, looked bright and chipper and raring to go, even though I knew she hadn't had any more sleep than Josh.

Charlie blushed, embarrassed though he had no reason to be, and took a seat in the wooden shellback deck chair I'd had made especially for him. The woman who'd built it hadn't even batted an eye at the oversized dimensions. Salt Spring Island was just crawling with artsy craftsy people who had turned their vocation into a booming tourism trade, and were more than happy to make anything for you if the price was right.

Drat, of course, couldn't be here—firstly because it was midday and the sun would turn him to stone, and secondly because he was currently on his honeymoon, which, as Charlie told me in a bit of TMI, lasts for about a day. Two if they do it twice. Don't ask.

"You're sure the Veil is failing?" Charlie asked, drumming his fingers on the armrest of the wooden chair.

"Well, there was that thing with the dragon this morning," Sabrina said.

"And the incident with Mike at the Market," Leanne added before disappearing inside the house after something.

Charlie frowned. I knew what he was thinking: on the face of it those two incidents didn't add up to the conclusion the rest of us had jumped to. Dragons are powerful—maybe even powerful enough to shake a glamour if they wanted to. Heckler seemed the type, too; a real attention whore if ever I'd seen one.

And the Market? If anything untoward was going to happen anywhere, it would be there, or thereabouts. Chinatown and Fan-Tan Alley, Bastion Square, the Empress Hotel, the Parliament Buildings—there were more ghost sightings and supernatural occurrences reported along that stretch of Government Street than anyplace I could think of. It was like Spooky Central. It was old, and had history, and not always the good kind of history, either. They used to hang condemned criminals in Bastion Square, right across from where the old courthouse used to be—where the naval museum is now. From what I've heard they buried them there, too.

Chinatown was crawling with opium dens and houses of ill repute back in the before. I can practically write my own horror stories given the combination of racism, drugs, and prostitution.

Every restaurant had a tale of how the previous owners had come back to haunt the premises, even the damn chocolate shop—although if I was going to have to haunt someplace...

What was I talking about again?

Right, ghosts. You might think that a lot of the tales were just local colour drummed up for the tourists, and in a few cases you'd be right, but in most, you'd be wrong. Take it from me, an Eternal, Victoria is one haunted city.

"I suppose it could be nothing, just a coincidence," I told Charlie. "But when have you ever known that to be true where I'm concerned?"

Everyone nodded their heads at that, which while it was nice they agreed with me, still kind of stung a little. "Hey, it's not like it's *all* my fault. *My* daughter isn't the Innocent."

Sabrina pursed her lips at that. I thought Josh might object, but at the moment he was head down and drooling on the table.

"Speaking of which, where *is* Alex?" I asked.

"She's over at Olie's," Sabrina said. "At least that's what the note she left this morning on my bathroom mirror said."

"Good, I think," I said. I wasn't fooling myself that the Forces of E-vil had given up on trying to corrupt the Innocent, but if Alex wasn't with me I couldn't think of a safer place for her to be than with the witches. And trust me, if she was at Olie's, you could count on the other two—Julie and Michelle—being there too.

I hadn't seen much of Alex last night after that whole Cael thing had gone down. The kid had stayed mostly to herself after that, or with her parents. The rest of the shapeshifters had given us all plenty of room. A free-for-all at a troll wedding is, apparently, *de rigueur*. A blood feud? Still frowned upon.

Leanne returned bearing a tray of sandwiches and tea, with a Diet Pepsi for me, and an entire mince-meat pie for Charlie. She set it down on the table, right in front of Josh's nose.

His nostrils twitched a couple of times and suddenly he was awake. "Is that ham on rye with havarti cheese, and just a touch of mustard?"

Leanne smiled. "Damn, he's good."

We all sat around, staring out at the ocean in silence, and eating our sandwiches, when Leanne said, "If Thomas were here he'd know what to do."

I took her hand in mine and she leaned her head on my shoulder. "Yes, he would," I said. Thomas—Thomas the Rhymer—had never been my favourite person, probably because he and Leanne had had a thing once upon a time. He could be pompous and condescending, and—frustratingly so—most often right. I'd never forget how he'd given his life to save Leanne's; never forgive him for dying without giving me a chance to thank him. I still missed him.

"So, worst case scenario, the Veil fails. What does that mean?" I asked, breaking the silence.

Charlie wolfed down the last of the meat pie, and finished it off with a sip of tea, even going so far as to hold his cigar-sized pinky finger out as he tipped the novelty sized twenty-cup coffee mug he used as a tea cup. "It means that Darkside and Summerland overlap," he said when he'd finished. "Or co-exist. It means no more glamour; the Darksiders will see everything as it is: ghouls, ghosts, zombies, vampires, shapeshifters, trolls, goblins, demons, dragons, the Sidhe and—ogres. It means a world where magic works, where humans have access to wishes and curses, spells and incantations, amulets and pentagrams and the calling forth of demons. All those things that merely leaked through before—all the stuff of legend and nightmare—will arrive full force, unchecked. Hungry."

I didn't even have time to let that sink in before Leanne piled on. "Magic and science don't work well together," she said. "Where one works, the other is as like not to. In those places where there was a stronger concentration of magic—along the ley lines or where the Otherworld folk congregated—there would likely be a breakdown in physics and the natural laws. Things like combustion engines and electric motors and generators may not function. Cell phones, GPS, computers—all useless, except for those pockets where science prevailed."

"So we'd be like the Amish, but with dragons," I said.

Josh nodded. "More or less."

I don't know about you, but I'm rather fond of the creature comforts of modern civilization, like the Bentley, and the 60 inch flat screen, and…indoor plumbing. And I'm not overly fond of vampires, or zombies, or demons.

"I think I speak for everyone here when I say that would suck!" I said.

Charlie shrugged. "Maybe it's nothing. Maybe you're right and it's just a glitch, but just in case I'll be in the library, if you don't mind."

"Of course not, Charlie," Leanne said, and kissed the ogre on the cheek. "Anytime."

Charlie blushed again and got up out of his chair, brushing the crumbs of the meat pie from the front of his jacket.

"Does he look thinner to you?" Leanne asked, her eyes tight with concern after the ogre had gone.

"He does," I said. "I don't think he ate a bite at the wedding last night."

"I'll send some more food into the library with him—and ice-cream. Lots of ice-cream," she said. "That should fatten him up some."

"I'll give you a hand," Sabrina told her, and the women wandered off back into the house leaving Josh and I to ourselves.

Josh seemed to have woken up some. Maybe the food and tea had helped. He was just reaching for the last sandwich when Bear popped in out of nowhere, snagged it off the table, and vanished again.

"Too slow," I said.

Josh just shook his head. I don't really think he was all that hungry now; he just hated to see food go to waste. "I'm surprised Bear still comes around, now that Leanne is a full-on Fae again," he said. Dogs didn't like the Fae much, and generally avoided them whenever possible.

I shrugged. "Bear's crazy about Leanne. She seems to be the only one who can look at him head on and still pet him."

The only other person I knew who could do that had been the ghost of my dead fiancé, Alison. But she was gone now. I mean really gone, and hopefully reincarnated. Leanne still held a tiny piece of Alison's soul within her. Maybe that's why Bear ignored the fact that she was Fae.

I looked at Josh and he looked back at me. We were both thinking the same thing, I'm sure. At the moment we were fairly useless. Charlie was in the library doing what he did best. Josh and I knew better than to try and help him. We would have just got in the way. Well, especially me. My Google-fu sucks unless you're looking for porn or penis enlargement offers.

Alex was off with her friends, and as far as I could tell, there was no Big Bad currently out to get her. Drat was on his honeymoon.

I know I shouldn't complain, especially after Dad had warned me and all. It's kind of pathetic when you think about it. I mean, here I am, an Eternal who can manipulate his matter just about anyway he likes, and transport myself instantaneously anywhere I want to be. I live with the most beautiful woman in the world at an ocean-side estate, driving fancy cars, and I have the best friends, ever. And I was bored.

"X-box?" I suggested hopefully.

"Sure, why not," Josh said.

Luckily I'm easily amused.

Josh was quite handily kicking my ass at *Call of Duty* when his cell phone went off. I didn't mean to listen in, honest, but my hearing is quite phenomenal now that I'm an Eternal, and I really couldn't help myself.

It was Alex. "Dad, could you come and get me? I'm downtown, just outside of Munro's."

The bookstore. Figures. Although she could have gone to listen to the buskers. It was a great way to kill time when you had nothing to do, and a lot of them were top notch. There were still a few about—not as many as there were during the summer months, but still. Knowing Alex, though, my money was on the bookstore.

Was it just me, or did the kid sound anxious?

I guess Josh thought the same thing. "Sure, hun. Be right there," he said.

"And Dad? Bring James."

We parked across the street from Munro's just outside the Bay Centre, even though it was a strictly no parking zone. There was a red Toyota parked a little ahead of us, and a van parked on the opposite side of the street in front of the Bedford Regency, so we weren't the only ones. It was a little after four o'clock and the sun was already setting. This close to Christmas the trees that lined the street on either side had been decorated with lights. Most of the stores had been strung with Christmas lights as well, with wreaths in the windows and cardboard Santas and reindeer adorning the sidewalks. Despite the trappings, it just didn't feel like the holidays to me without the snow, but at least the sky was clear with not even a sign of the constant drizzle that normally accompanied the winter months in Victoria. The moon was waxing gibbous tonight and still low on the horizon, big enough to light up the night once the sun set completely.

There were seven or eight kids, all Alex's age, sitting at the table under the tree on the sidewalk outside Munro's, but no sign of Alex or her friends.

"She must be inside," Josh said as he scanned the stone steps between the Tuscan columns that marked the entrance to Munroe's for any sign of his daughter.

We made it across the street without getting run over. Hey, *I* looked both ways; I can't say the same for Josh. The kids off to our right, five boys and three girls, gave us the patented sullen teenage stare as we entered the store—or maybe they were all just constipated. They sure were dressed nice, though. Even the kid with the tear in his jeans had probably spent a few hundred dollars on them. They probably came that way—pre-torn. I bet it costs extra to hire the guy to rip them before they ship them. Whatever, I'm pretty sure none of them shopped at Walmart, or K-Mart, or any store with a mart in it.

One of them mumbled something to the others and they all laughed. I don't know why, but I got the distinct impression they were laughing at us. If I were the insecure type it might have bothered me, but seriously, what did I care what they thought? Besides, I'm pretty sure my dad could take their dads any day.

Alex and her friends were waiting for us in the lobby of Munro's when we entered. She smiled nervously and gave her dad a big hug, which I thought was sweet. Most kids won't even admit they have parents when they're out with their friends, never mind commit to a public display of affection.

Alex's friend Olie gave me a big smile. "Hi, Mr. Decker." She threw her arms around me in a hug to match Alex's. Maybe she didn't want me to feel left out. That's my story, and I'm sticking to it. I gently broke away, and stumbled back a step or two to get my distance before Michelle and Julie could repeat the performance. At least they weren't all dressed in their schoolgirl uniforms.

Olie was the intellectual one—you could tell because she wore glasses. Okay, that and she was smart. She always reminded me of Audrey Hepburn—the yoga pants and purple MEC Truant jacket notwithstanding.

Julie probably had the most inherent talent of the three, meaning she did magic by accident that most witches couldn't manage after years of study. She was the athletic type, with her strawberry-red hair cropped short in a pageboy haircut, a sprinkle of freckles across her nose, and a runner's body, all lean and coltish, that even the baggy jeans and pullover she was wearing couldn't hide.

Michelle was a Spanish beauty, a dark complexioned Liv Tyler with the most raw power of them all, like a sexy Eveready battery. She was also the clumsiest.

I've always been awkward around beautiful women, even ones that were seventeen years younger than I am. These girls instinctively knew it, and took great pleasure in making me uncomfortable.

"So what gives?" I asked with some modicum of composure once I had them all at arms length.

I found it odd that Alex had called for her dad to come get her. Well, not odd—her parents and I had a standing rule that all she had to do was call, any time, any place, and we'd be there. A lot of kids had the same arrangement nowadays. It was a small price to pay—rather the inconvenience than the fear that someday a cop would show up on your doorstep with news of a fatal drunk driving accident. Of course given what Alex was and the unique dangers she might encounter, her drive requests covered a multitude of other scenarios. Still, I could tell that none of the girls had been drinking, and I'm pretty sure they'd all taken the bus downtown.

I took a quick glance about the bookstore. Munro's is probably one of the most elegant bookstores you'll ever see. It was designed as a bank way back in 1909, and the owner had restored it to much the same aesthetic; keeping the marble floors, the coffered ceiling with the brass hanging lamp, and the oval stained-glass window at the storefront that illuminated the rows of dark, wooden bookshelves. They'd added eight large fabric banners spaced about the store that gave the illusion of upper windows looking out over picturesque scenes of the four seasons. The place was beautiful, but as far as I could tell, definitely lacking in creepies and/or crawlies.

"Those kids outside are...well—" Alex stammered, eyes downcast.

"They're shapeshifters," Michelle blurted. "And they're giving her a hard time. I threatened to turn one of them into a newt, but Alex—"

Josh raised his little girl's chin so that she looked him in the eyes. "Is this true?" he asked, interrupting Michelle.

"Yes, Dad, but I told her no," Alex said.

Josh fought back a smile, and looked over at me. "I think she's been hanging around you too long," he said, then looked back at his daughter. "I meant about them giving you a hard time."

Alex looked down again, but nodded.

Josh's expression went dark, as if all the warmth and kindness had suddenly leeched out of him. "I think I'll have a little chat with them," he said, and turned to go, but Alex's hand on his arm restrained him.

"Can't we just go home?"

As the Innocent, sometimes I think the manifestation of just what Alex is tends to cloud her judgement. I've rarely seen her worry. There's always this air about her that everything will turn out all right. I think that's what she was hoping for now, that she could just leave, just walk away and everything would sort itself out, and everyone would see reason. I'm not really up on exactly what an Innocent is, or does. All I know is that if she's turned, humankind will be without hope for the next thousand years. So who knows, maybe she was right. Maybe because of what she is she could make that happen. But I wasn't about to take the chance.

Neither, apparently, was Josh. "This isn't about you, sweetie. It's all me. This is my past coming back to haunt you, and it's not fair."

"I say let your dad kick their asses," Julie said from where she was thumbing through the latest issue of *Chatelaine* by the magazine rack.

Josh frowned, and I said what he was thinking.

"You can't kick their asses, Josh, they're just kids. Sure, they're shapeshifters, but the cops don't know that. I'm pretty sure they frown on adults beating the crap out of teenagers. Well, at least as long as someone's looking, anyway."

Josh took his daughter's hand and put his other arm about her waist. "Are you sure this is the way you want to handle this?"

Alex seemed to relax somewhat. "Uh huh."

Josh stared thoughtfully at his daughter for a moment, then gave her another hug. "You girls need a ride?" he asked the others as he steered his daughter towards the door.

"Sure, thanks Mr. Faye." Michelle spoke for them all.

Josh just nodded. "You know, Michelle, your idea about turning them into newts doesn't sound half-bad."

The girls giggled at that, and I wondered if they really could do it. Leanne had told me that together these three girls were the most powerful witches that had come along in ages, and Leanne was old so when she said ages she meant it, but still. She'd gone to a lot of trouble to see that the witches ended up here with Alex, and were enrolled in Hogwa...er...Our Lady of Charity. As a matter of fact, with friends like Olie, Julie and Michelle I was a little surprised that Alex had called in the cavalry in the first place. Certainly Josh could have handled the motley crew that congregated outside Munro's. Why, then, had she made certain that I come along?

Then it hit me. I wasn't there to help Josh. I was there to help those shifter kids. If she couldn't talk her dad down, Alex had counted on me to do it. I looked over at the kid, and damned if she didn't give me the nod.

"You know things are really messed up when you're counting on me to be the voice of reason," I muttered under my breath.

The corners of Alex's mouth turned up slightly in what just might have been a smile, and she winked at me.

Damn, I hate it when I'm right.

We hadn't made it to the exit yet when that tall kid from the wedding, Cael, came charging through the doorway and almost bowled over Josh and

Alex.

I hadn't realised what a good-looking kid he was. Wavy, black, shoulder-length hair framed a face that was all high cheekbones and square-jaw, and his pale Nordic skin was somewhat offset by bright, if somewhat troubled-looking grey-blue eyes. He was tall and lanky, with broad shoulders, narrow hips and long legs. His baggy clothes—an over-sized denim jacket over a blue hoodie over a white t-shirt, loose fitting jeans, and dark brown Gore-Tex backpacking boots—failed to hide his athletic build.

There was something about him that nagged at me, until I realised he had that same quality that Josh had. Unless you thought about it, committed it to memory, you'd be hard pressed to describe Josh or Cael shortly after meeting them. Though both were undoubtedly good-looking—and I say that as a man secure in his…um…manliness—they were nondescript.

Cael's eyes flitted past us as he surveyed the scene and quickly fixed on Alex. "You're okay?" he asked her, ignoring the rest of us.

Apparently Josh and I weren't the only ones Alex had called.

"She's fine," Josh answered for her through gritted teeth.

Cael didn't relax until Alex nodded, smiling shyly. Of course, relax is a relative term. Josh didn't look too inclined to be overly friendly at the moment.

"I told them to leave you alone," Cael said, speaking to Alex as if the rest of us didn't exist, "but they're—"

"—assholes," Michelle finished for him.

"Your family has made it quite clear that they don't want you associating with my daughter," Josh said, his voice low and tone flat. "I think maybe it's best if you comply with their wishes."

Some of the bookstores patrons could sense the tension now. I could see a few of the staff, huddled in the corner and speaking in low whispers. No doubt one of them was trying to get up the courage to come over to see what was what. My vote was on the girl who looked to be no more than five feet tall and a hundred pounds. The little ones were always the feistiest.

Cael stared Josh in the eyes, and I couldn't help but note the similarity between the two of them. Both were…unyielding. "I'll be eighteen in a few months," Cael replied in the same tone Josh had used, "so as far as I'm concerned my family can shove it."

Josh said nothing for a moment, their eyes locked. Finally he shook his head as some of the tension drained from his face. He seemed tired, and not just physically. If I didn't know better, I'd swear he felt a little sympathy for the boy.

"It's precisely the fact that you'll be eighteen in a few months that you have no choice but to comply," he said.

I recognised the look that came over Cael's face, the *I've got you now* look.

I'd seen it on Leanne's face enough times.

"You mean like you did?"

Josh grimaced. "Yeah, well look how that turned out for me."

Cael smiled. It seemed genuine. "I dunno, you seem pretty happy."

Josh closed his eyes and pinched the bridge of his nose. All this obviously required too much hard thinking after a night of partying, and I don't think the poor guy was up to it.

"Come on, kid, let's get you home," he said finally. "Right now I just want to see my daughter safe and sound."

"Me too, Mr. Faye," Cael answered.

I'm sure that won him some brownie points with Josh. I know it did with me.

We stepped outside, with Josh and Cael on either side of Alex. Cael took Alex's hand and her fingers intertwined with his. I trailed behind the three of them with the girls and tried not to laugh when I heard Josh growl at the hand holding. Fathers.

It had gotten considerably darker in the few minutes we'd been inside, and the moonlight coloured everything in sepia tones. "That's right, run along home, cur," the kid with the ripped jeans called out.

Cur. It must be one of those Summerland insults. But hey, an insult was an insult. We might not be able to thrash the little bastards, but I was betting I could scare the bejesus out of them regardless. After all, what's the point of being an Eternal if you can't have a little fun? I'm sure Alex would let me know if I got out of line.

The expression on her face told me she wasn't inclined to stop me at the moment, and Cael clenched his fists and took a step in their direction, but someone or something else had other plans.

A blazing white bolt of fork lightning struck the street across from where the shapeshifters sat. The concussion pushed me back onto Munro's step, and blew the manhole cover up and into the Bay's storefront window. Current crackled along the power lines. The old-fashioned streetlamps exploded in a rain of glass as sparks traced along the cars that lined the street, setting of alarms and flashing headlights.

"Did you do that?" Josh asked, shielding Alex with his body.

"I wish," I said. I looked at the girls, huddled on the steps behind us. It was obvious they hadn't done it either.

"Well if we didn't do it, who did?" I shouted over the sound of wailing car sirens.

Something screamed under the street from somewhere down in the sewers. Whatever it was, it sounded—enraged. And big. Really big.

"Oh, that's who."

CHAPTER FOUR

The lights flickered on and off in the shops along Government Street before finally dying. The air seemed darker, as if something had sucked the colour out of the world. Whatever light was left failed to cast a reflection, not even in the windows or the shiny metal cars that bordered both sides of the street. It was as if the darkness greedily held onto any sliver of illumination it could find, absorbing it and giving nothing back.

I saw silhouettes in the vacant second story apartment windows, ghosts of the tenants who had died there and were now nothing more than disjointed, elongated shadows of who they had once been. Whatever was down in the sewers screamed again, and the shadows hid themselves, stepping quickly away from the windows and out of sight.

Apparitions appeared on the street. Pale and ethereal, they stood out in stark contrast to the inky blackness that surrounded them. Four men shuffled along in homespun clothes, heads hung low and covered in burlap sacks. The chains at their feet and manacles at their wrists rattled as they moved. I heard the resounding crack of a gavel and the men moaned, their ghostly voices echoing down the alleyway as they made their way toward Bastion Square.

A woman on the sidewalk down from where the shifter kids sat screamed, and clutched at her shopping bags. She pressed herself tightly against the café's storefront as a headless body staggered into her. The corpse was small, almost child-like, and dressed in a silk Chinese dress, embroidered with dragons and slit to the thigh. A young Chinese man appeared at her side carrying a bloodied cleaver. The woman screamed again and both apparitions faded away, only to reappear again further down the street toward Chinatown.

An elderly gentleman sporting a thick moustache and smoking a cigar sauntered along the sidewalk across the way. He was impeccably dressed in a dark suit jacket and pants, the knot of his silk tie perfect against the starched white collar of his shirt. Even from where I stood I could see where the side of his head had been bashed in by something heavy, perhaps a hammer or a mallet.

The thing in the sewers screamed again. The air seemed to shimmer with the sound, dissolving the apparitions momentarily, like sugar in water, until they coalesced somewhere further along in their travels.

A man and woman rushed past us, wide-eyed and frightened, into the relative safety of the bookstore. Victoria was crawling with ghosts, but odds are unless you had the Sight you'd probably never encounter one. Maybe a sudden chill you couldn't explain on a balmy night, a glimpse of movement out of the corner of your eye, or a feeling of unease. It was obvious that everyone saw what was going down on Government Street now, whether they'd been gifted with the Sight or not.

"Get the kids to the car," I told Josh. I saw that stubborn look he threw my way. "Get them to safety, then you can come back and help."

Josh bit his lip and nodded, then shoved the kids in the direction of his waiting Beamer. Cael looked like he wanted to argue, to stay and help, but his concern for Alex's safety won out in the end, too. They were almost run down crossing the street by a spectral Model T Ford that nearly clipped Josh in passing. I don't know if it would have actually hurt him, but none of us were taking any chances. Josh bundled the kids into the car. It was a tight fit, with Alex and Cael in the front and the three witches in the back. Even as accustomed to the supernatural as they'd become, the girls still looked frightened.

I saw Josh swear and pound on the steering wheel as the ignition clicked but wouldn't turn over. The battery was dead; the internal lights hadn't come on when he'd opened the doors either, come to think of it. It also explained why he'd had to use the key in the door. I guess the auto door locks hadn't worked. Leanne had said technology and magic didn't mix well. I guess this was what she'd meant.

The shifter kids in front of Munro's had changed form. I counted five werewolves, a couple of werebears, and one that reminded me of Josh when he changed—a sort of combination of both. It was a big no no shifting out in the general population like this, but I could hardly blame them. Given what was happening I understood the desire to be as big and bad as you could be, though I wouldn't want to have to explain to my mom and dad how I'd shredded my designer duds hanging around outside the bookstore. At least four of the shifters stood about with their big, hairy, clawed toes poking out through the ends of a pair of $300 kicks.

Josh got out of the car. I heard him tell everyone to stay put before joining me outside the bookstore. I guess the car was as safe a place as any right now. He arrived at my side just as a torrent of black, sooty smoke began to billow forth from the open manhole cover in the cobblestone walk across from the tobacconists.

"Why don't you kids get inside," Josh said to the shifters outside the bookstore. It wasn't really a question, or a suggestion either, and the kids didn't take it as one. The biggest of them looked hesitant, but then nodded. At least they had the sense to shift back before entering the store, tattered clothes and all.

"I don't suppose you have any idea what that is coming up out of the sewer?" I asked Josh.

Josh chewed on the inside of his cheek a moment. "With the kind of luck we have, I'd say it's whatever it is that's been doing all that screaming."

"So what, then? The Smoke Monster from *Lost*?"

Josh interlaced his fingers and cracked his knuckles, limbering up before the action. "Could be, although to be honest, I still don't know what *it* was either."

The smoke began to thicken above the manhole cover. It took on a vaguely human form, if humans were ten feet tall, with a build that made Schwarzenegger look like Sailor Moon. It seemed more concrete towards its center, increasingly smoky and insubstantial towards the edges, and the head was rudimentary—it had no neck, nothing more than two red burning slits for eyes, and a burning pit for a mouth. Its legs were shorter than its arms, like a gorilla, and it slammed a massive fist into the street sending spider web cracks radiating out through the pavement for a good ten feet. It opened its mouth and screamed, confirming Josh's hypothesis as to its identity.

I heard a knocking, and looked over to see one of the girls, Olie, tapping on the car window. She couldn't roll it down without power, but waved me over. It was obvious she wanted to tell me something. I was inclined to listen, her being a witch and all, and considering our predicament.

I ran to the side of the car and opened the back door.

"It's a ghost, Mr. Decker."

"*That's* a ghost?" Victoria is also known for the quality of its weed. It crossed my mind that maybe Olie had partaken in some.

She pushed her glasses up on the bridge of her nose. "Well, actually it's a bunch of ghosts—a vengeance spirit."

Michelle leaned across Olie. "That's what you get when you hang a bunch of people, bury them in a mass, unmarked grave, and let them stew for a hundred years or so," she said, as if the notion was obvious.

"Mr. Sinha told us that this area used to be crawling with opium dens and gambling houses," Julie added from the far side of the car, "and that all that negative energy—the stuff from the murders and the hangings and the like—was just building up and ready to pop."

"Mr. Sinha? Who's that, your defence against the dark arts teacher?"

Julie closed her eyes and took a deep breath. I think I was giving the poor girl a migraine. "No, algebra."

"Algebra? What kind of crazy shit are we teaching kids in school nowadays?" I asked. Apparently they thought I was kidding, because no one answered. "So why show up now, after all these years?"

"The Veil probably kept it in check," Olie said, and the rest nodded in agreement. "But, um...I don't sense it now. I think the Veil's gone, Mr. Decker."

Believe it or not I'd come to the same conclusion myself. "I don't suppose you have any idea how to kick this thing's ass?"

They didn't.

The vengeance spirit moved towards us and slammed a fist into the front end of the red Toyota Supra. The car flipped up on its side and wrapped itself around an antique-looking light post. I heard someone in the deli across the street curse. You know, the profanity that rhymes with brother trucker. I'm guessing it was his car.

"Maybe this isn't the safest place for you kids after all," I said. Everyone seemed to agree, and scrambled out of the car. "Hide in there," I said, and pointed towards the main entrance to the Bay Centre. "Get upstairs, to the food court. Draw one of your protective circles and keep everyone inside it until this is over." The food court was near the center of the mall. The vengeance spirit would have to toss something pretty hard to go through that much building. Besides, what self-respecting ghost would haunt a food court?

Cael looked dubiously at the vengeance spirit. "Maybe we could help?"

"Thanks, but you can help the most by making sure we don't have to worry about you." I looked Cael in the eyes. "Stay in the circle. I'm counting on you to keep the girls safe."

He looked to Alex and the others. I could tell they were all frightened, even Alex, but I'm sure if I'd asked they would have stayed. Finally, Cael nodded and the girls held hands as they all made a beeline for the door.

I turned my attention back to the vengeance spirit. So far Smoky had been content to rant, pound the ground, and trash a Toyota. Nothing I haven't wanted to do myself on occasion. Wraiths began to appear around it, at least a dozen or so in various states of decomposition and dress. A few looked to have been drowned.

"What, its got a posse now?"

"Something tells me that the dead of Bastion Square aren't the only spirits that are pissed off," Josh said. "I read somewhere that a bridge collapsed near here sometime near the turn of the century, killing fifty or so people. I think a boat sank, too, taking a bunch more with it."

"Mass hangings, murders, drownings—was this place built on a Helmouth or what?" I asked.

Josh looked at me like I had two heads.

"Come on, don't tell me you never watched *Buffy*?"

He looked really confused now. "You mean that little girl on *Family Affair*?"

Now it was my turn to look baffled.

"You know, with Mr. French, and Mrs. Beasley," he said.

I sometimes forget that Josh is way older than he looks. "I give up," I said. "Your show sounds way scarier than mine."

Smokey screamed again. He was getting stronger, and his voice shattered a host of windows along Government Street.

Josh cupped his hands over his ears and shouted. "So exactly how do you plan to take him down?"

"I don't suppose you have a giant leaf blower in the trunk of your car?" I hollered back.

"It looks kind of solid near the middle," Josh said, not dignifying my question with a response. "Maybe you can just kick its ass the old-fashioned way."

I looked sideways at Josh. It didn't escape my notice that he'd said "you" and not "we." Smokey stopped screaming. Why couldn't it have just been a giant Stay-puffed Marshmallow Man?

"Maybe I should try talking to it first," I said once the racket died down.

Josh cuffed me in the back of the head.

"What? Maybe it's just misunderstood, or at least in need of some extensive therapy."

"Fine," Josh said. "You try talking to it and I'll go see if I can find it a giant Zoloft."

I shrugged and took a step toward the vengeance spirit. "Yo, can't we all just get along?"

Smokey picked up the crumpled heap of the Toyota and slammed it down on the very spot I was standing. I raised my hands up over my head, as if that was going to help. The undercarriage crushed pretty much every bone in my body. I'm sure it smooshed my internal organs too, if I still had any. Trust me, even when you're already dead, that stings. I lay there in a mangled heap for a second, healing everything and trying not to whimper. When I'd finished, I grabbed the car by the right front axel and further down by the drive shaft, and pushed it off of me.

"I'll take that as a no," I muttered, and got to my feet. I tried to brush the dirt from my clothes but who was I kidding? They were covered in grease, road grime, and even blood in a few places.

"Two can play that game," I said, and grabbed the car by the front end. It was pretty smashed up now, so there were a lot more hand holds than usual. I think I heard the guy who owned it sobbing from inside the deli. And I thought my insurance company gave me a hard time about the car bombing.

"Give me a little room," I warned Josh, then did a turn, building up momentum like a discus thrower before releasing the Toyota at the height of its arc. The car flew straight and true, smack dab through Smokey's center and on through. It touched down about twenty feet behind the vengeance spirit and tumbled to a halt at the intersection of Government and View Street. What was left of the Toyota rocked back and forth a bit as the car alarm finally sounded.

"I guess he's not as solid as we thought," Josh said.

I shook my head. "Suddenly my leaf blower idea isn't looking so bad now, is it."

"Now what?" Josh asked, not taking my suggestion seriously. "To be honest I haven't had many dealings with ghosts, at least not the troublesome kind."

"I don't think we have time for a séance," I said. "We definitely don't have time to salt and burn their bones." Hey, it always worked on *Supernatural*. Of course the ghosts Sam and Dean dealt with were always conveniently buried in a cemetery out in the boonies somewhere, and not under the cobblestone market square in the center of the city, or lost out at sea.

Josh squinted his eyes, peering off into the darkness. "Have you noticed that Smokey hasn't moved around much since he came up out of the manhole cover?"

Smokey screamed again, almost as if agreeing with Josh.

"Come to think of it, he does seem a touch more frustrated than vengeful—other than that bit about clobbering me with the car," I said.

"Look, over there," Josh said, pointing to the Irish pub on the corner. "Right there, just above that corner window on the top floor."

"Something's glowing," I said. Even in the oppressive darkness that had swallowed up every flicker of light since the Veil had failed, something was glowing.

"Can you make it out?" Josh asked, still squinting.

"It's some sort of symbol, I think. Maybe Masonic."

Josh glanced at me sideways.

"Hey, I watched *The Da Vinci Code*."

He looked sceptical.

"I said watched, not read."

"Well, whatever it is, there's another one on the building across the street," Josh said.

It was a newer building, but sure enough, there it was on a corner brick near the top.

"You think they're some kind of spirit trap?" I asked.

"Maybe," Josh said, keeping an eye on Smokey.

The spirit screamed again, near rattling my teeth in my head. So far the ghosts that accompanied it seemed content to just stand there looking ghostly. And soggy.

"The pub's old, or at least the building is," Josh said. He opened his mouth wide and dug a finger in his ear to equalize the pressure in his head. "It was originally a Bank of Montreal."

This time it was my turn to look sceptical. Josh was smart—I'll give him that—but come on.

"It says so on the front of the building," he said, and had the nerve to stand there looking all smug.

I picked up a rock and threw it at Smokey. It passed through the one of the drowned ghost's forehead and on through the vengeance spirit's leg without doing either any damage. "Well, whoever built these buildings way back when seemed to know what they were doing."

Josh turned to look behind us. He pointed out two matching glyphs, one carved into the Scottish pub on Ford Street—another building that used to be a bank, by the way—and the second near the top row of apartments over the Irish linen store across the street from the pub. At least we had an idea now just how big the confinement area was.

"They're probably an insurance policy," Josh said, turning back to face Smokey. "The energy here was so thick you could have eaten it with a spoon, even before the Veil faltered. It was just a matter of time before something like this happened."

I stuck my finger in the hole in my sleeve where one of the bones—the ulna or radius—had popped through when Smokey had dropped the car on me. Leanne had bought me this shirt. She was going to be pissed.

"Great, so the spirits are trapped here," I said, still fiddling with the hole. "What do you suggest we do about it? Cordon off the block and put up signs that say *Here There Be Monsters*?"

Smokey turned, ignoring us now, and lurched toward View Street. The glyphs flared brightly, and Smokey screamed, then turned back towards us, confirming our theory.

"I guess we start by evacuating everyone," Josh suggested. "We get everyone out of the surrounding buildings and move them to a safe spot."

And just where might that be? The lights were still on in Esquimalt just across the harbour, and in the Parliament buildings at the south end of Government Street. Apparently the phenomenon was localised to no more than a few city blocks. Most of the buildings had back doors that let out onto streets that, while not free of whatever was happening, were at least further away from Smokey. As far as I could tell the other ghosts weren't all that dangerous. As a matter of fact, they didn't seem bothered by the confining glyphs either; that Model T had come at us from well beyond Ford Street.

I was just about to suggest we move everyone out through the back exits when the lights came on. Smokey's posse vanished instantaneously. The vengeance spirit raged as something seemingly grabbed it by its legs and toppled it face-forward, then proceeded to drag it back toward the manhole cover it had escaped from. Its fists pounded the street leaving tire-sized craters in the pavement, and it slammed a light post so that it crumpled a third of the way up and canted out over the street at a forty-five degree angle. Spectral fingers left jagged furrows in the cobblestone as it was inexorably drawn down into the sewers, still shrieking fury and defiance. Soon there was nothing left of it but a few stray wisps of smoke and soot.

"I guess it's true," I said. "If you procrastinate long enough, most problems will solve themselves."

"Spoken like a true slacker," Josh said, and started the Beamer with the remote. "And you've only been on the Island for a month."

"Let's get the kids and get out of here, before someone decides to blame us for all this." The only upside was that with the power out everywhere no one had been able to get pictures of anything. None of the security cameras would have functioned either. If I were one of the MIB, I'd show up with my flashy thingy with a story about a build-up of pressure in the sewers that blew off the manhole cover and did all that damage. The sewer gasses could have caused mass hallucinations, and...screw it, there was no way to explain what had happened to the Toyota.

I waited by the Beamer while Josh got the kids. Soon they were all loaded up and ready to go. There was no room in the car for me now, but I could teleport, so no biggy.

"I called Sabrina while I was in the mall to see if she was okay," Josh said. "It seems only Government Street was blacked out."

"This time," I said to myself as the car pulled away from the curb.

We'd been pretty ineffective. I had no idea what I could have done had the Veil not reasserted itself. What the hell were we supposed to do if it failed all over the city, or the island? What if it failed world-wide?

Dad was right. It made no difference if he'd been to the future or the past. His advice was relevant regardless. Enjoy the peace while it lasts, because it never does.

CHAPTER FIVE

I made it home a good hour before Josh arrived. I have no idea where Cael lived, or if he even lived in Darkside, but the girls were spaced out across the city so that it was a fair bit of running about to get them all home.

Josh and Sabrina had a penthouse condo in The Harbourside on Montreal Street that overlooked the ocean and city. They'd kept their place in Kingston, too. I don't know where Josh and Sabrina get their money, and I was raised to think it crass to ask. Neither of them appeared to have jobs, although Sabrina had mumbled something about investments once.

Olie and Julie both lived in military housing in Beaumont Park out near Colwood, and Michelle's mom had to be an officer because she'd bought a nice place by the water just off Sooke Road.

Josh must have dropped Alex off at home because she wasn't with him when he arrived. Their condo here was heavily warded, just like the place in Kingston. The moon wouldn't be full for almost another week, so Alex would be safe enough. By the time Josh arrived I'd gathered the others in the living room and filled them in on the night's events.

The living room—or parlour, as Leanne liked to call it—was on the first floor of the main wing. Floor to ceiling windows looked out over the back yard and the pool to the ocean. It was full on dark out now; green and red navigation lights winked on and off across the bay, which was kind of Christmassy if you thought about it. It had started to rain; nothing heavy, just the usual Victoria winter drizzle. It ran in rivulets down the paned-glass skylight in the living room's cathedral ceiling.

The room was painted in earth tones—light browns and beiges—and all the corners were rounded in what Leanne told me was a throwback to the

Victorian age. I'd helped Leanne stuff a big Douglas fir in the corner, and we'd decorated it all up with lights and tinsel and the usual cheesy Christmas stuff.

Charlie sat in the big easy chair near the fireplace. There was enough of a chill in the air that I'd lit a fire, and Bear lay sprawled out in front of it, asleep and snoring with all four paws in the air. Charlie shuffled the printouts he'd made of his research, and stuck his tongue out to the left and right as he highlighted passages with a big neon-blue highlighter.

I sat cross-legged on the sunken hardwood floor in front of the loveseat where Leanne lounged. "So, any ideas as to why the Veil is suddenly failing?" I asked when everyone was comfy.

Charlie peered over the edge of the paper he was highlighting. "There's a lot of buzz on the internet about 2012 and how the Veil is thinning because of it."

"There is?" I'd read all that crap about the Mayan Calendar and how the world would was supposed to end in 2012, but I didn't remember anything about the Veil.

Charlie nodded. "It's there, if you know where to look."

Sabrina reclined into her husband's arms, the both of them sprawled out on the white leather sofa. "You think maybe there's something to it?"

Charlie set down the papers and put the cap back on the highlighter. "The Mayan calendar completes its cycle on December 21, that's—"

"—Yesterday," I said. "Drat planned his wedding for the end of the world?"

Leanne ran her fingers through my hair, and smiled. "Actually, it was Tirade's idea, but yes."

Leave it to a troll. A wedding celebration or an end-of-the-world gala. Either way it's a party. Personally, I'd been so busy performing my duties as best man that I'd missed all the hoopla about the end of the world. Of course I'd missed the latest episode of *Archer* too. Luckily I'd DVR'd that.

"I bet there's at least a few people disappointed that the world didn't end yesterday," I said. I'd read numerous news reports of people stock piling food, and watched a special on TV about a company in the U.S. that made a fortune selling private underground blast shelters and countdown timers to December 2012. A lot of people had wasted a lot of money. Still, it was nothing near the frenzy inspired by Y2K.

Charlie finished his tea and set the cup down on the coffee table to his right. "What if yesterday was just the beginning of the end?"

I uncrossed my legs and stretched them out in front of me, leaning back against the base of Leanne's chair. "It's possible, I guess. Maybe the Veil failure is just a trigger, or the fuse that sets off the real fireworks to come."

Charlie shrugged. "Not everyone believes the Mayan calendar predicts an end. Some believe it signals a fundamental change in human consciousness, a spiritual evolution, or the dawning of Aquarius, as it were."

"Somehow I don't think that seeing ghouls and ghosties and things that go kill in the night was exactly the spiritual evolution the New Agers had in mind," I said.

Leanne stopped fussing with my hair and sat back in the chair. "There have always been places where the Veil thins," she said. "Places where the ley lines converge, or in-between places like crossroads and doorways. And it's naturally weaker at night, and during transitions like the solstices. We take advantage of these thin spots to create portals to travel back and forth between Summerland and Darkside. Maybe the failure is just a weak spot, like the hole in the ozone layer."

Josh pretended to spit on the back of his wife's hair, and Sabrina elbowed him in the ribs. "I thought the hole in the ozone was man-made?" he said, wincing.

"Somewhat," Charlie said. "It's always been there. The theory is that we've made it bigger."

"Could we have done the same sort of thing to the Veil?" Sabrina asked, nestling her head back into Josh's shoulder again.

Charlie nodded. "Anything's possible. Maybe we just punched too many holes in it traveling back and forth."

That didn't make sense. We'd been popping in and out of Kingston for months now. "Then why here? Why Victoria?" I asked.

Leanne dug her toes into the small of my back in a sort of impromptu massage. "The Veil doesn't just separate the two worlds," she said. "It's also the barrier between the living and the dead. Victoria's always been haunted. What if it's the weak spot in the fabric, and the first to tear?"

"Well, maybe it's just me, but I think that makes a bit more sense than tying it in with the Mayan long count," I said. I still had a hard time believing that over a thousand years ago a bunch of Mayan astronomers had predicted the end of the world, and the only note they'd made of it was to not extend their calendar past the cut off date.

"As I understand it—and I really don't," I said, "—the Veil is a worldwide phenomenon. Are there any reports of it breaking down anywhere else?"

Charlie frowned. "Actually, no. Not really."

"Not even on the rest of the island?"

"Not that anyone has reported," Sabrina said.

Josh broke into a wide yawn, and Sabrina reached back to cover her husband's mouth with her hand. "Maybe it's just a local phenomenon," she said.

Great, so we only had to worry about three hundred fifty thousand or so people instead of six or seven billion.

"Let's assume for the moment this has nothing to do with the Mayan calendar," Josh said, swatting Sabrina's hand aside. "Then we're right back where we started: why is the Veil failing?"

"And what can we do about it?" I added.

Everyone looked to one another, but no one had any bright ideas.

I got up and paced about the room for a bit. I think better when I'm moving. Charlie lost himself in his notes, while the rest of the gang pretty much stared into the fire, pondering. None of it seemed to help.

"Just where does the Veil come from in the first place?" I asked.

"Manannán mac Lir," Charlie mumbled, not looking up from his papers.

The rest of the gang perked up somewhat, although I don't know why. It sounded like Charlie had Tourettes to me.

Josh noted the puzzled look on my face. "Don't feel bad. This stuff isn't covered in Classic Comics."

"Manannán mac Lir is…well, a god," Leanne answered when I gave Josh the finger. "Or at least he was."

"A god? You mean like Tom Cruise?"

"Maybe not a god," Josh said, aware that I thought they were having me on. "But he was as close to being a god as it gets."

"He was here even before the Tuatha De Danann," Leanne said. I must have still looked lost—and I was—because she added, "The Sidhe go by many names. Manannán was here before even the oldest of us."

I sat down at Leanne's feet again. "Is he an Eternal?" Azrael had claimed to be many of history's greatest men, from Gilgamesh to Charlemagne. Maybe Manannán had been an attention whore too.

"I don't think so," Charlie answered. "He had power, real power. He had the gift of illusion, and prophecy, and the power over life and death. It was he who created Bran's Cauldron."

Charlie paused a second to let that sink in. Given our recent history, Bran's Cauldron was still a bit of a sore spot with me. "Manannán was also the guardian of the gateways to the Otherworlds," he said. "When the time came for the Sidhe to leave the world of man, it was he who led them into the earth."

By the way the rest of the gang was nodding, I guess I'm the only one who wasn't up on his Otherworld history. "What do you mean, into the earth?" I asked.

Charlie shrugged. "It's just a fancy way of saying he took them to Summerland, and created the Veil to separate the two worlds."

"Forced us, more like it," Leanne said. "It's not like we had a choice."

If I didn't know better, I'd say the girl was bitter. I don't know why. The Sidhe seemed to move pretty freely between one world and the next. All the Veil did was keep the mundanes in Darkside.

Something nagged at me for a moment. "I thought Azrael said *he* was the one who separated Darkside and Summerland, and banned the demons."

I heard Leanne laugh behind me. "Azrael may have *found* Summerland. He may even have banished a horde of demons to it, but it was Manannán mac Lir who created the barrier to…um…stop the cross-border shopping, so to speak."

I guess after a few millennia or so, even an Eternal could start to believe his own press. "And the vamps and goblins and dragons and stuff?" I asked.

"They just got caught up in the shuffle," Charlie said. "Ghosts, too."

Sabrina shifted on the couch and in Josh's arms until she was more comfortable. Josh blew at a wisp of her hair that was tickling his nose. "Magic has always existed here, even in Darkside," Sabrina said. "It's just weak here because of the Veil. That and technology; like Leanne said, the two don't mix well."

"Is that another one of the Stupid Rules?" I asked.

"Yep," Josh said. "And Manannán just might be one of the folks who wrote them."

I watched Bear kick his legs in the air as he chased dream rabbits, or goblins, or whatever it is that ghost dogs chased in their dreams. "Fine then," I decided. "If Manannán built the Veil, he can fix it. So just where do we find the great and powerful Oz?"

Leanne shifted in her chair, kneeing me in the back of the head in the process. "I'd start with Aine," she said, and massaged the spot where she'd assaulted me.

"You mean Queen Aine? What the hell for?" Aine, Queen of the Seelie Court, and the one who'd had Leanne turned all so she could have Thomas to herself. She wasn't exactly my favourite person. Leanne's neither, I'm guessing.

Leanne got up, then leaned forward and kissed the top of my head. "Because she's Manannán's daughter."

Josh and Sabrina headed home to feed Alex. She may have been an Innocent and all, but seriously, you couldn't trust the girl with a can opener.

Nobody felt like cooking so we ordered pizzas; one for Leanne and me, and four for Charlie. He was still pretty tired from the wedding and crashed soon after dinner in the guest room we'd done up especially for him in ogre-sized furniture. By the way, you haven't seen anything until you've seen Charlie in his Tranformers Pj's and bunny slippers.

I went to the library to do some more research after Leanne dragged me upstairs to have her way with me. What? I waited to leave until after she fell asleep. I take my responsibilities as cabana boy very seriously.

There was a lot of stuff on Manannán mac Lir on the web, but unless I felt like translating it from the original Celtic, most of it was pretty vague.

No doubt Charlie would, though, and I'd just read his cliff notes later. The one thing that did jump out at me was the constant reference to Manannán as a trickster figure, which I think is the ancient Celtic way of saying 'bully who pulls cruel pranks on unsuspecting rubes.' Picture the Three Stooges all rolled into one, and with god-like powers. I mean, how do you reason with a god who has a penchant for short sheeting your bed and putting shoe polish on your binoculars? Though if Josh was right earlier, it would explain the Stupid Rules.

Oh, and I also found out that none other than my old friend CuChulainn had had an affair with Manannán's wife. It's no wonder he'd been cursed to battle his dead enemies in that field over and over for the last thousand years. I had to hand it to the guy though, anyone who would fool around on his wife with Skatha, and then fool around on her, and with a god's wife to boot? I guess that's why they wore kilts in the old days; there's no way a set of balls like that would fit in a pair of pants.

Once I'd finished with the research, I booked us tickets on a flight from Victoria to the mainland in one of those little Buddy Holly killers. I thought about booking a helicopter, but the thought of flying in something that can't even glide if the engine cuts out still unnerves me. That, and the airfare is cheaper by seaplane. I know it's not my money, and Leanne has plenty of it, but still. Neither aircraft was big enough to hold Charlie, so he'd just have to sweet talk Drat into bringing him over by the Ways later once the honeymoon was over.

Leanne told me that Aine and her court wintered in Vancouver. I guess the island wasn't good enough for her. It still kind of freaks me out that half the Sidhe live in Canada. I love my country and all, but I can think of dozens of places offhand—warmer places—that I'd rather live given the chance, especially if I were filthy stinking rich like the Sidhe seemed to be. Leanne told me that the Sidhe like it here because it reminds them of the old country. I guess she means cold and wet. She told me that Canada has all of the modern conveniences of the civilized world, yet most of the country is still sparsely populated so the tech stuff doesn't mess with the magic as much. I guess that explains why none of the Sidhe live in Toronto.

I'd booked return tickets for Leanne and myself, and for Josh, Sabrina and Alex. I could have teleported, but there are some things that are just more fun the old-fashioned way, and a road trip is one of them. Worst case scenario: we don't find Aine and we all go shopping in Vancouver. Or maybe that's the best case scenario.

I nearly had a heart attack when a woman's voice behind me said, "What are you up to now?"

I spun my chair around to face her. "Damn it, Tammy! I'm going to get a bell and tie it around your neck to give me some advanced warning whenever you're around. Something dainty, like maybe the Liberty Bell."

Tam-Lien laughed. It sounded genuine, although I still got the faint impression she didn't really understand the humour, but laughed because she recognised the situation called for it. She'd come a long way towards becoming human again, but still had a ways to go. Kind of like Mel Gibson.

She held her arms out for a hug, so I figured what the hell. Tam-Lien was a just a little slip of a thing, but then I'm pretty sure she'd been Asian way back when she'd been alive the first time. If not, she certainly looked Asian now, or at least like WWII war bride. Her fashion sense seemed to be stuck back in the 40s or 50s somewhere, not that it didn't look good on her. As a matter of fact, Tammy was hot. Exotic hot, with luxurious, straight black hair that hung down to her waist, and jade green, almond-shaped eyes and cherry-red lips set against the stark contrast of her china white complexion.

She took a step back and did a little pirouette to show off her outfit, a blue floral print dress with cap sleeves and full skirt. She wore a broad black belt around her tiny waist that matched the three-inch stilettos—expensive ones, which is about all I know about women's shoes.

Tam-Lien reminded me of Nancy Kwan, the Asian sex symbol from the 60s. Go ahead, look her up. I'll wait.

"You look great, Tammy," I said, and meant it.

She smiled sweetly and perched herself quite lady-like on the edge of the library desk, crossing her legs and smoothing her skirt over them. "Thank you, James," she said. "You look rather dashing yourself."

Was she flirting with me? Nah, she was probably just messing with my mind. "So what brings you by?" I asked. "Not that you're not welcome anytime."

She tilted her head to the side, quizzically, something I'm betting she learned from Bear. "Do I still give you the—how did you put it?—oh yes, the heebie jeebies?"

Tam-Lien was the only other Eternal I knew. Supposedly there were seven of us, although Azrael's death may have created a vacancy. When we'd first met she was decidedly inhuman, and I have to admit it freaked me out that I might become like her. Seeing her here like this gave me hope. After all, if she could regain her humanity, why should I lose mine at all?

I laughed at her, and she pouted, just more proof that she was becoming more human every day. "Not at all, Tammy. I'm as comfortable around you as I am around any beautiful woman." Which is to say, not at all.

She smiled shyly, and I swear her eyes sparkled. It figures flattery would be one of the first human affectations she'd get a handle on right away. Women.

"The Innocent, Alexandria, you are still her champion?"

Champion? Well, I guess that was as apt a description as any. "Yes, I am."

My cell phone rang—Dark Moon Rising, so it must be Josh—and I excused myself a moment while I picked it up.

"Is Alex there with you?" he asked. I could hear the worry in his tone.

Tam-Lien uncrossed her legs, and stood. Apparently this was why she had come. "I thought you might want to know, the Innocent is in Summerland."

CHAPTER SIX

Josh paced his living room, stopping occasionally to stare out of the window at the city lights across the harbour. He carried a 9 mm Berretta in a shoulder holster under his left arm—an enchanted weapon the Sidhe smith Goibnu had made for him. The weapon never missed and never ran out of ammo, just like in the movies. The same went for the semi-automatic shotgun with a collapsible stock that hung from a sling under his right arm. An Italian Schiavona broadsword with its cat's head pommel and ornate basket hilt was slung across his back so that he could just reach the grip over his right shoulder. I had one just like it. The girls had given the swords to us as sort of a graduation present after our training with Skatha. They'd become our blade of choice ever since.

Leanne sat cross-legged on the sofa. It was only four o'clock in the morning and I'd felt terrible about waking her up, but in typical Fae fashion she looked as if she'd just stepped off a fashion runway all done up in her Kate Beckinsale leathers and longcoat. I knew she was armed—I'd seen the arsenal she'd set out on our bed before dressing—but save for the hilt of the rapier at her hip, I'd be damned if I could spot a weapon on her.

"You're sure she's not sleeping over at one of the girls' homes?" Leanne asked Josh.

"I called," Josh said, practically growling. "I woke their parents up at four in the morning and waited while they checked." He smiled, sheepishly. "I don't think they were too happy with me."

"And you're positive she was here when you went to bed last night," I asked.

Josh nodded, and turned to look back out the window. "I looked in on her. I always do."

Sabrina came out of the bedroom dressed in warm black yoga pants, a black fleece pullover with a stand-up collar, high-topped hiking boots, and with her hair tied back in a no-nonsense braid. I could tell she wasn't armed, but then again she'd never gone on one of our "missions" with us before. None of us was demented enough to suggest she stay behind now.

Josh gave his wife the once over and frowned, then pulled the Berretta from its holster and handed it to her. It was the perfect choice for someone who probably wasn't all that familiar with firearms, or swords for that matter. It didn't require training, and it never missed.

Sabrina made a face as Josh retrieved a Glock from a safe in the closet and holstered it, obviously not happy with her new acquisition, but tucked it away in the over-sized pocket of her fleece. At least she didn't try to shove it in the waist band of her yoga pants. "I really don't believe in violence," she said almost apologetically.

I shrugged. "I assure you, it exists. Stick around and I might even show you some."

She shook her head at me. "What I meant was I don't *like* violence."

"I know," I said. "To be honest, neither do I. I'm just really good at it."

"So, there were no signs of a break in," Leanne said, trying to get us back on topic. "You think she just up and left on her own?"

Sabrina bit her lip, and nodded.

"Then why go to Summerland?"

I was pretty sure I knew why. I guess Josh did, too.

"I think she went to see *him*," Josh answered. I swear if it weren't for the shag carpet Josh would have spit on the floor in disgust.

Leanne did the Mr. Spock single eye-brow raise thing, the show off. "The boy from the wedding?"

"Cael, yes," Sabrina said. "You don't think she's in any real danger, do you?"

I wanted to say, *Well it is Summerland we're talking about*, but thought better of it. "If she's with Cael she should be safe," I said. "The kid's royalty, after all."

Josh nodded. "He's a berserker, too. A young one, but still. To be honest I'd be more worried if they'd run off here, somewhere in Darkside."

Especially with the Veil failing and all, I thought.

Leanne tilted her head to the left and right, cracking the bones in her neck. "We all set, then?"

Everyone nodded. Charlie had already gone ahead to the portal and would be waiting for us on the other side. Ogres don't need much in the way of preparation. They just show up to a fight and pummel you with whatever they find handy.

It was only a short walk to the Empress Hotel from the condo. Josh led the way, his long strides eating up the distance so that poor Sabrina practically had to jog to keep up or be dragged along.

The Empress is an Edwardian, château-style hotel built in 1904, famous for hosting royalty and celebrities from King George and Queen Elizabeth to Shirley Temple and Harrison Ford. Nowadays it's as renowned for its old-world luxury as it is for its haunted history. Knowingly or not, the architect, Francis Rattenbury, built the Empress facing the Inner Harbour and atop the convergence of a whole whack of powerful ley lines. Maybe that's why his ghost is doomed to wander its halls along with all the other souls trapped there.

The lone receptionist working the graveyard shift gave us a nod. The receptionist was one of us—a brownie, I think.

"Has my daughter been by here this evening?" Josh asked.

"Yes, sir. Just a couple of hours ago," she answered.

"Was she with anyone?"

"Not that I could see, sir."

Josh slipped the woman a twenty for her help as we strode past the counter and up the arching stairway to the second level. It never hurt to cultivate friends among the Otherworld folk, especially here at the Empress.

This wasn't the first time we'd availed ourselves of the Fairmont entrance to tunnels that secretly honeycombed Victoria. And yes, they exist, no matter what anyone—especially the government—tells you. Besides, it's not the tunnels they should be worried about; it's the portals in the tunnels that should keep them awake at night.

The hotel was deserted at this hour, and we strode through the Victorian era Tea Lobby and past the shops to the Bengal Lounge. The room was a throwback to Colonial India, with polished hardwood floors, high ceiling fans, potted plants, and brass coat stands. Floor to ceiling windows looked out over the gardens, and the place smelled of wine, curry, and expensive cigars. Josh led us through the maze of antique-looking tables and comfy-looking leather chairs to the fireplace. He reached around behind the mantle for a moment until something clicked, then stepped back as the firebox rotated. A set of stone steps corkscrewed down through the floor and into darkness.

"After you," Josh offered.

"All right," I said, "But if there's any gollywoggles down there you'll never hear the end of it."

I ducked under the mantle and began the spiral descent. After only a few turns I could see the glow of incandescent bulbs. I reached the bottom of the stairs and moved into the tunnel entrance to make room for the rest of the gang.

Josh screamed behind me, a startled yell he tried to cut short. I turned to face him but he stared down at his feet and wouldn't meet my eyes.

"Gollywoggle?" I asked.

"Worse," he said. "Spider."

"At least he didn't shoot it like last time," Sabrina said, and winked as she passed by me and proceeded down the tunnel.

"That's 'cause he gave you his pistol. He probably thought the shotgun was over-kill," I said.

Josh shrugged as he pushed past me to trail after his wife. "I thought about it."

I shook my head at the big bad berserker. "Next time we come down here, instead of all that artillery you're packing, maybe you should bring along a rolled up newspaper or a shower sandal."

"Shaddup, you."

I don't know why, but I've noticed a lot of my conversations with my friends end that way.

We followed the tunnel south for a while. It was rounded, and covered in damp sand or clay as if made by the passage of a giant earthworm, but pale yellow light bulbs spaced along the ceiling every twenty feet or so confirmed that it was man-made. Or at least it originally had been. It smelled like wet mud and rotting vegetation, and water dripped from the small, sandy stalactites and formed shallow pools that we splashed through as we trudged passed the heavy wooden doors set into the walls about a hundred yards apart. The doors were locked—though there was no sign of a keyhole—and reinforced with rusted iron bands. Every now and then we could hear something that sounded like a far off scream from behind one of the locked doors. The rectangular, eye-level viewing slots set into the doors were barred to keep whatever was within from reaching out, though none of us had the nerve to peer through and look inside.

Smaller tunnels branched off from the main one at irregular intervals. A whole network of them ran under the city, especially Chinatown. We passed a door on the left, different from the others. It seemed new, the iron banding rust-free. Bright light shone from inside the room behind it. I knew this door, we'd used it before. It led to the same place the dumpster behind the MacDonald's in Kingston did—the land of the Fae. We were looking for another door now, though, the one that led to the Therians' land. Josh's people.

You know, it doesn't matter who or what you are, the tunnels are creepy. You never know what you might run into down here, and the sudden thought that maybe Smokey or his ghost buddies might show up had me more nervous than any dead guy had a right to be. We came to a fork in the way. The branch leading left and deeper into darkness led to Chinatown. We went right. Light spilled out into the tunnel up ahead from a door inset into the right side about a stone's throw away.

"This is it," Josh said, and we hurried for the far end of the tunnel.

I placed my hand against the door. "Any idea what we'll find on the other side?"

"Charlie, I hope," Josh said.

Like that was any help. I shrugged, and pushed the door open, then held my breath and stepped through. There was a bright flash and I stood outside in the warm night air under a cloudless, starry sky. Charlie was lying on a bed of ferns with his huge head pillowed on a rock, snoring loudly. I stepped out of the way to let the others through and the rest of the gang followed in short order. Leanne was the last, and closed the door set into the rock face of a hill at our back behind her. I nodded for Josh to go wake up Charlie while I got my bearings.

The moon broke over the canopy of tall trees, some over two hundred feet high, and cast a silver light over the uneven landscape of a temperate rainforest. Moss-draped vines strung themselves out across the lower tree boughs. Jagged hills covered in ferns and lichen, bare in spots where the underlying granite wore through, jutted up from the forest floor at random intervals to either side of us to create a meandering ravine. A light breeze set the treetops to swaying, and carried the scent of lavender, honeysuckle and…cinnamon.

I saw the lights of an ancient, stone-cut city in the distance, just on the other side of a wide gorge. I can see pretty well in the dark, but at this distance the city wasn't much more than a blocky outline surrounded by forest and covered in ivy and creeping vines. Tammy says I can seen in any spectrum if I want to—IR, magnetic, whatever—but I haven't figured out how yet. I still can't fly, either.

Charlie awoke with a start, but settled down quickly once he realised who we were and what was going on. "About time," he said, and yawned. I heard his massive bones crack as he stretched his arms out to either side. "I was starting to think maybe you got lost in the tunnels."

"And you were so worried about us you decided to take a nap?" I asked.

"We'd have been here sooner," Sabrina said, ignoring me, "but we had to wait for Josh to pick out a gun to go with his outfit."

Josh took his wife's hand and stepped off through the knee-high ferns in the direction of the city, assuming correctly the rest of us would follow. "I haven't been home in almost twenty years. I want to make a good impression."

I wasn't sure if he was being sarcastic or not, so I let the comment slide.

We followed the narrow, cobblestone trail that wound its way toward the city. The ferns and long grass on either side were wet and slimy with dew. I accidently stumbled off the path once and was instantly soaked to the hip.

"Do you know you squish when you walk?" Josh asked.

"Shaddup, you." Hey, turnabout was fair play.

Apparently I was too busy thinking up witty comebacks to notice the small boy that stood on the path no more than two feet in front of me. I stopped just short of tripping over him. I screamed, the kid screamed. We had a moment.

The boy was slight if not gaunt, and pale, with dark circles under his eyes and a shock of black hair to match the black clothing he wore. His lips were as thin and pale as the rest of him, and his jaw seemed distended. He looked like a Goth kid who'd been punched in the face a couple of times—not that that ever happens.

The kid screamed again, a shrill, piercing sound that immobilized me for a moment. He bumped me as he rushed passed and disappeared into the forest.

"What the hell was that?" I asked as I tried to recover some modicum of dignity.

"A wight," Charlie offered, digging a finger into his ear, probably checking to make sure the kid hadn't ruptured an ear drum or something. "A corpse with part of a decayed soul still animating its body."

"Like a zombie?"

Charlie tilted his head to the left and smacked it a couple of times. "Not quite. Instead of eating human flesh, it drains your life energy."

"Well, whatever it is I think the little creep stole my wallet," I said, patting my hands over my pockets. "Okay, who wants to help me chase the creepy looking Damien kid through the dark, spooky forest?"

No one raised their hand.

"I have your wallet," Leanne said as she pushed passed me and proceeded along the pathway. "As usual."

"Oh, right," I said, blushing in the darkness and glad that no one could see it. Leanne usually carried my wallet. You know, because she has a purse. Hey, it makes man sense.

The sound of rushing water in the distance grew louder as we approached the gorge. The trail led to a natural bridge—a kind of flat-topped stone arch maybe twenty feet wide spanned the gap where the rushing water had eroded the rest away. Moss, creeping plants and small, hardy shrubs grew all along its sides, dotted here and there with small white and purple flowers. A majestic waterfall thundered from the towering cliffs to the left of the bridge. White water churned under the bridge and through the gorge maybe two hundred feet below us.

The forest grew around and into the city, with towering trees spaced randomly among the cobbled plaza and growing up between the squat, squared buildings. None of the structures were more than four or five stories high, and looked to be made of massive cut blocks of symmetrically patterned or inlaid stone, giving the entire city a faux Mayan sensibility. Most of the buildings boasted terraces and rooftop gardens with artificial ponds. There were large, open windows everywhere—no glass—and tall, turn-of-the-century looking street lamps illuminated the plaza and the narrow, branching streets that ran through the city like a maze. Most of all, the city looked *clean*. And the air—this place had never been subjected to car fumes and industry smoke stacks.

People milled about or sat at one of the benches spaced about the courtyard: couples holding hands, children playing, others just standing about in small groups, chatting. Everyone looked—normal. Happy. It was like one big city on Prozac.

"Not quite what you expected, is it?" Josh said.

His voice seemed wistful to me, but when I glanced in his direction he looked—stoic.

This is where he grew up, I thought. I imagined him playing among the gardens, jumping from the rooftop into the pond, playing tag in the piazza, and lulled to sleep at night by the ever present sound of the waterfall. Hell, I know *I* would have missed this place, and Josh hadn't been home in twenty years. Exiled.

"Not at all," I answered. What had I expected? Something more medieval, I guess. Castles, or maybe a Viking longhouse.

Two guards awaited us at the bridge; two helmeted werebears in heavy plate armour, carrying the biggest double-headed axes I'd ever seen. Both resembled polar bears; the first in red armour that gleamed in the moonlight and bristled with bone horns at the shoulders, elbows, forearms and knees; the second in matching black armour. Both looked to top the scales at at least a thousand pounds. A fine mist drifted up from the gorge below, soaking the guards' fur. Wet man-bear is not a pleasant smell, just in case you were wondering.

The one on the right in the black armour gave the haft of his axe a quick spin in the palm of his hand so that the head twirled like a falling maple seed. He pointed the axe at Josh. "If you turn around now, we might let you live."

Josh waved, an exaggerated circular motion, palm outward. "Hey, Gord. Good to see you."

The werebear regarded us with narrowed eyes for a moment, then sighed and lowered the axe so that the head rested on the ground between his feet. "Why would you come back here? You know what I have to do."

I think Josh took some small comfort in the fact that Gord didn't look too happy about it.

"I think my daughter's here."

Gord's eyes widened. "The Innocent?"

"Yeah, she probably snuck in with Cael a couple of hours ago."

Gord gave the axe at his feet a twirl. "You ever think maybe you aught to rename that kid or something?"

Josh smiled "The thought had crossed my mind, trust me."

Gord looked past Josh to the rest of us. "Hey, Sabrina," he said, then nodded to Leanne. "Ma'am."

Me and Charlie he ignored.

"You're looking good, Gord. You too, Mick," Sabrina said to the second bear who so far seemed content to defer to Gord while pretending we weren't here.

Mick hefted the shaft of his axe against his shoulder and looked down at his feet, apparently embarrassed at his bad manners. It seems they all knew each other.

"So what makes you think she's here?" Gord said, turning his attention back to Josh.

Josh gave him that "are you kidding me" face. "Well, for starters, the fact that you two are standing here guarding the bridge. Not exactly normal rotation for a berserker, and the Captain of the Guard, at that. The only reason I can think of for Liam to put you two here is that he knew *I* was coming."

Gord and Mick looked at one another and shrugged before Gord answered. "I haven't been Captain of the Guard for quite a while now. Liam appointed one of his own lackeys to that position. He's got a bunch of sycophants hanging about him now, telling him how wonderful he is."

"Yeah, I think we met a few of those at Drat's wedding," Josh said.

"Still, as far as I've fallen, sticking Mick and I out here on gate duty tonight is a little extreme. I was kind of curious myself when the order came down an hour ago. I thought maybe His Majesty was pissed because he found out about…well…"

The way Gord rolled his eyes when he said "His Majesty" spoke volumes. "Is that the Eternal?" he asked, nodding at me. "He doesn't say much."

I reached back and adjusted my sword belt over my shoulder. "You know, you Coke bears were a lot friendlier when them penguins accidently dropped in unannounced," I said.

Josh grinned. "You asked for it."

Gord's lip curled, exposing a set of very white, very long, very sharp canines. I thought he was snarling at me but then I heard him chuckle, sounding exactly how you might expect a bear chuckle to sound. "Come on," he said. "I'll take you to see Liam."

We left Mick to stand guard and the rest of us filed in behind Gord. It took everything I had to refrain from humming the A&W Root Bear song as we crossed the bridge into the city. I'm pretty sure Leanne knew what I was thinking because she stepped up beside me and took my hand, then gave me that "Don't you dare" look. I did my best to look innocent and probably failed miserably.

Everybody stopped to stare at us as we traipsed through the piazza toward a set of massive doors set into the building at the far end. Or should

I say, they stopped to stare at Josh. For once I wasn't the center of attention, or at least not the one everyone was blaming everything on. It was kind of nice.

A quad of werewolves stood guard at the entrance to the building Gord led us to. They stood aside for us as we passed through the doors. While the buildings were all muted greys and slate coloured on the outside, the same couldn't be said for the inside. Everything was ochre and burnt orange and chamoisee, cinnabar, iris and jasmine, mulberry and puce and a whole host of other colours that can only be described in woman-speak. My default red, green, and blue simply wouldn't cut it.

A grand hallway, the ceiling tall enough for a were-asaurus to pass through—you know: part man, part T-Rex or something—led to a colossal inner chamber that just had to be the throne room. Okay, so maybe the thrones set on the raised dais at the center of the chamber gave it away. Four stone columns rose from floor to ceiling in a square about the dais, which itself was shaped like an Aztec pyramid with seven steps leading to the summit. Torches mounted in wall sconces bathed everything in warm, white light that softened the room's hard edges. There was none of that primitive burning rags on a stick, either, but ornate staves with little luminescent globes filled with smooshed glow-worms or ground up pixies for all I know.

Liam sat atop the dais in the ornately gilded and crimson throne. He didn't look happy, and not just because we'd probably got him out of bed at o'dark-thirty either. I guessed the grumpy looking woman seated on the throne beside him was his wife, the queen. She was actually quite stunning, with long, tangled red hair, tanned skin, plush lips, and beautiful sea-green eyes. Well, at least the eye that was open was. Both the king and queen had taken the time to dress, but you just couldn't hide that terminal case of bed-head.

Liam stared down at us, his sleep-encrusted eyes fixed on Josh, and smiled. "I ken tha sooner or later yood whack it up an I'd git tha chance tae keel ya ded"

At least that's what I think he said; his brogue was pretty thick.

"Says you, fur-face," I answered before Josh had the chance to.

"What he said," Josh added. "And what's with the accent? You're no more Scots than I am?"

"Tell me about it," his wife said, still half-asleep on the throne beside him. Her chin rested on her hand, her elbow on the armrest of the throne, and both eyes were closed now. "Some fool told him it made him sound more kingly."

"Well, I have to admit it's a sight better than that lisp he used to have," Josh said.

Liam's face clouded over, and I couldn't fail to notice the slight smile that tugged at his wife's lips.

"I was only ten," Liam snarled, all trace of the accent gone.

"Now that the pleasantries are done with, would you mind telling me whether or not you have my daughter?" Sabrina interrupted. She looked calm and collected, but I could see her hand in the pouch of her hoody clutching the berretta, and the way she thumbed the safety off.

"We do, and she's fine," the queen answered.

Liam scowled at his wife. I think he'd have let Josh and Sabrina squirm a little longer if he'd had his way, and she'd just spoiled all his fun. I bet she told the punch line to all of his jokes, too.

"I told ya ta keep her away from me bairn—er...my son," Liam said, and blushed when he realised he'd slipped back into his faux brogue. "Your daughter's fine, but I told you what would happen if you ever showed your face here again." The king nodded to someone in the shadows, and Gord and several large werebears stepped forward into the light and quickly surrounded us. Two of the larger guards pinned Josh's arms to his sides, restraining him, while the rest levelled pikes with gleaming sharp points and wicked looking barbs at the rest of us. Poor Gord looked positively glum.

I put a hand on Sabrina's wrist, preventing her from drawing her gun, and shook my head. "Not yet," I whispered.

Josh glared up at Liam. "I should have killed you twenty years ago."

Liam raised his chin, scratching at the beard there, and looked smugly down at the rest of us. "I could say the same about you. Difference is, come sunrise I mean to remedy my mistake."

CHAPTER SEVEN

I smiled sweetly up at the deranged king. "Oh yeah? You and what army?"

The guards pushed in closer, their blades all but pressed against me.

Charlie growled behind me, but didn't move.

"Oh, right. That army." I closed my eyes to see better. The darkness flared, filled with brilliant white spots all about me. Life announced itself as tiny beacons that shone bright in my vision. Some were merely specks like snowflakes whirled about in a maelstrom; insects and micro-organisms abound, and I concentrated on filtering them out until only the larger images remained. There were twenty people in this room, one hundred and seven in the building, a little more than five thousand in the city.

I'd developed this ability ever since the night I touched Bran's Cauldron. The cauldron had fed off me, and in turn connected me to every living thing that it touched. Thomas had said that my life energy is tied directly to the Wellspring; that it's unlimited, and in the end I'd overloaded the cauldron and revived those it had sought to drain. In doing so I had tapped the Wellspring, and now I could sense that connection whenever I closed my eyes. Maybe this was just another of those abilities Eternals have that I didn't know how to use, or maybe the cauldron had changed me.

A part of me was afraid of this newfound ability, afraid that I might snuff out those lights I saw in my mind's eye with just a thought, and I forced the notion from me whenever it cropped up. The upside was that I could now unerringly locate any living thing, be it man, animal, insect, Fae, or demon. I like to think of it as sort of a radar sense, but of course I'd never call it that or Marvel would probably sue.

I opened my eyes. "You know who I am," I said. It wasn't a question. "You know what I can do."

Liam paled a little, and his wife placed her hand over his.

"I am the Eternal, James Decker. I could end you and all your men here and now. I could wipe your city from existence. Pull its very walls down around me and emerge from the rubble unscathed. Aeons from now I would regale mankind with stories of how once there was a great race who called themselves Therians, and how, due to the folly of their king they are no more. End this nonsense and bring the Innocent to me."

Yeah, it was kind of high falutin', but these people seem to appreciate that sort of thing.

Leanne's brows knitted and she cocked her head to the side as if to say, "Seriously?" I glanced at her from the corner of my eye and quickly shook my head no. To be honest I was a little perturbed that she thought I might be, but then there'd been that incident where I'd trash-compacted a Chrysler 300 and threatened to kill the driver for running me over, so I guess I could see where she was coming from.

Liam bolted upright from his throne, his face beet-red. "What right do you have to interfere with our Affairs of State!" He was so mad spittle flew from his lips.

The man really was an idiot. "You really are an idiot," I said. "Just who did you sleep with to get this job, anyway?"

The queen sighed, and raised her hand. "That would be me."

"Oops, sorry."

She nodded, although I couldn't tell whether she was accepting my apology, or my condolences.

The guards had stepped back a pace. They were hesitant, glancing back and forth from their king to the prisoners. Gord stared off into the dark corners of the throne room as if wishing himself anywhere but here.

Liam glared down at us from the dais, slapping the head of the royal sceptre into the palm of his left hand, as if building up the nerve to jump down and beat us with it.

The queen stood slowly and smoothed her gown. She removed the diamond-encrusted gold circlet from her brow and set it on her throne. "Enough of this foolishness, Liam. Let it go. The man never wanted to be King." She looked down, and away. "He never wanted me." She raised her chin, a defiant tilt to her head, and faced her husband. "Now give him back his daughter and let them leave. I'm going back to bed."

Liam stood still and quiet as his queen took her leave. When she was gone, he stepped down from the dais. All the fight had gone out of him as he motioned to Gord. "Get his daughter. Bring her here. My son, too."

The guard made hastily for the exit. He, at least, had believed me when I said I'd ruin the place. Liam retook his throne, and the rest of us sort of milled about, waiting, while the king sulked.

Josh nudged me in the ribs with his elbow. "You laid it on a little thick there, don't you think?"

Josh had been the one who'd found me, slowly strangling the asshole who'd hit me with his car. I'd like to think I wouldn't have killed the man had Josh not arrived, but I'm not so certain. Apparently my friends weren't either.

"Acting!" I announced, and waved my hands in a theatrical flourish.

Charlie put a hand on my shoulder for moral support, which made me feel a little better. I'm not sure what worried me more: the notion that my friends thought I might actually carry out the threats I'd made, or the sudden understanding that I really could if I wanted to.

We didn't have to wait long. Alex and Cael entered the throne room hand in hand only a few paces ahead of their escort. Alex looked none the worse for wear—not a hair out of place—although I wondered at the backpack she wore slung over her right shoulder. Just how long had she planned on staying, anyway?

Sabrina threw her arms around Alex and hugged her daughter tightly. Cael wisely waited a few paces away. "You okay, honey?" Sabrina asked her.

"I'm fine, mom. It's not like they locked me away in the dungeon or anything."

Was that snark I heard? From Alex, the Innocent?

Josh looked down at his daughter, his face expressionless, his arms crossed. "We told you to stay away from him. What were you thinking?"

Alex broke from her mother and stared defiantly up at her father. "I was thinking that I wanted to be with Cael."

Now them's fight'n words. She might be an Innocent, but Alex was a teenager, too. Not that she'd ever acted much like one. I guess she was overdue.

Josh's eyes widened and he spoke through clenched teeth as he stepped in closer to his daughter. "Do you realise the danger you've put everyone in—that you put yourself in?"

Alex rolled her eyes. "Dad, I'm *always* in danger. If it's not demons or vampires, it's trolls, or...smoke monsters. How many times in the last few months have we been *this* close to death? And that's *with* James' help."

Josh said nothing. The anger washed from his face, his arms dropped slackly to his sides. Alex was right, of course, and Josh no doubt blamed himself. He was her father, and his little girl wasn't safe. Sabrina stepped up and put her arm about her husband's waist. I don't think Josh noticed.

Alex blinked back tears. She was fighting dirty now. "I wanted to see Cael. I *love* him, so I'm not about to stop seeing him just because you and his dad are feuding. This is my life, and for all I know I could be dead tomorrow. So here I am."

Josh spoke softly now. This was not an argument anyone wanted to have, especially not here. "Liam is not just someone's dad; he's the Therian King. There's more at—"

"I don't care if he's the Mamba King," Alex interrupted her father. "You're such a hypocrite. You gave up the *throne* for mom. How's that any different?"

Josh looked at Sabrina for a moment. A saddened smile touched his lips. He turned back to his daughter and shrugged. "I got nothing."

Liam pounded his fist into the throne's armrest and bolted upright. "THAT'S IT? YOU GOT NOTHING?" He stomped his feet, his fists clenched and face red, then stood still a moment and took a deep breath to compose himself. "Well I do," he said, once his emotions were relatively under control. "I may not be able to touch your *precious* Innocent, but I can still discipline *my* son." He nodded to the guards. "Tie him to the pole. Five lashes."

Gord stepped forward, probably to appeal to the king's reason, but Liam cut him short.

"One word from you and you'll join him at the post."

I'm not up on royal protocol and all, but I'm pretty sure it's not a good idea to go flogging the prince.

Cael glared at his father, but said nothing. He stepped up to the nearest pillar, pulled his sweater up over his head, and tossed it on the floor beside him. One of the guards approached him, suddenly panicked when he realised he didn't have anything to tie the boy with.

"Don't worry about it," Cael told the man, and wrapped his arms about the pillar as if hugging it. "I won't need it.

Cael was a good looking kid; tall, broad shouldered and narrow-waisted. Athletic. His back presented a broad, unblemished canvas to the guard who stepped forward holding the lash.

The lash in this case was three long strips of leather at the end of a leather handle. *At least it's not a whip*, I thought. I mean, this would hurt—no doubt—but it wouldn't really mar the skin. Then I noticed the little metal hooks weighting the end of the lashes. That was definitely going to leave a mark, though probably not a permanent one. Shapeshifters heal pretty fast; Josh had nary a scar on him. For all I knew Cael had been through this before.

Alex tugged at her father's arm. "Dad, you can't let him do this!"

Josh looked helplessly down at his daughter, who stared at him with tear-filled eyes that would have put Puss'n Boots to shame. "I can't..."

She went rigid, as if fighting the urge to scream and hit somebody. She turned toward the rest of us, a mix of anger and pleading. "James? Charlie? *Leanne*? Won't anybody help him?"

I could stop this. I just didn't know if I should. I mean, I don't believe in this sort of thing at all, but this wasn't my culture, my country—hell, it wasn't even my world. Who was I to impose my morals or values on these people? It would be kind of like violating the Prime Directive. And still—

I almost wished Liam was the Mambo King. Then we could have settled this whole thing with a dance-off. And I'd have won, too. Honest.

The guard stepped into it, the lash cracking as it snaked out. Alex turned her face into her mother's shoulder, unable to watch. Cael flinched, but didn't cry out as it left three bloody furrows in a diagonal streak from his right shoulder to his left hip. He turned to his father, his face a mask of contempt. "Nothing you do will keep us apart. Nothing."

I was starting to see what Alex saw in him.

Liam ignored his son, and nodded to the guard, who stepped in with a second lashing. Again the boy didn't make a sound.

I felt Leanne's hand in mine. I don't know if it was because she needed the support, or she thought I did. Maybe she was just making sure I didn't go all schizo-Eternal on everyone. I doubt my expression was a pleasant thing to look upon at the moment.

The guard pulled his hand back for another go. I heard the crack of gunfire and the three lashes parted from the handle. The guard jumped about, massaging his hand, though it seems the round had only hit the handle.

Sabrina stood with the Berretta Josh had given her, the pistol pointed up at the ceiling with her other hand at her elbow in one of those "Charlie's Angel" poses. "If you think I'm going to stand by and watch while someone whips my daughter's boyfriend, you've got another thing coming."

The pride I felt for her in that moment was cut short as I felt a rumble through the soles of my feet. Leanne noticed it next. Even Liam paused in the tirade I knew was forthcoming, and looked around, wondering what the strange noise was.

Whatever it was rocketed by overhead—you could trace its path by the sound as it buzzed past the city and out over the waterfall. It seemed to be turning and coming back for another pass.

"Is that...is that a.." Josh couldn't get the words out, the thought seemed so outrageous to him.

"It sounds like a fighter jet," I said.

Even Charlie looked dazed. "In Summerland?"

At least two more screamed by overhead.

Everyone ran for the door—us, Liam, the guard—everyone. Apparently Cael's punishment could wait. I saw the boy grab up his sweater as he took Alex's hand and the two of them followed the rest of us outside. I noticed he didn't put the sweater on though. The lashes still bled, but were clotting nicely. I guess I was right about the shapeshifters' healing ability. I hoped I wasn't right that Cael had been through this before.

Everyone in the plaza looked skyward, though as yet there was nothing to see. People huddled about in small groups, a mix of awe and panic on their faces. Most of them had probably been to Darkside and back numerous times. Technology wasn't new to them. But to see it here, in Summerland?

A jet broke low over the tree-line, back across the bridge near where we had entered Summerland. It was definitely a fighter, and it screamed towards us frightening birds from the trees.

"MiG-23," Josh said. "Syrian, I think."

I took his word for it. I wouldn't know a MiG from a Sopwith Camel, but Josh knew military hardware like a connoisseur knew vintage wines.

Everyone stared up at the fighter dumbly—until it opened fire, its machine guns tearing two parallel lines up the center of the piazza—then there was running and screaming and panicking, as one might expect. Sure, it's all fun and games until someone shoots at you with twin-barrelled 23 mm autocannons.

Liam stood dumbly, his mouth moving but nothing intelligible coming out. So pretty much par for the course.

"Get everyone under cover!" I called out. "Everyone inside." The whole city was built of heavy, quarried stone. As long as everyone stayed away from the windows I didn't think the MiGs would be able to shoot through them.

Gord grabbed the king and practically dragged Liam back into the building. No matter what the guard may have thought of his charge, at least he took his duty seriously.

Josh turned to Cael. "Get my wife and daughter to safety, somewhere deep inside."

Cael didn't bother arguing, and disappeared back inside the throne room pushing Alex and Sabrina ahead of him. Sabrina looked back over her shoulder at Josh, torn between protecting her daughter and staying with her husband. The last sight I had of her was her worried expression as she mouthed "I love you," to Josh. At least I'm assuming it was Josh, or things were going to get awkward. Sabrina was smart enough to know she'd be no use out here with us. Not that we were apt to accomplish much, either.

Our little group moved to just inside the entrance to the throne room and out of the MiGs' direct line of sight. "Do those things carry anything worse than machine guns?" I asked Josh. I knew most fighters carried missiles, but those were mostly for air-to-air combat. Could you even fire them at ground targets?

Josh craned his neck to follow the flight path of two more MiGs that rocketed by overhead. Neither opened fire. "Rockets and bombs," Josh said, "mostly unguided."

Not good. How the hell had those things got here. How the hell did they work here?

"The Veil must have fallen on this side as well," Charlie answered, as if reading my mind.

I stared at him, wide-eyed and incredulous.

"The Veil works both ways," the ogre said. "It keeps the Otherworld folk from Darkside, but it also keeps the Darksiders from Summerland."

"So it keeps the magic out *there*, and the Tech out *here*."

The ogre nodded. "Without the Veil, the two worlds seem to merge somewhat."

I'd say that was an understatement. I have no idea why a trio of Syrian MiGs should show up here, but then I don't know where Syria in our world is in relation to the Therian Kingdom. Kind of close, I'm guessing, in a quantum entanglement sort of way. I can only imagine the Syrian pilots were as surprised by their appearance here as we were. One minute they're flying a bombing run over some desert target, the next thing they know they're in a low level pass over the jungle with some freaky Mayan-modern city in their sights. Why they would open fire on said city is beyond me.

Speak of the devil. The three MiGs approached in a close, triangle formation. They were still high enough that you couldn't actually hear them fire, but they strafed the city, tearing chunks of stone from the piazza and surrounding buildings as they buzzed by overhead, then banked for another pass.

"Any idea how to stop those things?" Leanne asked, looking at me when she said it.

I, in turn, looked to Josh. Hey, he was our military expert. "I'm guessing you still can't fly," he said. "So short of turning yourself into an anti-aircraft battery or a stinger missile…" He shrugged.

"If this were Lord of the Rings we'd just call the eagles," I grumbled.

"Actually, there are eagles," Leanne said as she turned to watch the MiGs bank against the backdrop of the gibbous moon. "But they won't help. They're assholes."

"Aircraft are actually quite fragile," Charlie said. "Travelling as fast as they do, any little thing that hits them has the potential to do lots of damage. Especially if you hit the intake."

"So how do you propose I hit something travelling what? Seven or eight hundred miles an hour? And three hundred feet up."

"You aim for where it's going to be," Charlie suggested.

"If anyone can do it, you can," Leanne said.

At first I thought they were all pulling my leg, but they kept staring at me expectantly. "All right, what have you got?" I asked finally.

Josh motioned to one of the guards that stood along the wall of the torch-lit corridor to the throne room behind us. The guard nodded, stepped forward, and offered me his spear.

"You're kidding, right?"

Josh shrugged. "Hey, it's a pointed stick. It's not like we're asking you to take it down armed with a banana."

I looked to Charlie and Leanne, but they were no help.

"Maybe you should find him another one in case he misses with this one," Leanne suggested.

In case I miss?

I stepped out from under the overhang of the entranceway and moved toward the center of the piazza. I didn't have to wait long. The MiGs appeared over the treetops and began their strafing run. I don't know what they hoped to accomplish. They hadn't really hit anything yet, and everyone was inside. Everyone but me, that is.

That MiG pilot must have had damn good eyes, because he saw me and opened up. I stood there holding the spear at my shoulder as rounds tore up the cobblestone in front of me. I focused on the left intake and felt time slow. I could count the tracer rounds. The other two MiGs opened up, tearing into the piazza on either side of my position. Stone chips and dust blew inwards as the line of fire drew inexorably toward me. I could see bombs under the wings, or maybe they were external fuel tanks. I fervently prayed it was fuel tanks. If they dropped a bomb…"

I closed my eyes, sensing the connection between myself and the pilot, between his life force and mine. He appeared there in my mind's eye, a bright shining light approaching rapidly, and I pulled back my arm and let loose the spear with all the strength I could imagine.

I watched it fly straight and true. It careened off the nose of the fighter and ricocheted directly into the MiG's rectangular left intake. There was a loud 'clunk' and a bright orange spume of flame shot out from behind the left engine, followed by a lot of black smoke.

"No way!" I shouted as the rest of the gang jumped up and down, whooping and laughing.

The MiG pulled up, breaking off its run as the two fighters to either side of it peeled right and left. I grinned at Josh. "Let's see Rambo do that!"

Josh tried to look unimpressed. "Didn't Stallone kill a helicopter with a motorcycle in *Expendables 2*?"

"Shaddup, you."

The MiG I hit managed to extinguish the fire in its engine and levelled out, but it didn't sound too healthy. I'd like to know how he planned to explain the damage to his superiors if and when he ever got back.

The other two MiGs circled around and looked like they were about to make another run, when suddenly they disappeared.

"The Veil must have reasserted itself," Charlie said.

Good thing, too. I mean, what are the odds I could do that again?

"We should grab the kid and get back," Leanne said, ever the voice of reason. She looked worried. I don't like it when Leanne looks worried. What she said next was enough to worry us all. "If this is happening here, I wonder what's happened back home?"

CHAPTER EIGHT

I located Sabrina and Alex using my radar se—er—lifeforce locater thingy, and we got while the getting was good. Even if we had just saved the city, we'd overstayed our welcome—at least where its king was concerned.

"Hold up, I'm coming with," Cael called out as we were halfway across the bridge leading out of the city.

We turned to wait for him. I won't say Josh looked happy at the prospect, but at least he wasn't growling any more. Alex, on the other hand, was beaming.

"What's your father have to say about all this?" Sabrina asked him as he caught up to us and took Alex's hand.

Cael shrugged, then winced. The lashes across his back were still fresh, even with his super duper shapeshifter healing abilities. "He can beat me later if he wants to. Besides, I have an appointment in the city at ten."

I looked at my watch. It was almost seven o'clock. Of course it might not be seven o'clock back home. It could be weeks or months later, or a few seconds later than when we left. Time was wonky in Summerland. I hoped the kid knew what he was talking about, though. I'd have hated to miss Christmas.

"Come on, if you're coming," Josh said, and set off toward the portal without another word.

The conversation on the way home left much to be desired. I swear Charlie snored for most of the trip, as if he sleepwalked all the way home. It must be an ogre thing. No one said anything as we made our way back through the tunnels and up and out through the Fairmont Hotel. The receptionist gave us the nod as we exited through the lobby and out onto the street.

Victoria looked little the worse for wear. I'd half expected to find it a smouldering ruin, still in flames, the brunt of a dragon attack or something. I cocked my head, listening for the telltale sound of sirens. Nothing.

"Maybe the Veil didn't fail on this side," I said.

"It's possible," Charlie answered. "No one's really certain how it works. Maybe it's compartmentalised—a sort of a fail safe feature."

We talked as we walked back to Josh's apartment. It was only 8:30, so time had shifted a bit, but not much. It had started to snow—big, heavy flakes that stuck to your eyelashes. Odds are it would be raining before noon so no White Christmas for me, which was probably just as well. Victoria only has but the one snowplough, I think, and people here just aren't used to driving in anything but torrential rain.

"Maybe the Veil failed in Syria," I offered off-handed.

Charlie brushed the snow from his matted hair. "Maybe, but I don't think so."

"Why's that?" Leanne asked, then stuck her tongue out and tried to catch one of the flakes.

Charlie pulled his patchwork jacket a little tighter about his neck. "I don't exactly have a lot of data, but I *have* sensed a pattern."

I scooped some snow off the hood of a nearby parked car and made a snowball. "Don't tell me it's all my fault again," I said, before tossing the snowball at Josh who was at least ten paces ahead of us. I missed by a mile, too. Sure, I can hit a MiG with a spear. Oh well, at least I didn't accidentally hit Sabrina.

Charlie threw me a sympathetic smile. "Not this time. Actually, it's *their* fault," he said, pointing at Alex and Cael.

Alex turned about in front of us, walking backwards. "Who, me?"

Josh and Sabrina stopped and turned at Charlie's statement.

The ogre nodded. "And Cael."

"What makes you say that?" Sabrina asked. She had her hands tucked into the pouch of her hoodie to keep warm, or maybe she was just holding onto the Berretta. Josh had his arm about her and she was snuggled in pretty close, so I'm guessing it was the warmth.

"It was something Cael said," Charlie answered. "When the king had him at the post. He said, 'No matter what you do, you won't keep us apart. Nothing will.'"

Cael frowned, but Alex had gone pale. Charlie's statement had obviously struck a chord in her.

"Every time the Veil falters, you two are about. Both of you," Charlie said, talking directly to the kids now. "As soon as something threatens to separate you…"

Alex turned red. First shocked, then embarrassed. Interesting.

"Oh my god, it is our fault!" she said, though Cael looked at her, confused. Whatever she'd done it was a safe bet that he wasn't aware of it.

"It's the witches." Alex turned and buried her face in Cael's shoulder, trying to hide from us.

Josh and Sabrina had walked back to join us. Josh wisely let Sabrina do the talking for them. "What are you talking about? You mean your friends?"

Alex turned her head slightly and brushed the hair from her right eye so that she could see to look at her parents. "It was after all that to-do at the wedding," she said as Cael's arms encircled her protectively.

"I suggest we walk and talk," I said, "Before one of us freezes to death. And by one of us I mean Sabrina."

Sabrina nodded, her teeth chattering, and we all moved in the general direction of the condo.

"I told Olie about it the morning after the wedding. I guess I was kinda upset. Anyway, you know Olie. She got this look on her face and said, 'Don't worry, we'll handle it.' Next thing I know I'm standing in the middle of a chalk drawing and the three of them are dancing around chanting and burning locks of our hair."

Cael reached up and pulled on the hair that spilled over the right side of his face. It was evident now that it was slightly shorter than the hair on his left side. I guess he'd sacrificed a lock in the name of love. Everyone was staring at him now, and he blushed under the scrutiny. "How was I supposed to know she'd give it to the Threesome?"

We all raised an eyebrow or two at that one.

Cael looked down the snow-covered sidewalk to hide his embarrassment. "That's their nickname at school. You never see one without the other two."

I, for one, thought it the better part of discretion to accept his explanation of their moniker, mostly because I tried desperately to block the alternatives from my mind. From the awkward silence that followed I'd say the rest felt the same way.

We made it to the lobby of the condo, and everyone kept what they were thinking to themselves, at least until we were safely inside.

"Anyone up for some coco?" Sabrina asked after we'd finished brushing the snow off ourselves and were comfortably seated about the living room. Everyone was, especially the way Sabrina makes it, with whipped cream and little marshmallows and...anyway.

There really weren't enough chairs for everyone, not that it mattered. Charlie sat on the floor, cross-legged near the fireplace. Josh sat in the big armchair facing the sofa, his face, well, not exactly stern, but I wouldn't call it cheerful either. More like lost in thought.

Leanne and I sat on the sofa: me on the end and her curled up next to me with my arm around her. The kids sat on the floor at our feet, facing Charlie. And Josh. They held hands, though I'm thinking it was more for support than affection. Alex fiddled nervously with a charm about her neck, an amber pendant on a braided leather chord.

"Nice necklace," I said.

"Cael gave it to me," she said, and squeezed his hand. Cael raised her hand to his lips and kissed it lightly, then dropped it like a hot potato when Josh made a show of clearing his throat.

"So when exactly did the witches perform this spell?" Charlie asked once everyone was seated comfortably, or at least had brought the fidgeting to a minimum.

Alex screwed up her face, thinking. "Eight o'clock or so?"

"Right about the time the dragon appeared," I said, and Charlie nodded. "What happened around lunch time yesterday?"

The corner's of Alex's mouth turned down, and for a second there I thought she was going to cry.

"We met at that little Tea Shop in Chinatown," Cael answered for her. "I thought maybe if Alex hung out with me and my friends…anyway, the gang gave her a pretty hard time. The Threeso—um—Alex's friends showed up right about then, so she went off with them and I went with…" Cael looked down at the floor. "I should have stayed with her, but they're my friends, and—"

"Peer pressure, we get it," I said. "Don't beat yourself up kid. It happens to the best of us."

Cael nodded, but didn't look up. He squeezed Alex's hand tighter.

Josh closed his eyes.

Sabrina entered with a tray of steaming coco mugs, and Leanne fidgeted to sit upright as she took her mug. She blew over the top of the mug to cool it, then took a sip. "So that explains what happened in Chinatown," she said, and licked at the whipped cream moustache on her upper lip.

I took a sip of my own coco, and burned my tongue. "And just when things are starting to calm down Cael's friends show up outside of the bookstore and start causing trouble again."

Charlie drank from the soup bowl Sabrina had use for his hot chocolate. It was a little awkward, and he ended up with whipped cream all over his nose, but no one had the heart to tell him. "As for what happened in Summerland, I'd say that was pretty self-explanatory."

No argument there. The room got quiet for a while as everyone pondered the implications of our discovery—and drank coco. Sabrina made herself comfy in Josh's lap. That cheered him up somewhat.

"So now that we've determined it's all Alex's fault," I said once I'd finished my coco, "What are we going to do about it?"

Alex slumped up against Cael. For the manifestation of hope in the world, she looked pretty glum.

I nudged her with my foot. "Don't worry about it, kid. The upside to it being all your fault is that at least you're cute, so you'll probably get away with it. If I did this there'd already be villagers at the door with torches and pitchforks."

That made her smile, at least a little. "Fire bad," she grunted in her best Frankenstein monster.

Leanne gave me a light kiss on the cheek, probably as a reward for being sensitive or something. She's a big believer in positive reinforcement when it comes to my training.

"So the first order of business then would be to get a hold of the girls and find out just exactly what they did, and then get them to undo it," she said.

Alex bit her lip. "That could be a problem."

Josh tried to catch Alex's eye, but she looked down at her hands. "Now what?"

"Michelle left on the seven o'clock flight this morning," Alex said without looking up. "They're spending Christmas back in Kingston with her grandparents."

"When do they get back?" Sabrina asked.

"Not until the 30th."

"Well at least we can talk to the other two. Maybe whatever they did won't require all three of them to undo," Sabrina said. She looked doubtful, though.

I had my doubts as well. I might not be as savvy as they others when it came to magic but even I knew that it must have taken a hell of a lot of power to mess with the Veil, and would probably take just as much or more to fix it. I guessed they'd need the power of three, at least.

What? Hey, I've watched *Charmed* too you know.

What really blew my mind was the Threesome had more likely as not done it accidentally.

"In the meantime," Josh said, "As much as I hate to say this, I suggest we make certain that Alex and Cael stay together. Cael, I don't think you should go home anytime soon."

Alex perked up, but Josh was a dad. She wasn't going to get off that easy. "You can stay with James and Leanne," he added, looking our way for confirmation. We both nodded, and Alex pouted, but it was just for show.

Sabrina leaned back into her husband, who wrapped his arms around her. "Is there anyway you can let your mom know you're safe here with us?" she asked. "I'd leave your dad out of this as much as possible. I don't think he's inclined to be reasonable right now."

"If ever," Josh mumbled.

"Yeah, I can get a message to her," Cael said.

"I suggest we all get some sleep, then," I said. "We've got a flight to Vancouver leaving at noon today. I figure we can skip across to the city, talk to Queen Aine about this Manannán thing, do some shopping, and be back before seven."

The girls perked up at the thought of shopping in Vancouver, even Leanne. I was afraid she'd raise a stink about seeing Aine—the two of them didn't exactly get along—but I guess a big city shopping excursion trumped awkward meetings with your mortal enemy.

"You'll be coming with," I told Cael, who shrugged. I doubt the thought of shopping held quite the same allure for him, but the thought of spending the day with Alex probably mollified it somewhat. I'd have to buy another ticket for him. I suppose I could have just given him mine and teleported, but like I said before it kind of takes the fun out of a road trip when I do it that way.

That settled, Leanne and I collected Cael and headed home. Alex held onto his hand until the very last minute, almost refusing to let go as he pulled away at the doorway.

"For crying out loud," Josh growled. "He's just going to Leanne's place; he's not off to fight the Huns. You'll see him again in a couple of hours."

Alex stuck her tongue out at her dad, then gave Cael a quick peck on the cheek before closing the door on us.

It was nine o'clock by the time we were all bundled up in the Bentley and headed for Leanne's. It had warmed up some, and the snow had already changed to rain.

"Maybe you should just drop me off downtown if I'm going to meet my appointment at ten," Cael said from the back seat.

"Do you have your driver's license?" Leanne asked.

"Yes, ma'am."

Leanne's mouth tightened at the *ma'am* part, but she let it slide. "Then why don't we take you home, get you situated first, and then you can take the car into town for your appointment,"

I watched Cael in the rear view mirror. His eyes widened at the thought of driving the Bentley.

"Ha, not a chance, kid," I said. "She barely lets *me* drive this, and I'm sleeping with her. There's a Murano in the garage. You can use that." Actually, there were several cars in the garage, as well as a few motorcycles. You know you've got it made when the least expensive ride you can offer the kid is a Murano, and a fully-loaded one at that. Apparently the kid thought the same thing because he was grinning from ear to ear.

We got him home and I showed him to his room, one of the big ones in the west wing with its own ensuite and Jacuzzi.

"This is *nice*," he said, "and that's from a kid who grew up in a palace."

I grinned. "Does your phone have a GPS in it?"

He nodded, and fished an iPhone out of his pocket.

"Remind me to give you the coordinates to get back to the kitchen before I leave." I was only half-kidding. "Make yourself comfortable. You have full run of the house. If you're hungry, eat. Don't be shy. If you eat everything, we'll buy more." I noted his distinct lack of baggage, but then he hadn't known he'd be staying with us when he left home. "I guess we'll have to pick you up some clothes when we're in Van," I said. "At least another couple of shirts and pants and whatnot, and maybe some PJs." I don't know if the kid even wore PJs. And honestly, I didn't want to know. "There's a closet in the hallway with stacks of tooth brushes, tooth paste, mouth wash and whatever. Sometimes I think Leanne is stocking up for the Apocalypse. Anyway, help yourself."

"Thanks, Mr. Decker," Cael said. He sat on the corner of the big sleigh bed, gave the mattress a test bounce, and nodded in approval.

"That's James," I said. "And if you want to live I wouldn't call Leanne "ma'am" again either, or she'll kill you and use your blood to maintain her beauty."

The poor kid didn't know whether to laugh or run screaming. I guess not everyone was aware that Leanne wasn't part vampire anymore, so as far as Cael was concerned, that last quip was a distinct possibility. I considered explaining the situation to him, then figured to hell with it. We grown ups have to find our fun where we can.

"When you're ready come on down to the kitchen. I'm sure Leanne will want to feed you while I see if I can dig up the car keys." I turned to go and give the kid time to get the feel of the place, but my curiosity got the better of me. I stopped in the wide, double doorway.

"What's the deal with Josh and your dad?"

Cael stood, pretended to examine the landscape painting on the wall. "Mr. Faye never said?"

"Not really."

He shrugged, and ran his finger over the painting in the bottom corner, looking for the artist. "It goes way back, but mostly it had to do with succession—who'd be king next. Josh was next in line, but he gave it up to be with Sabrina. Dad got it by default. He got mom that way too, I guess."

I leaned up against the door jam. "Sounds complicated."

"It is, although they never got along, even growing up." He turned from the painting to face me. "I guess that's brothers for you."

"Brothers?"

"You didn't know? Yeah, dad and Josh are brothers. Well, half-brothers anyway. Different mothers, same father."

"So why do they have different last names?"

Cael wandered into the ensuite, and whistled. When he answered, his voice echoed, making him sound almost god-like. "Therians are a matriarchal society. We take our mother's last name. The crown passes down through the female line, too. Dad and Josh were both in line for the throne—Josh first because he was older by three months—but only if he married my mom."

"And he was in love with Sabrina."

Cael stepped back into the bedroom, and nodded. "A double no no. A mortal woman. Therians are a dwindling race, and Josh is a berserker—good family, good breeding stock."

"Can a shapeshifter and a mortal have shapeshifter kids?"

"Yes, but it's rare. Whereas two Therians always have Therian offspring."

"I'm not sure, but I think Innocent trumps shapeshifter."

The boy shrugged. "Depends on who you ask, but hey, I'm not complaining. If all that had to happen to bring Alex into this world, then I'm good with it."

I turned and headed for the stairs, calling over my shoulder, "No doubt Josh would agree."

I liked the kid. I bet Josh did, too. It was probably just the "dad" thing. No boy is ever good enough for your daughter, and you probably never see your kids as all grown up despite all evidence to the contrary.

It occurred to me that if Josh and Liam were step-brothers, that made Cael and Alex cousins, or half-cousins. Second cousins? I'm sure it had occurred to the others as well, but it didn't seem to bother them. Maybe everyone was so wrapped up in the whole Josh/Liam blood-feud thing that a little matter of cousins dating didn't seem all that important. And we're talking about royal blood lines here. Royalty's been frequently known to marry among closer family ties than part-cousin, so I guess it wasn't that big a deal.

Josh never talked about his family much. I didn't even know if his parents were still alive. Sabrina neither for that matter. Or Leanne. All I knew about Charlie was that he had a sister named Rosebud somewhere. I thought about that as I rummaged through the key press in the garage looking for the keys to the Murano. It was oddly disconcerting that I knew so little about the people who had become so important in my life. I swore I'd remedy that, though in my defence you have to realise that I'd only really known them all for a few short months. The fact that I had become this close in such a short period of time still amazed me. After all, I'd always been somewhat of a loner. Like I keep saying, dying had done wonders for me.

I found the key on a black leather Murano key chain—it was pretty hard to miss, with its laser cut Nissan Murano logo engraved on a silver plate. Talk about idiot proof.

By the time I got back to the kitchen, Cael was just finishing the last bites of what had no doubt started out as a foot-long hoagie under Leanne's watchful eye. I tossed the keys to him, gave him my cell number, and he made his escape before she could convince him to have some cake, or pie, or cake *and* pie. I valiantly sacrificed myself and ate the desert for him, both of them.

"I feel for the kid," I told Leanne as I pressed my finger to the last cake crumbs on the plate, then put my finger in my mouth. "It must have been rough, growing up with that tool for a father."

Leanne nodded, and took the plate from me, no doubt rightly worried I'd lick it clean. "Rumour has it Liam isn't his real father anyway. I don't suppose that made it any easier on Cael. And from what I know, his mother isn't much better. I've met vampires with warmer hearts than hers. When it comes to her son, she might best be described as—disinterested."

"It's a miracle he turned out so well."

Leanne gave the plate a quick rinse and set it in the drying rack. "With neither parent particularity interested in his upbringing, Cael was raised by an assortment of nannies and palace guards. Good people, like Gord, who cared about him, and were obviously a much better influence on him than the king and queen would ever be."

Leanne kissed me, then left to go pack, the fact that we were only going to be in Vancouver for a day apparently irrelevant. Left alone with my thoughts, I couldn't help but wonder: If Liam wasn't Cael's father, who was?

CHAPTER NINE

We left from the Victoria Inner Harbour airport at 11:40 A.M. on a DeHavilland Twin Otter. The manifest said it could seat up to eighteen people; it didn't say anything about seating them comfortably. Two rows of seats ran down the right side of the plane with a single row running down the left. The aisle was barely wide enough to squeeze through. We probably could have saved air fare if Leanne had just sat in my lap for the trip. She practically did anyway.

The float plane was packed with passengers trying to get that last minute shopping trip in before Christmas. Leanne's luggage consisted of little more than a backpack—okay, so it was a Luis Vitton backpack, but still—which was a good thing because there really wasn't much room for storage. Our return flight was booked for 5:00 PM—the last flight of the day—so odds are the trip back would be worse, what with everyone trying to store their gift purchases.

I had a window seat. An orca spouted out near the entrance to the harbour. I bet that's something you wouldn't see flying out of Toronto International.

Leanne and I sat together near the front of the plane with Alex and Cael just behind us, and Josh and Leanne just behind them. The young guy that sat across from Leanne and I wore a rumpled suit to match his rumpled face, and smelled like cheap cigars and vomit. Probably flying home after a hard night's partying.

The crew pulled a little curtain across the entrance to the cockpit to make sure that I couldn't see the pilot sleeping, or playing Angry Birds. The flight was only about thirty minutes long. By the time we reached cruising altitude, it was time to start the descent. The water was calm today so the takeoff and landing went relatively smooth. An orca surfaced just to our left on landing and I wondered if it was the same one. The show-off probably raced us across the strait. I bet that's how killer whales get their kicks.

The rental guy handed us the keys to a metallic-black Cadillac Escalade at the terminal and we rode in comfort into the city. I felt guilty about riding in such a gas guzzler until I realised it was a hybrid, then I just felt guilty that it cost so much. It didn't seem to faze anyone else, but then again I was the only one in the car who hadn't grown up rich.

It was just a short hop to Gastown, and we dropped everyone off by the steam clock on the corner of Cambie and Water Street. Leanne and I had decided we'd visit Aine on our own. No sense subjecting the rest of the gang to the Sidhe Court. Besides, Leanne thought it might give Josh and Sabrina a chance to get to know Cael better. Sometimes I think Alex had rubbed off on her, and Leanne was just a little too optimistic. Cael would have probably agreed with me at the moment; the kid looked nervous. I saw him in the Escalade's rear vision camera as we pulled away, looking like your dog does when he realises you just tricked him and he's really going to the vet to get neutered.

Aine lived on an ocean front estate just off of Marine Drive, so we had to backtrack after dropping everyone off and take the Lions Gate Bridge over to West Vancouver. And I thought Leanne's neighbourhood was ritzy. Aine's property was extensive, with a ten-foot high stone wall running back from the beachfront and along the roadside. Thick, creeping ivy camouflaged most of the wall so that that weathered grey stone only showed through in a few places. A heavy, black wrought-iron gate reinforced with dark mahogany panels provided an effective barrier to the private drive that led up to the estate. We could just glimpse the house through the round, iron moon gate with a stylized world-tree at its center.

I pulled the Escalade up to the call box perched on a post at the gate's entrance. I didn't see a camera anywhere, but after a few minutes the call box buzzed and a male voice asked, "How may I help you?" in a tone that told me he really had no interest in helping us at all.

"James Decker to see Aine," I said, trying to sound as bored as he did.

"One moment, sir," he replied. Maybe it's just me, but I thought he sounded a tad more respectful that time. After a short pause, he added, "Come right in, sir. You can park at the main entrance. The queen will meet you in the Great Hall."

I heard the intercom click off, and the iron gates slowly slid open to the left and right like giant sliding doors. I nudged the Escalade up the stone-paved drive toward the house, although now that I could get a good look at it through the tree-lined drive it would be more accurate to call it a castle. It reminded me of Cinderella's Castle at Disney World, with its tower and turrets, gables and balconies, except this castle seemed more—functional. Functional if you were prepared for war, that is. I don't recall Cinderella's Castle sporting ballista, or arrowslits.

No matter that it was what passed for winter in the rest of Vancouver, on Aine's estate it was perpetually spring—and fall. How else might you explain the apple and cherry blossom trees in full bloom lining the drive, or the maples, oaks, and elms that dotted the rest of the grounds in resplendent fall foliage? I parked the car near the steps leading to the portcullis—that's a "latticed grille made of wood, metal or a combination of the two"—I looked it up on Wikipedia. I got out of the car and moved around to open the door for Leanne because my mom raised me right. The Escalade chirped as I remotely keyed the lock, and we walked down a short tunnel through a second portcullis to the inner courtyard.

The courtyard grounds were covered in pale, coral stone. Courtiers sat about fountains and Koi ponds on white, roman-style scroll benches under autumn-coloured shade trees. The Fae, dressed in blue, peach, green and lavender pastel, stared up at us as we passed, forcing a lull in their conversation.

"As you were," I ordered. I guess they took me at my word because they all went back to conversing. Leanne and I made a beeline for the entrance to what I hoped was the Great Hall. In all honesty I just followed her. She seemed to know where she was going, but then I guess she'd probably been here before despite her feelings for Aine. Thomas, after all, had been Aine's bard.

The Great Hall looked like something right out of a Three Musketeers movie—the good ones, with Michael York, Oliver Reed and Fay Dunaway. Everything was white and gold. White marble, white marble columns, gold filigree, gold moulding. Even the furniture was inlaid with mother-of pearl. The high, arched ceiling was adorned with painted frescoes of the Fae doing Fae things, like hunting, and dancing. There was a minstrel's gallery, and a big honking fireplace with an elaborate overmantle decorated with what I can only assume was Aine's coat of arms. At the far end of the hall was a raised dais where Aine awaited us upon her throne. There was only the one throne. If Aine had a husband or an escort, apparently he wasn't entitled.

Aine looked stunning, as usual. Photoshop perfect. Long, golden hair in loose curls cascaded gently over her shoulders. Her complexion was flawless, milky white; her eyes like blue sapphires against a field of snow; her lips cinnamon-red. She wore an ankle-length, sleeveless, arctic-blue dress with a plunging neckline that looked like it might have been airbrushed on. A stunning necklace of golden flowers offset with diamond centers—probably from the "We're Way Richer Than You Are" collection—adorned her neck, and a matching armlet entwined about her upper left arm. Apple blossoms rained lightly down about her from out of thin air. Two small Sprites flitted about her head trailing sparkling faerie dust.

She stood to greet us, or should I say me. Leanne may well as not have even been in the room.

"James, we were just talking about you."

"We?"

"Yes, dear Liam and I."

Liam stepped out from behind the throne.

I didn't have to act surprised. "What, were you hiding back there? And you didn't even give me a chance to try and find you. Here, I'll close my eyes and count to ten, and you go hide again."

Aine stepped down from the dais. "I'm sure you can guess why he's here."

I glanced at Liam's smug, hairy face. I never wanted to punch anyone so bad. "I'm hoping it's for a little manscaping, but something tells me that's not it."

"I want my boy back," Liam said tightly, with no trace of the Scots brogue he had affected.

Straight to the point. I'm guessing diplomacy was not his strong suit.

"Yeah, sorry we had to interrupt his beating," I said dryly, "but there's a little wrinkle you may not be aware of."

Aine smiled her saccharine smile. "You mean that separating Cael from the Innocent is causing the Veil to falter?"

She must have read the surprise on my face, because she added, "I am my father's daughter."

And that's why I don't play poker.

Leanne advanced on the Queen, her face pale. I hadn't seen her this white since before the demon had been burned out of her. "You understand this, and yet you aide Liam in his effort?"

Aine stepped back up to the dais and took her seat on the throne, crossing her legs daintily as she sat and smoothed the wrinkles from her dress. "Some of us do not see the tearing of the Veil as the tragedy you seem to, my dear. We did not go willingly to this Summerland after all, but had it forced upon us."

Leanne glared daggers at the queen, but said nothing. Hadn't she alluded to the very same thing last night?

Well, maybe Leanne could see Aine's point, but I couldn't—or didn't care. I wasn't Fae, and no matter how you sliced it humans were going to get the shitty end of the stick if the Veil fell. Not that Aine would care about that one way or the other. As a matter of fact, I couldn't quite figure out why she did care.

"What difference does it make to you if the Veil remains intact?" I asked. "The Sidhe travel practically at will between the worlds anyway. As it stands, all it does is keep the humans away from Summerland. Well, mostly."

The sprites flitting about Aine's head became agitated. I don't think they liked the tone I took with their mistress. "True," she said, "but it also serves to keep from us the comforts we've become accustomed to. Comforts only technology can offer."

The selfishness of the Sidhe never ceased to amaze me. "So you mean to tell me you're willing to rain down death and destruction just so the Fae can have flush toilets and big screen TVs in Summerland?"

The queen smiled sweetly. "Well, I wouldn't put it exactly that way, but…yes."

I wondered if my disgust showed on my face. I certainly hoped so. "Let's see how you feel about it when some Darksider Conglomerate strip mines Candy Mountain, or whatever you call your Sidhe holy place. And don't think this will be a cakewalk, either. This isn't the dark ages. Humans have learned a thing or two about killing. If I recall, the Fae are severely allergic to lead, and my kind have developed lots of ways to toss it about willy nilly, and at high speeds."

Aine shrugged, as if the possibility didn't concern her.

Liam plopped himself down on the edge of the dais, ignoring the frown the queen threw his way. "You could always send the girl to us," he said. "I'm sure we could use another scullery maid."

I communicated my thoughts on the matter non-verbally, using only the third finger of my right hand.

Aine pursed her lips, her eyes narrowed as if scolding two naughty schoolboys. "You could keep the boy," she said, giving up on her attempt to chastise us when she saw it had no effect. "The Veil will remain intact. Of course then the Sidhe would have to join Liam and his people in a vendetta against you and your friends. We will not stop until every last one of you is dead, and you, my dear Eternal, are confined."

It was my turn to smile now. "You're welcome to try."

Liam crossed his arms over his chest. "Of course if the Innocent were the cause of a vendetta—as she would be if we go to battle over the boy—well then, she wouldn't be the Innocent any more, would she?"

"She…wait…wha?" I said. I can be incredibly articulate at times.

Leanne clutched at my hand. "It's true, James," she said. "Even if only indirectly, Alex would be the cause of much death and destruction. The Corruption would strip her of her Innocence, and the world would be without hope for the next thousand years."

I looked around for someplace to sit down, but the only chair was up on the dais and I wasn't about to sit on Aine's lap. "So you're telling me if I hand Cael over, the Veil falls and the world goes to hell?"

Leanne nodded.

"And if I don't the Sidhe declare jihad on us, Alex stops being the Innocent, and the world goes to hell."

Leanne stared solemnly down at her feet.

"Talk about damned if you do and damned if you don't."

"You have until midnight tonight, Christmas Eve, to decide," Liam said. "If the boy's not home by then, we go to war."

We left Aine and Liam gloating in the Great Hall, and headed back to the city to find Josh, Sabrina, and the kids. I doubted Aine would be forthcoming about finding Manannán mac Lire for us after divulging her diabolical plans, so there wasn't much point in hanging around.

Truth was, this wasn't my decision to make anyway. Maybe this was something Alex should decide for herself—she was the Innocent. Who was more qualified than her to decide this sort of thing with the fate of the world hanging in the balance? Still, I couldn't help thinking—Innocent or not, she was a sixteen-year old girl. And Alex wasn't my daughter, though maybe the possible repercussions took the decision out of her parent's hands, too. Hell, who were we to choose for the world? Maybe this was something that should be brought to the Prime Minister? The President? The UN?

Screw that. I didn't trust them either. They'd probably propose some sort of Veil Tax and debate over it for years while the world crumbled around them.

Leanne held my hand as we drove back over the Lion's Gate Bridge toward the city. "We're looking at this the wrong way," she said out of the blue, as if thinking allowed. "Who says there are only the two options?"

I breathed a sigh of relief as I realised she was right. Thankfully there was someone smarter than I was working on our predicament.

"There's no reason our previous plans won't work," Leanne said. "We're just operating under a more restrictive timeline now."

More restrictive timeline? The woman should run for politics, I thought. She definitely had the talk down.

"If we can get the Threesome together and break the spell we can send Cael home—no harm, no foul," I said, and squeezed her hand. "I'm sure it's not the ideal situation as far as Alex and Cael are concerned, but they'd be no worse off than they were before all this. And Cael will be eighteen soon; after that it won't matter."

Leanne leaned her head against my shoulder. "Barring that, all we have to do is find Manannán mac Lir and convince the god to repair the Veil. So what if no one's seen him in over a thousand years."

"And we have a whole ten hours to do it in," I said, my elation at our options somewhat faltering. "How hard can it be?"

We found the gang holed up in a shoe store on Robson Street—thank you Google Maps. I even found a parking spot right outside the shoe store;

proof that Karma had blessed our quest, I hoped. Alex and Sabrina were trying on shoes while Josh and Cael sat on the low, pleather-covered benches provided. The guys were surrounded by an embarrassment of colourful shopping bags in various shades of pink, orange, and tiffany blue. Our visit to Vancouver had been a success as far as shopping went, at least.

"So, how'd it go?" Josh asked, and nodded his approval at a pair of suede, knee-high boots Sabrina was modeling in front of the mirror. "That bad, eh?" he added when I remained silent.

"Let's just say I'm afraid we're going to have to cut our little shopping trip short," I said.

"Oh, how terrible," Josh said, his ear-to-ear grin belying his words.

Cael showed no signs of elation or regret, but I think he may have already been in a coma. We'd probably have to slap the stupor out of him to get him going again. I once said there were three kinds of zombies, but I guess I forgot to mention the male shopping zombie; pretty much only good for carrying bags, and maybe a wallet.

"I'll tell you all about it once we're in the car," I said. I thought the girls might put up more of a fuss, but apparently they'd bought enough already to take the edge of their shopping habit. Leanne even managed to buy herself a pair of open-toed sling backs while I'd been talking to Josh. These girls were pros.

We got everyone loaded into the Escalade and headed back to the port. Leanne had already called ahead and changed our tickets for an earlier flight. The airline was only too happy to oblige. It seems everyone wanted the last flight of the day out, whereas the 3 A.M flight? Not so much.

We explained the situation to everyone on the ride to the harbour. Josh and Sabrina looked grim at the news. Alex burrowed herself deeper into Cael's shoulder. I could see her in the rearview mirror, her eyes misting.

Cael looked determined, his jaw locked and eyes narrow. "I'll be eighteen end of April," he said, stroking Alex's shoulder, "then nothing will keep us apart. Not the Veil. Not the threat of a Fae war. Nothing."

I believed him. I think Josh and Sabrina did too, though I'm not sure how they felt about it. Alex was only sixteen after all, though she would be seventeen in March. Whatever their feelings, they kept their mouths shut about it.

"It won't come to that," I said, catching Alex's eye in the mirror. "We'll fix the Veil, one way or another. With that threat eliminated, Aine and Liam will lose any leverage they have. You two might have to spend a couple of months apart at worst."

"Promise?" Alex whispered from the back seat.

I sighed, experiencing that sinking feeling in the pit of my stomach. That wasn't fair. How could I promise such a thing? What if I couldn't deliver? I was an Eternal, not a genie. Hell, I wasn't even a very good Eternal.

I remembered how I felt when I was sixteen, all raging emotion, everything in black and white, wonderful or horrible. Life is harsh to a teenager, all your feelings insanely amplified. Two months is forever.

Who knows what Liam might do to Cael in two months? I'd never heard him call Cael "son." It was always, "the boy." The Therian King had already proven himself a vindictive bastard.

I watched Alex's tear-stained face in the mirror, saw the way Cael stroked her hair to comfort her.

"I promise," I said.

Leanne squeezed my hand as we pulled into the harbour parking lot.

Alex relaxed and closed her eyes, as if those words from me were all that mattered. I had said it, and I would do it. Black and white.

But I was an adult, and I knew better.

CHAPTER TEN

The flight home was uneventful. Even the killer whale had abandoned us. It was decided that everyone would stay at Leanne's place—our place—until this was over. It was just easier to keep track of everyone that way, and the estate was heavily warded. More so than Josh and Sabrina's place in the city. It's not like we didn't have plenty of room—although Josh insisted on staying in the wing opposite the one Cael stayed in, or more exactly, he insisted Alex did. Once a dad...Of course if we didn't sort this all out by midnight it really wouldn't matter who stayed where. It was 5 P.M. now. We had seven hours.

Everyone but Charlie was in the kitchen. He'd insisted on eating in the library. We'd stopped and picked up Thai food on the way home, mostly because it was one of the few restaurants that was still open on Christmas Eve. I was just shovelling some sticky rice onto my plate when there was a knock at the door. "I'll get it," I called out and trooped through the house to the front door. I opened it to find Drat and Day.

"I'm back!" Drat announced. He tapped at the cigar he was smoking, dropping ash on the hardwood doorframe. "Did youze miss me?"

"We did," I said, smiling, and stepped aside to invite them in. "Well, *I* did, anyway."

Day pushed passed me, giving me the evil eye as she did so. She was still dressed in full battle armour, a spiked club hanging from her belt and her hair pulled back into a no-nonsense braid. She stopped just before stepping down into the sunken living room, scoping out the exits and looking for signs of potential threat. I hoped she didn't plan on securing the entire house before letting Drat in, or he'd be left standing out on the step for weeks.

"Is that Drat?" Sabrina called out from the kitchen.

Drat tamped out the cigar against the side of the house and shoved the stoggie into his coat pocket before Sabrina could catch him with it. "Damn, she's good. I wonder how she knew it wuz me?"

Sabrina entered the living room from the hallway carrying coffee in one of those trendy Starbucks coffee tumblers. She looked the troll up and down. "When it comes to you I have like this third sense."

"Don't youse mean sixth sense?"

Sabrina wrinkled her nose. "No, third. I'm pretty sure a sense of smell pretty much covers it." She held out her hand, fixing the troll with a no-nonsense look.

Drat rolled his eyes, dug the cigar out of his pocket, and handed it over.

"Evening, Day," Sabrina called out as she turned on her heel and headed back toward the kitchen.

"Ma'am," the troll answered, and smiled.

"Am I the only one she doesn't like?" I asked, and escorted Drat into the kitchen on the heels of his bodyguard.

Drat grinned, showing off most of his over two hundred teeth. "Yep, pretty much."

"Pull up a chair, there's plenty to go around," Leanne offered, giving both trolls a big hug.

"Don't mind if we'se do," Drat accepted for the both of them.

At least Day didn't insist on tasting all his food for poison beforehand. Come to think of it, Trolls probably considered poison a seasoning.

"So, how was the honeymoon?" Josh asked around a mouthful of Pad Thai.

"Awesome!" the troll answered, beaming. "We did it *tree* times. I even took pictures. I'll show youse all later if ya want?"

"NO!" everyone said, and all at once.

Drat shrugged, not in the least offended. "Do youse have any wine ta go wit dis?"

Josh handed the troll the bottle from the center of the table.

Drat poured a glass for Day, then took a swig straight from the bottle and belched loudly. "So, what'd I miss?"

Sabrina excused herself while Leanne filled the trolls in on our current predicament. Drat listened attentively, or as attentively as a squirrel with ADHD, which was still pretty good for him. When she was finished, Drat nodded, blinked a few times, then asked, "Are youse going ta finish dat chicken?"

Leanne smiled, and handed him the carton. "Help yourself."

I know he was paying attention. I'm pretty sure he understood the graveness of the situation, but Drat was a troll. There were few things that couldn't wait until after a good meal, and if they were that important, why, you'd just have to eat afterwards. There's an old troll saying: "It's better to die on a full stomach."

Sabrina returned, looking a little concerned. "Did you know there's a humongous spider in the bathroom? Whatever you do, Josh, don't go in there."

Josh looked unconcerned. "There's eleventy-four bathrooms in this place. I'm sure I can find a spider-free one."

Day looked up from her chicken. "Why didn't ju just keel it?"

Sabrina grabbed a few of the empty cartons from the table, and walked them to the garbage pale. "I tried smacking it with an umbrella that was drying in there."

Leanne gave her a hand clearing, a bemused look on her face. "How'd that work out for you?"

"It took it."

I laughed, which quickly became awkward when no one laughed with me. You know life has gotten strange when it dawns on you that that sort of thing is actually possible now.

Drat finished his chicken, burped again to show his appreciation, then asked, "So what do youse plan ta do about dis whole Veil mess?"

Priorities.

"I thought I'd pop back to Kingston and see if I can talk to Michelle. Meanwhile you guys can try to get a hold of Julie and Olie here. Hopefully they're at home, it being Christmas Eve and all."

"What do we do if it requires the three of them together to fix the Veil," Alex asked. She'd been pretty quiet ever since we'd returned. She hadn't eaten much, either. Cael, while no more talkative, seemed to have Drat's appetite, but then he was a growing were-boy-bear-wolf-thingy.

I looked around, hoping someone else had a bright idea. Problem was, there was no way Michelle could fly back from Kingston in time. I could teleport there no problem, but I couldn't teleport her back. It seems living things—real living things—couldn't survive the trip. I'd tried it with a couple of goldfish, and a mouse. The three of them were buried out back, under a tiny cross Alex had made for them.

Charlie entered the kitchen carrying his empty plate. "Hey, did you know there's a spider in the bathtub? I tried to rinse it down the drain, but it has this umbrella."

Everyone laughed but me this time. Damn, but I never know when they're having me on or not.

"We were just trying to figure out what to do about the Veil if it requires the Threesome here to fix it, what with Michelle in Kingston and all," Josh told Charlie. "Any ideas?"

The ogre rinsed his plate off in the sink, then placed it in the dishwasher. I realised he was making me look bad so I got up and followed suit.

"Maybe Drat could bring her back through the Ways?" Charlie

suggested.

Drat patted his pocket, looking for the cigar that was no longer there, and frowned. "It'd be tight," he said. "An hour or so dere, and da same back. If we leaves now we could jus make it in time."

Day didn't say anything, but her eyes narrowed to slits. No one had ever come right out and said it but I always had the impression that there was something dangerous about the Ways. Day's reaction further reinforced what my gut had been telling me.

Sabrina dropped the empty Thai food containers into a hefty bag and tied the bag off at the top. "Or we could just take her through the portal to Summerland in Kingston, and from there back through the one here, at the Empress," she suggested.

"Problem is even the brief time spent in Summerland could mess up her timeline here," Leanne explained. "She might arrive here ten minutes after she left, or ten days."

"Can we be excused?" Alex asked, speaking for Cael.

"Sure, just...don't go far," Josh said, and gave his daughter a quick kiss on the forehead. I'm sure what he meant to say was, "Don't go getting naked," or something to that effect, if the evil eye he fixed Cael with as they left was any indication.

Cael looked a little hesitant, but left with Alex. I got the impression that he would have preferred to stay, to be in on the planning stage. What we decided directly affected him, after all. Or maybe it was just a King-In-Training sort of thing. He'd been brought up to be a leader. He probably already knew more about leadership than I did. The fact that he didn't argue the point, but simply left with Alex once she'd decided her course of action told me he definitely knew more about women than me.

"What do we do if the Threesome can't help us? How do we find this mac Lir dude?" I asked.

"We could always try a summoning," Drat said. "What?" he added as all eyes fixed on the troll. "Hey, I has good ideas every now an den, too."

Most of the gang looked dubious. I looked to Charlie for expert advice.

"You can summon any of the Fallen, if you know their true name, and have their sigil," the ogre agreed grudgingly. "The problem here is that we don't even know if Manannán mac Lir is one of the Fallen. He may be something else entirely. He's certainly more powerful than any I've ever heard of."

Leanne shook her head. "It's nonsense anyway. You can't summon the Fallen; you can merely call them. They may appear or not, as the whim takes them."

"So it's sort of like phoning someone with call display. They might pick up, or they might just let it go straight to voice mail."

Leanne smiled. "Close enough."

"Well, it's a start anyway," I said. "I'll head to Kingston and see if I can locate Michelle. Drat and Day can take the Ways, just in case, and the rest of you can try and hunt down Julie and Ollie while Charlie works on locating mac Lir. Try the summons thingy, and if that doesn't work, try something else."

"I'm glad he said it's a start, and not a plan," Josh mumbled to Sabrina, "because as plans go it's pretty weak."

"Shaddup you," I said. He did, but only because he didn't have a better plan. No one did, and we all knew it.

I left before the others, and with little fanfare. There wasn't time. Just a kiss on the cheek from Leanne, and I was gone. I materialised in the center of the living room at her—our—manor in Kingston. I could have materialised anywhere, but it's easier if I do it someplace I'm familiar with. On arrival, however, the manor didn't seem familiar at all. I'd always thought the place creepy enough before. Now, empty and with tarps covering most of the furniture, it seemed downright sinister. Goblins waited to pounce from every dark corner and zombies clutched at me with rotting hands from under the dust covers—or so it seemed.

Man up, you big chicken, I thought. I was an Eternal, top of the food chain. What did I have to worry about?

The fact that you may not actually be top of the food chain now, are you? The thought came unbidden, as if someone else had whispered it at my shoulder. "Yeah, well close enough" I mutter to the empty room.

There were always the other Eternals to worry about. Tammy seemed friendly enough, but Azrael had caused more than enough trouble. I had yet to meet the other five, and Tammy never talked about them.

And of course there was the Fae—the Fallen. As Sidhe they were pretty powerful. Hell, they did magic! Even without the consequence of Alex loosing her Innocence, Aine's threat of war was something to take seriously. But I was pretty sure there was a lot more to them than maybe even they knew. Being Fae or Sidhe was just a manifestation of what they truly were. I'd seen Leanne in her true form when Bran's Cauldron had burned away the façade she and the rest of her kind presented to the world. The mere sight of her had seared me to ash.

And Manannán mac Lir? For all I knew he was a god, or at least had god-like powers. Even the Fae thought so.

"Bite me, creepy house," I muttered, and headed upstairs to the library. Self-doubt could wait; right now I had to find Michelle.

While the estate in Victoria boasted every technological marvel one could imagine, most of the phones in the manor didn't even have call display or speed dial. The only phone that might have Michelle's number in memory would be in the library. I suppose I should have asked Alex for it before I left.

I pulled the tarp off of the chair behind the big oak desk, and uncovered the computer while I was at it. I gave both tarps a good shake to clear them of dust, which started a sneezing fit. Luckily there was a box of Kleenex under the tarp by the computer, and I blew my nose and got down to business. The phone sat in its cradle in the charger, and I thumbed it on and flipped through its contact list. Sure enough, there was Michelle's number. I dialled, thinking it couldn't be this easy. I was right; no one answered. Worse yet, after a moment an automated message informed me that "the number you have dialled is no longer in service." Then it dawned on me. Michelle didn't live here anymore. Not everyone got to keep their home in Kingston when they moved to Victoria like Josh and Leanne had. I'd been hanging out with rich folk for too long.

Hadn't Alex said something about Michelle going back to Kingston to be with her grandma? That's where they probably were, but how was I going to find them? Hell, I didn't even know Michelle's last name, never mind her grandma's. If it was Michelle's grandma on her mother's side she wouldn't have the same last name anyway. I really hadn't thought this through, so I decided to do what I always used to when I'd messed up and didn't know what to do next.

I called Greg.

"Hey old man, what's up?" I said when he answered the phone on the seventh ring. Come to think of it, *he* probably had call display.

"Merry Christmas to you too," he said. There was something about Greg's voice—something in the inflection—that always led you to believe everything he said was a joke. You just never knew whether the joke was on you or not.

Greg was the newly appointed Chief of Detectives of the Kingston Police Force. He'd been my dad's partner when dad was killed in action, and a surrogate father to me ever since. He was probably the best detective I'd ever met. I bet he'd have given Sherlock a run for his money, but then I'm biased.

"Yeah yeah, Merry Christmas. I'm looking for Michelle's grandma; do you know where I can find her?" I asked. If I was short with him, it was because time was of the essence. I knew being the man he was Greg would figure it out, and understand.

"Sure. I've got her dossier in my office."

"You do?"

"Of course I do. Don't you?"

See, that's what I mean. Now I wasn't sure whether or not he was making fun of me, or whether he really did have her dossier. Knowing Greg, though, I'm guessing the latter. Once he'd found out what Michelle and the other girls were, he'd probably run complete background checks on the three of them. Just in case.

I hated to think what he had in his dossier on me.

"Why don't you…you know…pop in while I dig it out?" he said, confirming my suspicions. "I'm sure Maggie and Erin would love to see you."

"Sure," I said, "I'd love—," but he hung up before I could finish. That's Greg, straight to business.

I pictured Greg's front step, with its flowerpots and the bronze, antique-style wall lamps, and the big black numbers "52" on the doorframe beside the burgundy-painted, six-panel steel door. There was no glass in that door, either. It was decorative, but you wouldn't be kicking it down any time soon. All of the lower windows were covered by wrought-iron grates, too. Greg was a cop, after all, and knew how to burglar-proof his home. Or zombie-proof. Whatever.

Kingston wasn't Victoria. It had snowed here—at least a couple of feet of the stuff. It was piled up on both sides of the sidewalk leading up to the house, and in a big heap at the end of the drive. I probably would have froze to death out there on the step if I'd still been alive, and materialized a short leather jacket and plaid scarf for myself just to keep up appearances.

There were several cars parked in the driveway and on both sides of the street. Greg probably had some of his cop buddies over for a little Christmas Eve soiree. The door opened before I had the chance to knock.

Greg stood there, a drink in one hand and a folded piece of paper in the other. His hair was buzzed short and he still had that affected razor stubble look that everyone sported nowadays. It was hard to look the tough guy, though, in the garish green and red striped sweater he wore. It must have been a Christmas present from his daughter, Erin—maybe last Christmas, and probably a practical joke.

"Come on in," he said, stepping aside. "You got time for a drink? I think Maggie stashed away a few Diet Pepsis just in case you showed up."

"Sorry, no," I said and pushed past him into the vestibule.

Maggie stood at the top of the stairs, a slight, dark-haired, dark-eyed Italian cutie who could still probably pass for twenty-something even though she had to be close to fifty now. She, at least, was tastefully dressed, in a crisp, white shirt with lace cuffs and collar, and a black, knee length skirt.

She smiled her infectious smile and met me at the bottom of the staircase, throwing her arms around me in a big hug. "What do you mean you can't stay?" she said, her voice tinged with genuine disappointment.

I heard cheering coming from the den in the basement. Greg's guests were probably all playing Pictionary or Trivial Pursuit or something. Maggie let me go and stepped closer to her husband, putting her arm about his waist.

"I have to catch a nine o'clock flight back to Victoria," I lied. It was already eight o'clock in Kingston, what with the time difference and all. "There's a charter waiting for me at the airport."

"Ooh, Mr. Bigshot," she teased, but I could tell she was pleased by my apparent success. If Greg had become my surrogate father, Maggie had taken on the role of surrogate mother, and it didn't matter that I still had one of those, either.

"Leanne says hi," I said to the both of them. As far as Maggie was concerned I'd shacked up with a rich woman and helped her run her Antique Clearing House. At least the shacking up part was true. Yep, still felt like a gigolo.

Maggie frowned. "I still haven't met her yet, you know."

"You guys should come up for a visit sometime," I said. "Trust me, we have the room."

"We just might take you up on that," Greg answered for the both of them, but his smile belied the worried look in his eyes.

I understood. Greg knew what I was. Leanne too. He also knew the kind of trouble we routinely ran into. He'd helped us out of the last mess. Consorting with us was just asking for trouble. No matter what pleasantries we exchanged here, I doubted I'd see Maggie or Erin in Victoria any time soon.

Speaking of which. "Where's Erin?" I asked.

Greg shook his head, as if disappointed. "In her room, *studying*."

"On Christmas Eve?" Maybe studying was a euphemism for surfing internet porn or something.

"Yeah, sometimes I think there's something wrong with that kid," Greg said, and Maggie punched him in the arm.

"Maggie, what's the number for that pizza place again?" someone called up from downstairs.

"Coming!" Maggie answered, and stepped in for another hug and a kiss on the cheek before scurrying downstairs. "Next time drop by when you can stay longer," she called over her shoulder. "And bring Leanne."

"Yes, dear," Greg and I answered simultaneously.

Greg looked me up and down with a critical eye once Maggie had disappeared. "So, what's up?" he asked, and handed me the paper he held folded in his hand.

I opened it up and saw a name, address and phone number there. Michelle's grandma, no doubt. I'm surprised he didn't list the GPS coordinates. "You really want to know?"

"Do I?" he asked.

I didn't want to spoil his Christmas, but I probably already had. If I didn't tell him he'd just worry anyway. I took a deep breath, then gave him the reader's digest version. Greg listened, not interrupting, just taking it all in and processing it.

When I finished, he chewed on the inside of his cheek for a moment. "So this Veil only fails where the kids are, when they're separated?"

That's Greg. No wasted time. He'd skipped over the whole "this is incredulous" part; the "this can't be happening" denial that would cripple any sane person's though process, and moved directly to the comprehension/planning stage.

"So far," I said. "But it's getting worse. Last time it happened there was only the *threat* of keeping them apart."

"And you're afraid it'll become a world wide phenomenon."

I nodded.

He thought for a moment. "If it came right down to it, what do you think would be worse? A world where Darkside and Summerland overlap, or a world without hope?"

I tried to imagine the world where the supernatural was an everyday commonplace occurrence. Where magic ruled. We'd survived it once, back before Manannán had created the Veil. We humans were tough, and we didn't give up without a fight—as long as we had hope.

"A world without hope, I guess."

"Me too," he said, and put a hand on my shoulder. He pushed on the door, holding it open for me, knowing time was critical. "Just see to it you don't have to make that choice."

CHAPTER ELEVEN

Michelle's grandma lived in a little brownstone on Elm Street, a side street just off of Division Street in one of the older areas of Kingston. I had to think about how I was going to do this. After all, I couldn't just appear on her grandma's doorstep, knock on the door, and ask for Michelle. If I were her dad I know I would have had issues with some grown man with an urgent need to see my daughter on Christmas Eve—well, unless that man was Santa Claus, then maybe.

There was a church on Colborne Street a couple of blocks from her grandma's place. I'd been there for a co-worker's wedding back before I'd been downsized, and the whole Eternal thing. I teleported into the parking lot behind the church where hopefully there wouldn't be too many people yet. It was still early for midnight mass. Still, I didn't want to freak anyone out by appearing in front of them out of thin air. I thought I'd use the walk to Elm Street to come up with a plan to see Michelle, but by the time I'd arrived I still had nada.

I stood out front of the house by a barren old oak tree, just lurking, when Michelle solved my problem for me. The porch light came on and the door opened. Michelle stepped out onto the step swaddled in a thick, black wool pea coat. A long scarf was wrapped about her neck and shoulders at least twice, the ends still reaching half-way down to her knees. A big woolly toque covered her head. Black, furry earmuffs protected her ears, and matching fur-lined gloves covered her long, slender hands.

The door opened behind her again as she made her way carefully down the steps. Her father's head poked out from the doorway. "Don't forget the eggnog," he called after her.

Michelle waved him off. "Dad, I'm not a moron you know."

Her dad pursed his lips, apparently considering the validity of her statement, but decided against further rebuttal and closed the door.

I waited until Michelle left the yard and proceeded down the sidewalk, then approached her quietly from behind.

"Hey, Michelle," I called after her.

I probably should have approached her from the front where she could see me coming. I could have at least waited until she was under a well lit street lamp, I suppose, instead of in the darkened gloom of a row of pine trees that blocked out the light.

Michelle screamed, and actually jumped, her legs flailing as if she were climbing imaginary stairs. When her feet finally touched down, she spun quickly and pointed a fur-lined glove at my face. I barely got out of the way in time as a fireball exploded against the mailboxes behind me. It could have been worse, I suppose. She could have turned me into a newt.

Michelle squinted into the darkness, her gloved hand still pointed at my head, just in case. "Mr. Decker? Is that you?"

"It's me," I said, stepping into the light.

Michelle clutched her hand to her chest, no doubt trying to keep her heart in place as she tried to calm her rapid breathing. "Damn it, Mr. Decker, you're lucky I didn't turn you into a newt!"

I smiled, trying to put her at ease. "And a charbroiled one at that." The mailbox behind me was still smoking, the paint blistered and peeling.

Michelle stepped nervously from side to side. Or maybe she was just trying to keep her feet warm. "What are you doing here?" Michelle asked, once she'd caught her breath.

"You headed to the store?" I asked, and she nodded. "Come on, we'll talk as we walk."

Michelle fell into step beside me, towering over me. She was tall to start with, and the five inch heels on her winter boots put her well over six feet. Although, seriously—heels on winter boots? It's a good thing the sidewalk ploughs had been by already or I doubt she would have gotten ten feet in those things.

"It's about the spell you girls put on Alex and Cael," I told her.

Michelle tucked her hands into her pockets, gloves and all. "What about it?"

Well, at least she didn't try to deny it. "It's destroying the Veil."

Her brow knitted, puzzled.

"The one that separates Summerland from Darkside."

She looked down at her feet as she walked. I could almost see the thoughts churning in her head. "How's that possible, Mr. Decker? It was just a little spell to keep them together?"

I thought about telling her to call me James, but the girls were already a little confused about me, and perhaps a little too familiar what with me appearing as someone their own age the first time I'd met them. I decided a little distance was probably best. "Your little spell is keeping them together, all right," I said. "Whenever anything threatens to separate them, the Veil falters, merging the two sides. You can imagine the kind of havoc that's caused: a dragon spotted over Mount Baker; Big Foot sightings in China Town; vengeance spirits tearing up Government Street. Three Syrian fighter jets attacked the Therian kingdom last night."

Michelle stopped, her face pale under the waning yellow light of the street lamp. She still wouldn't look up from her feet. "We didn't mean...I mean...how..."

I thought she was going to cry. She'd probably freeze her eyes shut in this weather.

"We know you didn't mean it," I said, jamming my own hands in my pockets even though I didn't feel the cold. "But we need you to fix it. Can you do that?"

"I don't know. Maybe." She looked up at me. "Not by myself, though. It has to be the three of us."

"We figured that," I said. "Drat's on his way here to take you back to Victoria through the Ways. He should be at the Manor in about twenty minutes or so."

"You mean I have to go back now? What do I tell my parents?"

Michelle was practically still a kid. Here I was telling her to leave her friends and family behind—on Christmas Eve, no less—to run off with me and save the world. It was a lot to ask of anyone. After all, it wasn't like I was Doctor Who.

"If everything goes well, we can get you there and back in a couple of hours. You'll be back before midnight. Is there somewhere you can tell them you're going? A girlfriend's house or something?"

Michelle thought about it for a moment. She looked worried, and with good reason. I wasn't about to add to it by telling her what would happen if she failed.

"I could tell them I have to go see Beth, I suppose. She's been really depressed lately."

"Sure, if you think that would do it," I said as we arrived at the corner convenience store. I held the door open for her and a bell chimed as we entered. The kid working the counter didn't even bother to look up from the comic she was reading.

"Yeah, mom would understand," Michelle said, and stepped into the brightly lit interior. She moved between the rows of confectionary items to the coolers on the right, then rifled through the cartons of eggnog, examining them carefully for expiry date. "Mom's a volunteer suicide prevention counsellor for the base."

"This Beth, she's going to be alright, right?"

Michelle found a couple of cartons that met her standards, then grabbed a couple of bags of chips on the way to the counter. "Oh, sure," she answered. "She hooked up with Brent Taylor last week and now she's all good."

Teenage girls, seriously.

I carried Michelle's purchases for her as I walked her back to her grandma's. Michelle didn't say much on the way back, probably mentally rehearsing what she would tell her family. I handed her back the bag and waited out by the curb while Michelle went inside to put her plan into action. While I was waiting I called a cab. The Manor was too far away to walk. I glanced at my watch. If we timed it right we should arrive a few minutes before Drat and Day.

After about ten minutes the porch light came on again and Michelle appeared at the door. "I'll be back before midnight," I heard her say as she closed the door behind her. The yellow cab pulled up just as she made it to the sidewalk. She carried a plate in her hands, covered in aluminum foil. Steam rose in wisps from under the makeshift lid. I opened the door for her.

"Have a brownie," she said as she climbed in the back, offering one to the cab driver as well. "Grandma thought they'd cheer Beth up."

Grandma was probably right. I know I felt better. I think the cabbie did, too.

The cabbie dropped us off at the manor. I gave him a nice tip, and three more brownies.

We didn't have to wait long. I think Drat smelled the brownies all the way from the Other Realm and hurried faster.

I answered the knock at the door. Drat and Day stood there, an open portal shimmering at their backs. "Grab da goil, and don't ferget dem brownies," Drat said.

Michelle did as told, and we stepped through the portal into the Ways. We were only a few feet in when the opening snapped shut behind us.

The Ways looked exactly like they did the last time I'd travelled them. A narrow path, more of a mountain trail—all beaten grass dotted by the odd boulder and shrub along its route—wound its way through the darkness before and behind us as far as the eye could see. Everything else was stars, clustered in nebulas, spiralling in misty shades of pink, and lime green, purple and red. As far as I could tell there was just the one path, but to a troll, it branched off at irregular intervals, leading to only they knew where. And the gods forbid you should fall off the path, or step off, or you could be stuck falling—sideways—for all eternity. Or until you died of thirst if you were human, I guess.

"Lead on," I told the trolls.

Drat and Day walked side by side just ahead of us, with Michelle and I bringing up the rear. Day kept her hand on the worn, leather handle of the battle axe at her belt. Even Michelle noticed, and it only made her all the more nervous. The trolls chatted idly to themselves, but in low tones so Michelle couldn't hear. Good thing, too.

"She's hawt," I heard Day tell Drat. "Too tall, but I'd do her."

Drat chuckled, and turned to glance at Michelle. He grinned, aware that

I had overheard their conversation, his smile brimming with chocolate brownie-covered teeth.

I really don't know much about the sexual proclivities of the troll race, and if I had my way I never would no matter how long I lived. Maybe Day was gay, or maybe all trolls were bisexual. All I know is Drat had never made a pass at me, but it could be I just wasn't his type.

After about ten minutes, Michelle removed her coat and scarf, jamming the toque and gloves into a side pocket. The Ways seemed to be climate controlled; at a guess I'd say a balmy seventy-two degrees. I offered to carry her coat for her, and slung it over my left arm. After the cold she had just experienced in Kingston I bet even the burgundy cowl-neck sweater seemed too warm for her. She'd probably have changed her jeans in for a comfy pair of shorts right now if she could. She should have changed out of those ridicules boots, but she sauntered along at my side and never complained, so who was I to argue?

I wrinkled up my nose, distracted from my mental musings by the strong stench of rotting, wet wool and damp mud. At first I thought it was just Drat, or Day. After all, we had fed them Thai food just prior to our little outing. They both stopped short. The trolls must have smelled it too. Michelle covered her nose with her hands as the miasma overwhelmed us.

"Goblins!" Day called out, and loosened her battleaxe as Drat followed suit. I pushed Michelle between us and turned to cover our backs, sandwiching her between the trolls and myself.

Goblins are like the mob cleaners of the Otherworld, disposing of the corpses of those supernatural creatures unfortunate enough to die in Darkside. They don't need body bags, or bleach, or…chainsaws, however. They simply eat the remains. Everything, until there's not a trace left to alert the unsuspecting human populace that anything untoward had ever happened.

I could hear them wailing now, a cacophony of screams that rose and fell in pitch like the keening of a tribe of banshees.

"Dere must be a whole scourge a dem," Drat growled. "Deys only howl like dat when dey travels in a pack."

A scourge of goblins. Kind of like a murder of crows. It seemed fitting.

"I hates goblins," Day said. "Dey don't even taste good."

The ground churned in front of me as something dug its way toward the surface. A clawed hand pushed up through the earth, followed quickly by the creature's head and shoulders. The Goblin scrabbled forth, hunched on all fours, resting its knuckles on the ground. It shook itself roughly to clear its fur of sand and dirt.

Goblins shared an affinity with dogs, only in that it's hard to focus on them. Your eyes want to slide off them, as if refusing to converge on something that can't be real. What you can see of them is baleful yellow eyes and a maw of mucus-encrusted teeth amidst a hazy mass of putrid black fur and a tangle of oddly disjointed and twisted limbs.

More goblins dug their way forth on all sides of us. I could see others, their hate-filled yellow eyes glowing in the dark as they loped towards us from off the path, seemingly above and below us, and to either side. Trolls weren't they only ones who could travel the Ways, it seemed.

The one that had dug its way up in front of me hadn't attacked yet. It swayed from side to side on its haunches, occasionally keening to its brethren who answered in kind from all around us. It was bigger than the rest. The average goblin standing erect might reach a height of about 5'5" and weighed maybe a hundred pounds. This one would have topped six feet, and weighed at least two hundred.

"*Your fault*," it whispered, its voice hoarse and raspy as if not used to speaking.

I'd always thought of goblins as some sort of dumb animal, like a hyena, or a shark. It had never dawned on me that they might be intelligent. "What the hell—they talk?"

"Oh, dey talks alright," Day said. "Is jus no won leesen to dem."

The goblins surrounded us, appearing at varying heights as if we stood at the basin of a great, invisible amphitheatre.

"What do you mean, my fault?" I asked it. Hey, if there was a chance in Hades that I could talk our way out of this mess, I was willing to give it a shot.

The goblin king tilted its head, or seemed to. I still couldn't get a good look at it.

And I called it the goblin king only because it seemed to be their leader, and goblin king sounds cool. Of course for all I know it could have been the goblin queen.

"*Not you. HER*," it hissed, and jutted its jaw toward Michelle. The goblins that surrounded us keened louder in response. "*She has broken the world.*"

Drat spat on the path. "Yeah, what's it to ya, ya Sesame Street reject?"

And that's why trolls usually hire ogres to do all their diplomatic work for them. Although to be fair, the goblins did kind of remind me of Grover on crack.

"*WE HURT!*" the goblin screeched. "*No place to belong. Not here, not there. Krahata gone, like never were.*"

I glanced back at Drat. "Krahata?"

"It's what dey calls demselves," Drat said.

I think I understood. The witches had messed with the fabric of existence, the curtain separating one reality from another. The goblins were...um...reality-impaired to begin with. The Veil falling may have affected them even more profoundly. Rather than merging their worlds, some of them had simply ceased to exist.

What I found intriguing was how they had figured out it was the Threesome that had done it in the first place. And how they had tracked us here, in the Ways, of all places. And had they tracked Julie and Olie as well? Were they under attack too?

"We're taking her to fix it," I said. "The three of them together can right what they have done." At least I hoped they could, but I didn't say that out loud for obvious reasons.

The goblin stood up on its hind legs, stretched out its neck with its nose pointed high, and sniffed, as if it could smell the magic emanating from Michelle. "*We fix now. Kill, now.*"

"Dere's jus two problems wif dat," Drat said without turning to look at the goblin king. "One, kill'n da witches won't break da spell."

The goblin king sat back on all fours, the backs of its knuckles resting on the ground, and blinked, waiting for Drat to finish.

"An two," Drat gave his battle axe a practice swing. The blade cleaved the air with a whooshing sound, just like in all those bad kung fu movies. "I'd likes to see ya try."

The wailing rose on all sides. I guess Drat had insulted them. Who knew goblins would turn out to be so sensitive.

Day tapped the head of her battleaxe against the palm of her hand and stood shoulder to shoulder with her king. She didn't say anything, which was just as well. I have a hard enough time understanding Drat sometimes.

The goblin King stood again, stretching itself out to its full height and towering over the rest of us. Well, except for Michelle and those damn heels. The rest of the goblins went silent.

"*Midnight*," it said. It stood quietly, watching us for a moment as if to make sure we understood, then suddenly bounded off the path and vanished. The rest of the goblins took up their keening again, then disappeared. Their insanely malevolent eyes blinked out one by one as the sound of their wailing faded.

"Midnight?" Michelle whispered behind me once the last of them had gone.

I turned to face her. She looked scared, pale, young,—too young to be a witch. Too young to have the fate of the world on her shoulders. Still, there was no sense sugar-coating it.

"We have until midnight," I said. "After that, they come for you."

CHAPTER TWELVE

Julie and Olie were waiting at our place in Victoria when Drat opened the portal into the living room.

Leanne looked disapprovingly at the troll. "Drat, you know you should knock first," she said, which I guessed meant "No opening portals in the house."

The troll shrugged. "I figured since it wuz James' place too it wuz no biggie."

Leanne arched a brow at me.

"What she said," I told the troll. "It's a privacy thing."

I'm sure that lost Drat entirely—trolls seemed to have no comprehension of the concept of privacy whatsoever—but he nodded. "Sure, okay."

He and Day wandered off toward the kitchen. "Sheesh, it ain't like I walked in on her when she was on da toilet."

Day nodded. "I doan tink she's forgiven you for dat yet."

Michelle joined Julie and Olie on the couch. Everyone else just sort of huddled around them.

"Any trouble getting away from home?" I asked.

"Nah, we just told our parents we were going carolling," Olie said, curling her legs under her. "Easy peasy."

Now I know why they call her the smart one—besides the glasses. It sure beat the story Michelle and I had come up with. It might also explain why the two of them were wearing matching Santa outfits, you know, if Santa were a Vegas showgirl.

"So can you do it? Or... undo it?" I asked Olie. She usually did the talking for the three of them.

Olie looked back and forth at the other two girls, then up at me. She bit her lip. "We're not sure. We don't really know how we did it in the first place. It shouldn't have worked that way."

"Exactly what did you do?" Leanne asked, her left foot tapping impatiently against the hardwood floor.

Olie adjusted her black-rimmed designer glasses against the bridge of her nose. "Well, we started with a couple of effigies. I used my old Dance Club Devon doll for Alex, and a G.I. Joe I got at a yard sale for Cael."

"Did it have the kung-fu grip?" I asked.

Sabrina laughed, and did the facepalm thing. "I doubt that's relative, James."

"It is to me," I said, and tried not to sulk.

The girls looked at me oddly—even Leanne, but I bet Josh understood.

"Anyway, we tied locks of hair to the dolls to bind them, wrapped them up in an old silk scarf, and placed them in a small pentagram," Olie said, ignoring me.

Julie tucked her feet up under her and pulled down on the skirt of her Santa suit. It still only reached to about mid-thigh. "I placed some glyphs around the pentagram, and then we all sang *Tear My World Apart*, you know, by *Greeley Estates*," she added. She looked down at her hands, embarrassed to look me in the eye. The song's title said it all.

"Um…in Latin," Michelle added, almost whispering. "Olie translated."

I told you she was smart.

"Then we burned everything," Olie finished, coming full circle.

"What glyphs did you use?" Leanne asked.

Julie adjusted the Santa hat on her head and pushed a strand of strawberry red hair back behind her ear, then closed her eyes. "Um…I used the square for Cael at the left base of the pentacle, because it represents male, and a circle for Alex at the right base."

Leanne nodded. "The square also represents the physical world; the circle, the spiritual one."

Julie frowned, still with her eyes closed. "On the left arm I used an Infinity glyph for…um…forever—"

"It can also mean a balance of different forces," Leanne interrupted her.

"And on the right arm I used the arrow, for sexual attraction," Julie went on. She actually blushed when she said that last one.

"Or war," Leanne said.

"I topped the pentacle with an Anarchy glyph, to represent the whole 'do what you will' thing."

"Or…I don't know…anarchy?" I added. You didn't have to be versed in magic to figure that one out.

Julie opened her eyes. She looked as guilty, as embarrassed and ashamed as the rest of the threesome.

"The scarf they wrapped the effigies in no doubt doubled as the Veil," Sabrina added, getting in on the act.

Leanne knelt at the foot of the sofa, putting her on the same level as the girls. "There's no way you could have known," she said, all trace of the agitation she had displayed earlier gone now. "Magic has a dual nature. Any dealings in it can have unexpected consequences, especially for someone as powerful as you three. It's why we arranged to have you schooled here in the first place."

Michelle scrunched up her face. "We really didn't mean it," she said. All three girls had tears in their eyes.

"Of course not," I said, and Leanne leaned in and hugged Michelle. Soon they were all one big group hug, crying their eyes out.

I got the box of tissues from the end table beside the sofa and started handing them out. "The important thing is you're going to fix it, right?" I said once all the sniffling and nose-blowing had died down.

"Of course," Olie said, her eyes red rimmed as she reached for another tissue. "We'll do whatever we can. But we'll need a few things."

Leanne patted Olie's hand. "Make a list," she said, then stood, leaving the girls to themselves on the sofa. "We'll get you whatever you need."

The threesome nodded in unison, then huddled again, all talking at once. I couldn't make out half of what they were saying. It didn't help that they were talking in teen-speak, where every other word is some sort of texting abbreviation. I mean, WFM? FML? Less than three? They carried on like that for a couple of minutes before I realised they weren't going to finish anytime soon.

"I'm going to go check on the kids," Josh said, obviously thinking the same thing.

Alex and Cael had made themselves scarce. They hadn't even made an appearance when the Threesome had arrived. Sabrina told me that they'd gone to the library to help Charlie with his research.

Now seemed as good a time as any to check on the ogre's progress. "Hold up, I'll come with," I told Josh.

Charlie stood halfway up a ladder leaned against the stacks on the south wall. The big, hairy toes of his left foot barely squeezed between the ladder's rungs. His other foot dangled in mid-air, and he clutched at the ladder with his right hand while his left reached up for a book from a shelf just slightly out of his reach.

The ladder was on rollers that locked in place at the base. Like any self-respecting guy the ogre couldn't be bothered to climb back down to push the ladder that couple of extra required few feet, and instead risked a serious fall. Charlie must not have heard us come in, because he screamed like a little girl when I gave the lock bar a kick and pushed the ladder to the left.

"Thanks, James," he said, blushing as he easily retrieved the volume he had been reaching for, and scurried down the ladder.

Josh glanced around the library, stepping aside to get a good view down the aisles of books, and standing on his tip-toes as he scanned the upper levels. "Where's Alex?"

Charlie sat down heavily behind the desk and thumped the book down.

The ogre was tired. I could see it in his posture, the way he slouched. He blinked often, trying to moisten red, dry eyes. "They were here just a minute ago," Charlie said, flipping the book open to the index and running his finger down the listings. "I think they said something about playing *BioShock Infinite*."

"Is that some freaky new version of doctor?" I asked.

Josh shook his head. "Thankfully, no. It's a PS3 game."

"Kids," I said.

There was a big seventy-inch monster TV in the games room where we'd connected all the games consoles. "I'll just go look in on them," Josh said, and left me alone with Charlie.

I wrinkled my nose at the smell of Lemon Pledge. Charlie must have dusted the desk before he sat down. There's nothing worse than an ogre with OCD.

"I bet he's gone to make sure they're not playing doctor," I said.

"If they are, no doubt Cael will be in need of an actual one soon," Charlie mumbled without looking up from his book.

"How's the research coming?"

The ogre thumbed through a few pages, then stopped, stabbing a huge index finger down on a black and white illustration at the bottom of the page. "Got it!" he said.

"Got what?"

"They symbol for Manannán mac Lir." He rubbed at his eyes with the back of his hand, leaving them even redder than before.

I looked down at the page. Three interlocking spirals in a circle. I'd seen enough episodes of *Supernatural* to know that what I was looking at wasn't angelic script, and said as much.

Charlie leaned back in his chair, stretched his arms overhead, and yawned. "Sorry," he apologized.

"No need," I said. "You've been working too hard. You should take a nap."

"I will, and you're right, it's not script," Charlie said, effectively changing the subject. "But if Manannán is one of the Fallen, I can't figure out which. He's certainly a lot more powerful than any of the Sidhe I've met. Maybe he's not one of the Fallen at all, but an archangel, or a dominion, or even a cherubim."

"So you think maybe he's some sort of super-angel?" I asked. As if the regular kind weren't bad enough.

Charlie opened the lid on the photocopier/printer beside the monitor and slapped the book illustration-down against the glass. "Maybe. The writings refute that all the angels who came to earth were fallen; some simply '*came down from the mountain.*' Whatever that means."

He printed out a copy of the illustration and inspected it. Satisfied, he closed the lid on the copier. "It's not like any of the writings agree anyway. Judaism, Christianity, Old Testament, New Testament—they all have different versions. Some don't mention them at all. Others list their names and crimes in detail. According to the Quran they weren't angels at all because angels cannot disobey God; they were jinn."

"Can't we just ask Leanne?" I said. I still couldn't shake the image of her, burning bright when Bran's Cauldron tried to suck the life out of her. "I mean, she should at least be able to tell us what *she* is."

Charlie interlaced his fingers and stretched his arms out in front of him, cracking his huge, hairy knuckles. "Actually, she can't," he said. "The Sidhe don't remember. All they know is that they weren't always Sidhe, and that they've changed—involuntarily, I might add—over the centuries to conform to what humans thought they should be."

"Or they're lying," I said. It seemed as likely to me, given my past associations with them. Leanne was the only one of the bunch I really trusted, and I know she keeps things from me. Most likely for my own good.

The ogre closed the book and placed it on top of another stack to be put back in their proper place later. "Leanne talks about herself as being *this manifestation*, but only has a hazy recollection of ever being something else."

I shrugged. I was willing to concede that maybe even the Sidhe didn't know their true nature—for now. "So if you can't nail down who mac Lir is, then you can't find the script to summon him," I said.

"Not as one of the Fallen."

So what's that?" I asked, pointing to the copy of the illustration.

"It's a triskelion; a pre-Celtic symbol," Charlie said, tidying up the desk. "They found it in Ireland, carved in a megalithic tomb built around 3200 BC. It's what's known as a sacred triad, representing the Land, Sea and Sky; Underworld, Midrealm and Heavens; and Gods, Dead and Sidhe, at least in the Celtic culture. And get this." Charlie ran his finger along a line he had highlighted at the bottom of the page. "It is especially *the sign of Manannán mac Lir*, the God of Magic, the Lord of Journeys, Keeper of the Gates."

"Sounds good," I said. "You think we can summon him with it?"

Charlie picked up the stack of photocopied papers. "Let's hope so, because if not I don't know what to do next."

Neither of us mentioned that even if it was the correct symbol, and we did the rites perfectly, there was no assurance that mac Lir would bother to answer.

Someone hollered my name from the living room. It took me a moment to realize it was Leanne. I don't think I've ever heard her yell before. Not even when she was in imminent mortal peril. So when I heard her call from the living room it was like the room suddenly went cold. Then again, maybe I made that happen. It does, sometimes, when I'm really upset.

"JAMES, WE NEED YOU, NOW!"

I didn't bother to run, as fast as I am, but teleported to where everyone was still gathered in the living room. The threesome still sat on the couch. Everyone stood around the witches in a circle, but all eyes were on Josh.

He looked haggard. Everyone suffered from lack of sleep. Well, except me. I hadn't slept since becoming immortal. And Leanne, because apparently the Sidhe have a tougher constitution. But everyone else was dragging. Even Drat looked droopy, but of course he was worn out from his honeymoon and…no, I don't want to go there. Day seemed fresh too, but I think she was faking it. She twiddled with her braids as she watched from the doorway.

Josh held a piece of paper in his hands, a letter, by the look of it. "I found this tacked to Alex's door," he said.

I guess she hadn't been playing *BioShock* after all.

He read from the letter:

Dear Mom and Dad;
Sorry we have to put all of you through this, but Cael and I have talked this over and we think it's for the best.
I know you're trying to fix the Veil, and it's nice and all that it solves your problems, but what about us? Best case scenario is it gets fixed and Cael is sent back to his dad. You've already seen what he can expect when he gets home. And no matter what, we wouldn't be allowed to see each other again. That doesn't work for us, so we've come up with another way.
Cael and I have run away together.
Now it won't matter if you can't fix the Veil because it's safe as long as Cael and I are together, which is what we want anyway. And Cael's dad can't start a war if you don't turn him over, because you don't have him in the first place. It's not up to you. All he can do now is send people after us, and trust me, he won't find us.
I don't want you to worry about us. I know Cael will keep me safe.
I love you all.
Alex. <3<3<3

Sabrina put her arm about her husband's waist and buried her head in his shoulder. "What was she thinking?"

I think she sounded more hurt than shocked. She and Alex are close. Hardly like mother and daughter at all. More like friends. Sabrina had once told me Alex had a habit of over sharing. There were just some things that as her mother she'd rather not know, not that she would have ever told Alex that. I guess Alex hadn't told her mother everything, though. It was all just part of growing up. Sooner or later parents always become "them."

"She's thinking that she's a teenager in love, and that she wants to be with her boyfriend," I said. It all sounded a little too *Romeo and Juliet* for my liking. Not that I worried that either of them were about to commit suicide. And I had to hand it to her; their solution did solve all of our problems. Not that we'd let it stand.

"How hard can she be ta find?" Drat spoke up with his usual tact and diplomacy. "She's da freak'n Innocent. Her aura's so bright it's like starin' at a arcwelder wifout da goggles."

I was about to agree with him, when I noticed Julie raise her hand.

"You need to go to the bathroom?" I asked the witch.

"Um...no Mr. Decker," she said, squirming. "It's just that...well...I don't think she'll be that easy to spot after all."

My right eyebrow rose, almost involuntarily. "Holy shit! Did I do it? The Mr. Spock eyebrow raise?"

Leanne patted my hand. "No, dear."

"Damn! Anyway, you were saying?" I said, privately dealing with my failure.

All of the witches squirmed now.

"What did you do?" I asked them in that tone of voice that leaves no doubt that you know they've done *something*.

"Well," Julie said, and took a deep breath. "Alex was complaining that her and Cael could never really be alone. Her mom and dad watch her like a hawk, and the teachers at school, and...like, you could pop in anytime, or one of the ghosts you have watching her. So we kind of...um..."

"We made her a sort of an invisibility spell," Olie finished for her. "Except it just hides her aura."

Josh's face went dark. "Do you have any idea what kind of danger you've put her in," he said, probably more harshly than intended. At least I hoped so.

Olie stood up, not the least bit intimidated. "Actually, we probably saved her life. Maybe you can't find her right now, but neither can Cael's dad, or any of the creepy crawlies."

I was impressed. I don't know many people that have the nerve to stand up to Josh that way, especially knowing what he is. It probably would have been even more impressive if she didn't look like Hooker Santa at the moment.

Still, there was nothing to do but put her claim to the test. I closed my eyes, concentrated on Alex's aura, certain that I'd be able to locate her. Nada. There were thousands of pinpoints of light in the vicinity as I widened my search, but nothing I could identify as her, or Cael, for that matter.

"She's right," I said. "I can't find her."

"How'd you do it?" Leanne asked, quietly, trying to diffuse the situation. "How'd you make her invisible?"

It worked. Josh relaxed, and mouthed a sorry to the witch.

Olie simmered down. You could see the tension leave her body. She sat back down beside her friends. "Well, it had to be something she could turn on and off, so we tied it to something she could wear. But it had to be something she could wear so that nobody would notice."

Made sense so far. Then why the hesitation. Even Olie looked uncomfortable now, and nothing much rattled that girl.

"So we put a cloaking spell on her...um...underpants."

"Let me get this straight," I said, and paused for effect. "You gave the Innocent...Panties of Invisibility?"

Olie covered her mouth, trying to stifle a laugh, so Michelle answered for her, all wide-eyed and innocent. "Uh huh. One pair for every day of the week."

"Well at least she'll 'ave clean Panties of Invisibility if she gets in a car acceedent," Day offered.

"Will everyone just stop calling them that," Josh blurted.

I heard giggling that broke into outright laughter. Sabrina turned from her husband, wiping tears from her eyes. "Oh, come on. It's funny," she said at Josh's disapproving look. "And I think she really is safe. Sure, she's not safe here, with us, but she's safe never the less. Even James can't find her. And Alex is right. This does solve all our problems, or at least gives us some breathing space to really find a solution. Your daughter is smart, dear. Maybe smarter than we are. I'm pretty sure she's been planning this since we first told her about Liam's ultimatum."

Josh pulled his wife in closer to him, and kissed her forehead. "Why do you say that?"

Sabrina looked to the corner of the room, where the Christmas tree stood. "Because she took all her presents with her."

CHAPTER THIRTEEN

Mike towered over Alex and Cael as they stood in the cedar-chip driveway of his split-level home facing Green Timbers Park in Surrey. The Sasquatch leaned up against his flowers-and-butterfly painted Volkswagen kombi van. He'd been napping when they knocked at his door, and had answered dressed only in khaki cargo shorts and pair of humongous worn sandals.

He held the keys to the van out to Alex.

"You're sure this is all right?" she asked him.

Mike grinned, showing several large, blunted teeth. "Yeah, no problem, dudes. I'll just drive the Beamer."

The couple looked up at him, their scepticism clear.

"What? I'm an investment banker," the Sasquatch added.

Alex stepped in and wrapped her arms about the Bigfoot's waist in a hug. Her head only came up to his belly button. Mike smelled like old wood and coconut, and not like dog fur as she'd half-expected. "Thanks," she said. "But remember, you can't tell anyone we were here."

"Yeah, I know," Mike said, returning the hug as best as he could. "Fate of the world and all that."

Alex stepped back and took Mike's keys.

Mike scratched the crown of his head with big, callused fingers. "Not even the Eternal?"

"*Especially* not the Eternal," Cael said, taking Alex's hand.

Mike shrugged. "Okay." He didn't sound too certain, though.

Alex pulled the handle and slid the side panel door aside. The bulb under the yellowing plastic cover in the van's ceiling flickered on. Mike had done a nice job on the interior. A big, brown leather bench seat took up the back half of the van. It folded down into a double-sized bed if you removed the Maplewood table that sat on its chrome post just in front of it, and hid the mound that covered the kombi's engine. Along the right side of the van was a set of cupboards—also done in maple—that came up to the bottom of the van's windows. There was a small black and chrome gas burner set into the countertop, and a tiny stainless steel refrigerator just behind the passenger seat. All the windows in the back had tie-dye curtains you could pull shut for privacy.

"You have money?" Mike asked, and reached for his wallet.

"Yeah, were good, Mike," Alex said as she climbed into the driver's seat and adjusted the seat forward. Way forward.

Cael threw the bags that had accompanied them with the taxi onto the bench seat. He slung a backpack over his shoulder, slid the door closed, and walked around to the passenger seat. "I took some money out this afternoon," Cael said as he buckled up. "We've got enough for a while."

Mike hesitated, but left his wallet where it was.

Bear appeared between the kombi's bucket seats and barked in that ghost dog way of his.

Alex adjusted the rear view mirror. "Yes, Bear, I told you you could come, but you can't tell James."

Bear whined, but turned in a circle and lay down with his head on his paws in the back of the van.

"We should get going," Alex said. It was a little after nine o'clock by the old wind-up clock set in the kombi's dashboard.

Mike nodded and stepped away from the van as Alex closed the door. She pulled on the choke and pumped the gas a few times before turning the key in the ignition just like the Sasquatch had told her. The kombi sputtered a few times, but then the engine caught and settled into a quiet rumble as she eased up on the choke.

Alex waved as she backed the van out of the driveway. The last thing she saw of Mike was the Bigfoot waving back as she drove off. She rolled the passenger window up and waited for the van's heater to do its job.

Cael pulled a map from his backpack and traced their route with his finger in the dark. "You sure they can't see you?"

"Pretty sure," Alex said, not taking her eyes off the road. "I figure if they could, James would have been here by now."

Cael nodded in grudging agreement. "You still wearing your magic panties?"

Alex smiled to herself in the dark. "Just you never mind about my panties."

Cael laughed. Alex could see his teeth flash even in the van's darkened interior. "Yes, ma'am." He looked back at the map and did a few mental calculations. "The last ferry left at nine. We'll find a place to park overnight and then catch the first one in the morning at seven. We should be at the Inn by noon tomorrow."

That was the plan. They'd borrowed the van just to throw everyone off their trail. Alex had no doubt that Mike would tell her parents she'd been there. Maybe not right away, but sooner or later he'd crack. Adults were like that. Now everyone would be expecting them to be camped out on the mainland somewhere, maybe at a rest stop or campground.

Cael had booked them a room at the *Wikaninnish Inn* in Tofino. No one would be looking for them on the island now, and she'd always wanted to stay there. Cael had fake ID, and she knew she could pass for at least twenty.

Cael reached out and covered her hand on the stick shift with his. She'd watched James and Leanne drive like this, and it had always touched her. It was such an unwitting display of affection. She had to admit, she liked it. She glanced at Cael from the corner of her eye as he read the map, and inhaled slowly to hide her nervousness.

She'd had a few boyfriends before. Mundane boys. She'd even kissed a couple of them, not that her dad ever knew. She smiled to herself at the thought of what he would have done had he known. *Probably snuck into their homes in the middle of the night and appeared in front of them in full were-form standing over their beds. That and a little verbal warning ought to scare them off*, she thought.

Cael was her first real boyfriend; the first guy that knew what she was, and wasn't intimidated by it. Even the kids at Our Lady of Charity seemed somehow frightened of her, although she couldn't imagine why. Most of them were Otherworld and a lot scarier than she could ever be.

If she were honest with herself, she had to admit she liked her old school better. Sure, it couldn't teach her the things she needed to know about Summerland and the Other Realm folk, and it probably wasn't as safe, but at least there she was just another kid. She wasn't the Innocent. She had been popular there.

Now, not so much. If it weren't for the Threesome she didn't know how she would have managed. If it weren't for Cael.

He'd found her sitting out under a tree in the schoolyard during a spare they shared in the afternoon schedule. Alex had her ukulele from music class and was practicing Mr. Sinha's assignment—Bobby Ferrin's *Don't Worry Be Happy Happy*. She was just starting in on the second verse when she heard a sweet baritone voice ring out seemingly from out of thin air.

"Here's a little song I wrote. You might want to learn it note for note." Cael walked around from behind the tree, looking like Jared Padalecki—but not like Sam Winchester. More like back when he was Dean on *Gilmore Girls*, with his long hair spilling into his eyes and a big smile plastered to his face.

Alex smiled back, then fixed him with a glance that dared him to keep singing as she strummed the next chords.

He'd taken her up on the dare, and she'd harmonized with him on the second verse. He'd even done the whistling part. They'd sounded pretty good if she said so herself, or if the scattered applause from those in earshot was any indication.

They'd sat together cross-legged under the tree after that, and talked.

And then every day following. She'd told him all about being the Innocent, and about Aeshma, and Azrael, and her mom and dad, and James and the whole gang. And he'd told her about who he was, and his family, and some of the things he'd told her made her cry.

That's when I fell in love with him, she thought. Because he had such a sad life, yet he was so sweet, and kind, and funny. And cute.

She felt bad about feeling sorry for herself. She, a spoiled rich kid, growing up with dance lessons, piano recitals, and trips to Disney World. No matter what happened to her, at least she had family that loved her. And by family she meant all of them. James and Leanne, Drat and Charlie, the ghosts, Bear. She felt a sad twinge at the thought of Thomas, and Alison. She hadn't known them very well, but she'd liked them.

"We're almost there," Cael said, interrupting her reverie. "Just make a left up here."

Alex saw the street he pointed to and turned into the lane for the underground parking garage. She stopped at the yellow and black striped gate, took the ticket from the automated teller, and drove through when the gate raised. She followed the lane down a couple of levels and backed into a spot near the rear of the garage. This time of night, and it being Christmas Eve, there were lots of empty spaces. She shut down the engine and glanced over at Cael.

This was the part she was really nervous about. Being alone with him. All night. Sharing the pull-out bed. Sure, they'd made out before. She'd even let him put his hands up under her shirt. But it was one thing when you were worried that someone might walk in on you at any moment, or appear out of thin air. It was one thing when you knew you had to leave and get home. It was another thing entirely to know that you'd be spending the night—all night—in the same bed.

She glanced over at Cael in the passenger seat, his face half lit by the garage's sparse, too-white fluorescent bulbs. Was she imagining it, or did he look nervous, too?

"I'll get things ready in the back," he said finally, and stood, hunching low and moving between the kombi's bucket seats to the back of the van. She heard him fussing with the table, storing the top on the counter.

Alex knew Cael had been with girls before. One of them—Kim something-or-other—had made it perfectly clear that she'd slept with Alex's new boyfriend, and would do it again if she had the chance. She smiled in spite of herself at the Threesome's reaction to the news. Olie had cast a spell on Kim—more of a curse, if she was being honest with herself—a kind of reverse glamour so that every time she looked in the mirror she saw her face covered in acne, her hair falling out, and her teeth turning brown. Kim had stayed far away from Alex, Cael, and especially the witches after that.

Alex watched Cael retrieve the blankets from one of the cupboard drawers. She had never been with anyone before, and Cael knew it. He hadn't pressured her either, which was another reason she loved him. But she knew he wanted to.

And so did she. Physically she did. Damn, did she ever. Mentally? It scared the hell out of her. More so than Aeshma had.

Anyway, she'd be damned if her first time was going to be in the back of a Volkswagen kombi. Sure, it was kind of romantic to be on the run and all, but still. What had her really worried, though, was what excuse was she going to use when they got to the *Wikaninnish Inn*? It had to be one of the most romantic places on Earth, in either realm, looking out over the ocean, with a fireplace and Jacuzzi, and room service. What excuse could she offer? How would she stop herself? Why should she?

Bear growled suddenly, his eyes red, his shape all shadow-spikey. Something rocked the van violently from side to side.

Alex smashed her left shoulder into the door and grabbed the steering wheel to keep from being thrown to the right. Cael wasn't so lucky, and hit his head on the side panel door handle before careening to the right and into the kombi's cabinets.

Bear disappeared through the side of the van, snarling. Something howled in agony. Alex was sure it wasn't bear. *Good dog*, she thought, and tried to get a glimpse of whatever it was in the side-view mirror.

"Hold on," she told Cael, who had managed to crawl up onto the bench seat in the back. "I'm getting us out of here." She turned the key and cranked the gas, then slammed the gear shift in reverse as the kombi coughed to life. She cranked the wheel to the left and felt the thud as the back of the van came into contact with something less solid than one of the garage's musty, concrete pillars, but certainly more solid than any living being had a right to be.

Shadows flitted across the hood of the van and across its roof and blotted out the pitiful garage lighting, creating a strobe effect.

"Goblins." Cael said, as if the word were a curse, and pulled his shirt off over his head. "I got this."

Alex watched him in the rear view mirror. She had never seen him morph before. She wondered if she should avert her eyes, then realised she had more pressing concerns as the van rocked again and she fought with the stick shift trying to find first.

She could hear Bear snarling, saw his red eyes flash past in the darkness as several goblins retreated from the dog's relentless attack.

The van rocked back and forth again. Whatever was behind it shoved it forward a good three feet, even though Alex stomped on the brake.

A goblin couldn't do that; they're not big enough, she thought as the gears ground and she frantically pumped the clutch. *There's got to be something else out there with them.*

Cael must have found the handle because she heard the side door slide open. She caught the barest glimpse of brownish-red fur as his image flashed past in her rear view mirror, then felt a moment of elation as the stick shift slipped neatly into gear.

Alex stomped the gas peddle into the floor and the van lurched ahead. "Get back in here!" she hollered after Cael. Whatever was out there, she was pretty sure it couldn't out run the kombi. Well, reasonably sure. Maybe.

"Son of a—" she heard the beginning of Cael's curse, but something choked it off. She glanced into the side view mirror. What she saw turned her cold.

Cael was in full were-form—part bear, part wolf, part man—a slightly smaller version of her father when he changed. Something held him aloft, his feet dangling several inches off the ground as he pounded ineffectually at the fingers clutched about his throat.

The semblance of a man, massive and misshapen, and formed out of wet sand or clay, stood at least seven feet tall at the rear of the van. He looked like something a deranged beach artist might have made, some sandman from a childhood nightmare, all bulky and asymmetrical. Its head jutted forward on a short, thick neck, its blocky face devoid of features save for a rune inscribed across its forehead. Its arms were too large for its body, long and thick with the fingers of its left malformed hand brushing the pavement even though it stood erect.

Golem, she thought. She recognised it from a picture Mr. Sinha had shown her in history class. But who would send a golem after them? Definitely not the goblins. There was no way they had the power, the know-how, or the will to build one. And hadn't Mr. Sinha said something about how only a very holy man could conjure a golem?

At the moment she didn't care if Ghandi himself had called it forth; it had her boyfriend by the throat.

Bear kept the goblins busy, tearing into them with shadowy teeth, but the ghost dog seemed to have no effect on the golem. Alex understood why as Cael clawed at the construct's massive forearm, leaving deep scars along its length that quickly filled in and smoothed over as if they never were. Cael kicked out, planting the heels of both feet against the golem's colossal chest. The golem let go, and Cael dropped to the ground.

"Get in the van!" Alex shouted.

Cael dove through the side door and Alex floored the gas pedal. The kombi lurched ahead, then stopped as the rear end was lifted off the ground. The kombi's engine squealed as the tires spun without friction, and Alex let off the gas.

A goblin appeared in front of the van, much larger than the rest. It did its best to stand upright, but the stance was unnatural for it and only made it look all the more grotesque. Bear stood between it and the van, panting, his head hung low.

I guess even ghost dogs get winded, Alex thought.

Goblins surrounded them on all sides now. The large one motioned for them to get out of the van. "*Come, if you want to live*," it said. Its voice was hoarse, as if it were unused to speaking.

Alex looked to Cael. He was back in human form, and rubbed at the welts about his throat.

"It could have killed me," he said. "When I kicked out. It was strong enough to hold on—I felt it. But it would have crushed my throat. It chose to let me go."

She saw something in Cael's eyes, recognised it as failure. He thought he had let her down, that he couldn't protect her.

"There's nothing you could have done," she said, and took his hand. "There's nothing anyone could have done." *Well, maybe James*, she thought, but kept it to herself. That wasn't Cael's fault. This had been all her idea and she had chosen to keep James out of the loop. If anything, she had failed Cael.

The golem moved around to the front of the van and stood by the large goblin. They seemed to be in no hurry, and waited patiently for the two of them to exit.

Alex shrugged. What was the point in fighting? She knew when she had lost. She nodded to Cael, and the both stepped out.

She moved forward and placed her hand on Bear's neck, scratching him behind the ears. The dog whined. "Bear, go find James," she said. "Go get help."

Cael shook his head. "He's a ghost dog, not Lassie."

Bear vanished, but she knew Cael was right. It would do no good. Even if Bear could make James understand, by the time he arrived she and Cael would be gone, and James still couldn't lock onto her.

A portal opened in the garage wall behind the large goblin. She had always wondered how goblins travelled. Apparently they used the Ways, just like the trolls.

The goblin leader approached. It stopped, its face mere inches from Alex's. It reached out suddenly and tore the amber pendant Cael had given her from around her neck. The beast snorted, and tossed the pendant to the ground contemptuously before it dropped to all fours, then stepped through the portal. It didn't look back to see that she and Cael followed. There was no need.

Alex stared at the pendant on the pavement. Her lip trembled, and she sniffed back tears. Cael had given it to her, his first present. His mother had given it to him when he was only three.

Cael took her hand, and squeezed it lightly. "It's okay," he said. "It's only a necklace." He put an arm about her shoulder guided her through the portal.

The sadness she felt at the loss of the necklace was replaced by a sense of stifling unease. If this was the Ways, it was different than any she had known. The sky was black, starless—a void. Alex could barely make out the path. She felt the golem at her back, blocking out what little light still filtered through from the garage. The portal shut behind them leaving them in utter darkness, alone save for the goblins, and the golem.

CHAPTER FOURTEEN

We all gathered outside on the stone tile patio beside the pool. Except for Charlie. Leanne had sent him to bed. The ogre had protested right up until his giant head hit the giant pillow we'd had made for him. He struggled briefly against the nap attack, and lost.

The Threesome stood in the center of a pentagram they'd drawn in chalk. It was chilly—the wind whipped across the strait carrying the scent of salt air and seaweed. The girls were wrapped warmly in borrowed fleece windbreakers and yoga pants from Leanne's closet. Olie shivered violently, her lips blue and her fingers tucked into the sleeves of her jacket, but then she was the thinnest of the three. Not that any of them weighed more than 115 pounds soaking wet.

"We still need the dolls—for the effigies," Julie said, and wiped at her runny nose with the back of her hand. "Um...they kind of have to be the same type of dolls."

"You mean a Barbie and a G.I. Joe?" I asked.

"Dance Club Devon," Julie corrected me.

Where in the world were we going to come up with those, at this time of night, on Christmas Eve?

"There's an antiques and collectable shop just off Ford Street," Leanne said. "They have a huge inventory of dolls from the seventies and eighties. Maybe they'd have some."

"I'll gets 'em," Drat offered. "Just toss me da keys to da Bentley."

I gave the troll a look that told him what the odds of that happening were. "You can't even see over the dashboard."

"I'll steer, an Day can work da pedals."

"Um...no."

Drat shrugged. "Eh, it was worth a shot. Probably just as well. I couldn't tell dem dolls apart anyway."

"Really?"

"Uh huh. Youse all look alike to me. I wouldn't know youse from Leanne if it wasn't for youse smelled different. "

"I'll go," I volunteered as I let Drat's revelation sink in. I could just

114

teleport. It'd be faster that way.

"Speaking of Leanne, where'd she get to?" I wondered aloud. She'd been right here a second ago.

"She's going through Cael's room to see if he left anything behind—like a few strands of hair," Sabrina said, her hands tucked into her armpits while she rocked back and forth from heel to toe.

Odds were Leanne would find plenty. The kid had a lot of hair, not that I'm jealous. Oh, maybe before I became an Eternal, but now I could have as much hair as I wanted to, and...where was I again?

Right, the antique shop. I took a moment to Google the exact location on my phone. "Be right back," I said, and appeared in the alley just outside the store. No sense popping inside on the odd chance that someone was working late on Christmas Eve.

I needn't have worried. The interior of the store was dark. Not even a safety light left on. I looked around to make sure no one had seen me, then teleported inside. The room smelled musty, lined with cheap wooden shelves that reached almost to the ceiling and were packed so close together that I had to turn sideways to move between some of them. The old hardwood floor creaked as I passed shelf after shelf stocked full of old ornaments, china, Ninja Turtle collectables, radios, Hello Kitty stuff, cameras, and finally, Barbie. There, about a third of the way down the shelf, I found not one but three Dance Club Devon dolls. I picked out the best one in the dark and began my search for G.I. Joe. Joe was even easier to find, and I grabbed one from a stockpile of Joes—one of the ones with the Kung-fu Grip—and left fifty dollars beside the register before teleporting home. The dolls weren't exactly in mint-still-in-the-box condition, and I never thought to read the tags wrapped around their feet until I got home. Seems I slightly over-paid.

"Got 'em," I told everyone after teleporting out near the pool and making my way to the others on the patio.

"Awesome," Olie said, and took the dolls from me. Leanne handed the witch the strands of hair she'd managed to find. Olie's hands shook from the cold even though someone had lit the patio heaters while I'd been gone, warming the area considerably. I thought the hair was going to slip through her fingers and get caught on the wind. It would probably end up in Portland before it touched down again. Olie managed to hang onto it though, and wrapped a few strands around each doll, and then a couple of strands around both to bind them together.

"We still need a scarf," Julie said.

"I've got one," Leanne said, and handed her a silk scarf, midnight blue and patterned with tiny gold suns, moons, and stars.

Julie wrapped the dolls Olie held out for her up in it. "Perfect! Um...does anyone have any lighter fluid?"

"Just a sec," I said. "I think there's still some charcoal starter fluid for the barbecue around here somewhere." I'd bought some for the charcoal grill we hardly ever used; the big natural gas monstrosity we had was just too convenient. I searched futilely for a few seconds before Leanne "tsked" and found it in the cupboards under the in-counter grill—exactly where one might expect to find lighter fluid, but certainly not where *I* left it. Women.

"Ready?" Olie asked hesitantly, once all the ingredients were together.

Everyone nodded, but no one said anything.

"There's something I don't get," I said. "How is doing the exact same spell going to reverse the original one?"

"Well, it's not exactly the same," Olie said. The Threesome stepped into the pentagram and formed a triangle in the center as they all held hands. "The first spell was performed during a waxing moon; the moon is waning now. The colour of the pentagram is different. The first time it was red, 'cause that's the only chalk we had. Maybe not he best choice of colour, in hindsight. Anyway, this pentagram is white—a more pure colour. That, and we're going to do a different chant. Trust me, it'll work."

"The trappings aren't as important as the intent," Leanne whispered, not wanting to interrupt the girls. "They serve as more of a focus."

Made sense, I guess. I'd read a lot of spell books recently, and for the most part no two spells were alike from book to book. Oh, there were certain things they agreed on, like what the different colours represented, and what the various phases of the moon meant. Red symbolized action, confidence, courage, vitality. The waxing moon was good for bringing things to you; the waning for pushing things away. That sort of thing. But when it came right down to the nitty-gritty mechanics of the spell no two books were alike. Each spell was personal; unique.

"Just one thing bothers me about all this," I told Leanne as the Threesome placed the dolls in the center of the pentagram.

"Only one?"

"Okay, seven. But what's bothering me right now is that if the intent of the spell is what is really important, then how did the first spell go so wrong?"

Leanne took hold of my hand. "That's magic for you. The universe has a tendency to take you literally. And sometimes it gives you what you want, not what you ask for."

That's the double-edged nature of magic, I guess. The "be careful what you wish for" aspect of it. I thought about what Leanne was. Whether she was a fallen angel or not, or whatever else she might be, she was also the Lhiannan-Sidhe. Her gift was that she brought inspiration to those she loved. Thomas the Rhymer owed much of his vaunted gifts of music and prophecy to her. That magic had been twisted when the Korrigan had taken her and made her vampire, so that while she inspired, she also fed off the life force of her lovers, aging them prematurely. Now that she was no longer a vampire, had her gift had returned to its true, pure form? If it had, I don't think it worked on me. Like I said, double edged.

"And sometimes the universe is just a bitch," I said. Leanne squeezed my hand in agreement.

The Threesome began to chant, in Latin. If I didn't know better I'd swear they were singing Captain and Tennille's "*Love Will Keep Us Together.*" These three were way too young to remember that one, though, unless someone had recently done a death-metal hip-hop grunge rap cover of it that I didn't know about.

I couldn't tell if it was working or not. How would we know? Would a big bell sound, like a microwave timer letting you know it's done? About the only thing I did notice was that the wind had really picked up. And it didn't seem to be blowing at us from any one direction any more. It circled *around* us. Lightning flashed across the strait, over Mount Baker. Thunder rumbled in its wake. Even in Victoria where winter means rain and lots of it, that was unusual.

"IS THIS SUPPOSED TO BE HAPPENING?" I hollered over the maelstrom.

"I DON'T KNOW," Leanne yelled back. "I DON'T THINK SO."

The ocean was choppy, the waves crashing against the break wall only thirty feet away and dousing us in wet spray.

The threesome stopped chanting. They held hands in the center of the pentagram and looked confused. "SOMETHING'S NOT RIGHT," Olie yelled, her words almost lost in the din of wind and thunder. I as much read her lips as heard her voice. "IT SHOULD BE WORKING, BUT IT'S AS IF SOMETHING IS…FIGHTING US."

I winced in pain. Leanne held my hand, her grip crushing in intensity. Her eyes were closed, her face pale as the wind whipped her long black hair about so that it seemed alive.

"SHE'S RIGHT," Leanne yelled, barely audible though she stood by my side. "WHATEVER IT IS, IT'S MORE POWERFUL THAN ANYTHING I'VE EVER SEEN BEFORE."

Lightning seared the sky overhead. The Threesome screamed as a bolt struck the patio. It forked down through the night sky and incinerated the dolls at the center of the pentagram. The concussive blast hurtled the witches in opposite directions. I caught Michelle as she slammed into me; Julie careened through a pile of deck chairs before coming up hard against the rail; Olie was tossed like a rag doll clear of the patio and into the swelling ocean.

"I got her!" Josh called, kicking off his shoes before taking a running dive across the patio and up and over the rail. Sabrina stood with her hands covering her mouth and watched her husband swim out to where Olie floated face down in the tossing waves. He got an arm around her, pulling her face up in the water, and swam strongly for shore.

Michelle blinked up at me as I cradled her in my arms, her pupils' mere pinpricks.

"You Okay?" I asked.

"I think so," she said, but didn't move.

"You look okay." No limbs bent at impossible angles, no blood or scorch marks that I could see.

"Dis one's fine!" Drat called out from where he and Day had run to check on Julie. "At least she don't smell dead."

She didn't look dead, either, by the way Day was helping Julie to her feet. Dead people tend not to move around much. Well, most dead people.

The wind had died down and the rain stopped as Josh climbed over the rail carrying Olie. She lay limp in his arms, and he laid her gently down on the patio table as Sabrina rushed out from the house carrying blankets. "She's still breathing," Josh said, ignoring the blanket his wife offered him.

Sabrina covered up the unconscious girl, partly to protect her from the cold, and partly because soaking the Stripper Santa suit the witch wore had made it positively indecent—er.

Olie bolted upright, eyes wide open. "MOTHER FU—"

"Let's get everyone inside," Leanne interrupted the girl, and pulled the blanket tighter about Olie's shoulders. "No sense freezing to death out here."

Or standing about waiting to be struck by another bolt from the heavens, I thought. Though by the time we collected up everyone and got indoors there was nary a cloud in the sky.

We took a few minutes to verify that the Threesome were really alright. Julie seemed to have gotten the worst of it, slamming up against the rail the way she had, but other than a few bruises she seemed none the worse for wear. Olie was jittery, super-charged, but otherwise okay. Not even a burn mark. Leanne took her upstairs to find the girl some dry clothes, while Michelle sat on the couch and held Julie's hand. Both girls looked even more frightened than they had before the failed ritual.

Sabrina came downstairs with some dry clothes and a towel for her husband. You'd never know the ocean was just this close to being one big slushie the way Josh stood there stoically dripping salt water all over the hardwood floor. Josh excused himself and left to change, returning shortly in a pair of navy sweats.

Leanne and Olie sauntered down the stairs about thirty minutes later; Olie had taken the time for a hot shower, and had done her hair and makeup.

"Can anyone tell me what just happened," I asked once everyone was settled, drinking tea and hot chocolate, and a whisky on the rocks for Josh cause he's a manly man.

"It didn't work," Olie said, staring off into space. I think maybe she was still in shock, literally. She still smelled faintly of ozone.

Michelle huddled herself around a steaming cup of tea. "It's not that it didn't work, it's more like something stopped it from working."

"Something, or someone?" I asked.

"Someone," the Threesome replied in unison.

"I agree," Leanne said from behind me, and put her arms about my waist—probably to stop me from pacing. "I definitely felt a presence, though I couldn't tell you whose." She pressed in close to me, and not just because I was generating heat like a furnace at the moment. "I'm certain of one thing, though. It's not one of the Fae. Not even Aine is that powerful."

"So if it's not Aine, then who Spielberged us?" Michelle asked.

I didn't have time to answer—or figure out what she was talking about. Bear appeared in front of me, barking in frequencies that only ghost dogs could muster, and fading in and out through at least a few different planes of existence. "What's wrong, boy? Is little Timmy trapped down the well?"

He barked again, shattering Julie's teacup, and grabbed at my shirt sleeve.

"Alright, already. Lead the way," I told him, and he vanished, covering my sleeve in ghost-dog ecto-slobber.

I shrugged at the others. "I'll be right back," I said, and followed the dog, closing my eyes and picturing him mentally. It doesn't always work. Normally I have to picture a location, and one I already know at that. Sometimes I can picture a person and appear where they are. Sometimes I only appear at the place where I have the strongest memory of them. Sometimes nothing happens at all. It tends to work better with people I have a strong connection with.

I materialized in an underground parking garage, beside a Volkswagen van. I recognised that Van; it belonged to Leanne's hippy Bigfoot friend, Mike. The van was backed out into the laneway and all the doors were opened. The rancid scent of goblins assailed me.

Bear barked excitedly.

"What is it, buddy? Did the goblins get Mike?"

Bear growled. I took that as a no.

I frowned, and scented the air. My nose was pretty good now that I was dead. Not as good as Josh's, but still. I picked up a musty smell, a mix of sandalwood and coconut. Mike's scent, but faint. He hadn't been here recently. Someone else had driven his van. There was another scent, almost as strong as the goblin reek; like wet sand, maybe a little swampy. I couldn't place it, but I knew the scent they masked. A faint aroma of orange body wash, the citrus smell of shampoo, a touch of *Eternity* perfume. "Alex."

Bear whined, confirming my suspicion. I followed the scent, hoping she and Cael were still here, but it died abruptly at the south wall. My stomach churned at the thought of Alex with the goblins. They had issued an ultimatum. Had they jumped the gun on the deadline? I inhaled, searching for even the faintest whiff of blood, and found none.

I didn't know what had happened here, but I was pretty sure they hadn't killed her—yet. What I did know was that I wasn't smart enough to figure this out on my own, or to come up with a plan to get them back. Like I always said, I'm not the brains of the outfit, and I'm smart enough to know it.

I checked my phone for my current location. Its GPS isn't the most accurate, especially in an underground garage, but then it doesn't have to be. How many underground garages could there be within the block or so it might have been off? Sure enough, there it was, listed with a yellow pointer about a building or two from where the GPS said I was.

"Come on, Bear, let's get the others," I said.

Everyone looked to me expectantly as I teleported into the living room, curious as to where Bear had led me. How was I supposed to break this news to them?

"Is everything okay?" Sabrina asked, her face taking on the same worried expression I probably wore.

I hesitated, but looked her in the eye when I answered. No sense beating around the bush. "I'm not sure. I think the kids have been captured."

Josh stood so abruptly the loveseat he'd been sitting in skidded back on the hardwood floor a couple of feet, even with Sabrina still on it. "I'll kill that bastard! If Liam—"

"I don't think it was Liam, or Aine either," I said quietly.

Josh scowled. His canines appeared, sharp and glistening. "We'll if Liam didn't take them…"

"I think it was the goblins, and something…else."

Sabrina stared up at me from the love seat, her arms wrapped about her knees as she hugged them to her chest. "What the hell do you mean, something else? Christ, James, what have you gotten her mixed up in now?"

I looked away from her, stared at the Christmas tree. I watched the lights blink on and off for a second. "I don't know. But I'll get them back. I promise."

Sabrina was on her feet now. "You sure? You'll save her? Like you saved Alison, and Thomas?"

"*Sabrina!*" Josh reached out for his wife, but she pulled away from him. Everyone else in the room was silent. A few held their breath.

I turned away from the tree, back toward the couple. Sabrina's face was pale, her eyes red and brimming with tears. She looked horrified, shocked at what she'd said, even if it was the truth.

"I'm sorry, James," she said quickly, stumbling over the words. "I didn't mean it. I'm just worried, and none of us has slept and…you know it's not your fault, right? No one here blames you."

I smiled, and took her hand. "Of course," I lied. "You're just overwrought. What's important now is we figure out who took them, and where."

Sabrina wasn't going to let me get off that easy. She stood, and wrapped her arms around me in a hug, sobbing softly into my shoulder. "I'm sorry. Really, I'm so sorry."

I hugged her back. "It's okay," I told her. I closed my eyes, relishing the darkness, letting the nothingness of it swirl around me. I let all the negative emotion drain from my body, diluted by the abyss, and opened my eyes. It still hurt, but I could fake it now.

"Now cut it out," I said, forcing my usual irreverent tone. "If you make me cry, Josh here will have no choice but to revoke my standing in the He-man Woman Haters Club."

Sabrina pulled away, and wiped at her eyes with her sleeve. "You're an idiot."

"Yes, but he's our idiot," Leanne corrected her. It was her turn to hug me now.

"This is nice and all," I said finally, kissing Leanne on the forehead, "but we don't have time to worry about hurt feelings."

Everything's normal, I told myself. If I act like everything's normal, then soon everyone else will pretend everything's normal. Pretend long enough, and presto, eventually everything is normal. And yes, this is the way it works for guys.

"We need to find the kids." I turned to look at the Threesome where they sat on the sofa. "And we need to get them home for Christmas." It was just after ten o'clock. "Drat, if you leave now, you can get Michelle back before midnight."

'Uh uh, no ways," the Troll said. "I ain't goin nowheres. Day can takes her."

"But boss," Day began.

"No buts. It's a order," Drat said.

Day snapped to attention and clasped her fist to her chest in a roman salute. "Yo, Chief," she said.

I can't be certain, but I think she was mocking him. Regardless, she followed orders. "Come on, ju," she said, nodding at Michelle. "Maybe I kin get ju 'ome and make it back before I miss da good stuff."

"But you need us," Julie said. "Who's going to summon Banana Man Mac Lire for you?"

Maybe it's just as well we were sending them home. I doubt the god would appreciate being called Banana Man.

"I'll do it," Leanne said, smiling down on the girl who was still huddled with her friends on the sofa. "Me and Charlie. We don't need the power of three for a simple summoning."

"Besides, magic is too dangerous right now," I said. "The last spell you tried just about turned the three of you into Lite Brites."

"Go home. Spend Christmas with your families," Josh said. "If we need you, we'll call."

"Promise?" Olie said as she stood, digging around in her purse for her car keys.

"Promise," Sabrina assured them as Day opened a portal in the living room.

"Oops," Day muttered at a scowl from Leanne, and shrugged. "Let's move," she told Michelle as the girl hugged her friends and Day shoved her through the open portal. Michelle waved goodbye over her shoulder and Day stepped in behind her as the portal snapped shut.

Josh and Sabrina held the door open for Julie and Olie. They hugged the girls and everyone called out their goodbyes, but Josh still practically had to shove the witches out before closing the door.

"What now?" Josh said once they'd rejoined us.

"Now we go to the scene of the crime," I said. I turned to Drat. "Can you track a portal once it's been closed?"

Drat pulled out one of his cigars and chomped down on it, smart enough not to light it in the house. "Maybe, if da trail's not too old. Goblin portals is hinky, though," he said, and shrugged.

"Can you get us here?" I asked, and showed Drat the map with the location of the underground garage.

"Piece a cake," the troll said.

"There's one thing I'm certain of," I said, as Drat opened another portal in the living room and Leanne threw up her hands in surrender. "The goblins didn't do this on their own. They had help. The question is, whose?"

CHAPTER FIFTEEN

It took us less than five minutes before we were back at the underground garage. Josh had taken the time before we left to arm everyone from the duffle bag in his Beamer's trunk. Whatever we found, we'd be ready.

Josh did pretty much what I'd done when I'd arrived at the scene; he scented the air and followed the trail to the back wall of the garage. "They went through there," he said, pointing with the auto-shotgun at the brick wall covered in soot-stained, glossy white paint. "Alex and Cael, the goblins, and...something else."

"I smelled it too," I said as the others gathered near the wall.

Something glinted in my peripheral vision on the ground near Josh's foot. I bent down and picked up the amber pendant Alex had been wearing, a gift from Cael. The leather cord was broken, as if it had been torn from her. I showed the pendant to Josh and he nodded in silent acknowledgment. I stuffed it into my pocket before Sabrina saw it. It was proof the kids had been here, but the broken leather strands hinted at violence. No sense panicking until we knew for sure. Well, no sense panicking Sabrina, anyway.

Drat switched his battle axe to his left hand and ran his right hand over the wall, trying to sense the remnant of the portal the goblins had used.

It was cold in the garage. Leanne danced back and forth with her hands tucked into her armpits even though she wore a black, down-filled jacket. She wrinkled up her nose. "It smells like wet sand, kind of like the beach," she said.

Josh nodded. I saw his nostrils twitch as he fought to place the unfamiliar smell. He squinted, turned his head from side to side, and set off in the direction the scent took him. After a moment, he stopped. There was a puddle at his feet formed where the condensation on the overhead metal beam had pooled. A thin crust of ice had formed on the water's surface. On the outer edge, where it had frozen all the way through, was a large, sandy footprint: a circle for the heel, a larger oval for the ball of the foot, and four oblong blocks where the toes should be.

"Mike?" I wondered aloud. I had thought the bigfoot's scent too faint to allow that he'd actually been in the garage when the kids were taken, but maybe I was wrong. The imprint was huge; definitely something at least Mike's size.

"No, he wasn't here," Josh said, agreeing with my earlier assessment. "Besides, Mike has all five toes."

"So we'se looking for what?" Drat asked, still over by the wall. He pressed a hand hard against it, but it didn't give. "A four-toed sandman?"

Josh shrugged. Whatever it was, he'd never seen its like either.

"I have an idea, but it's kind of far fetched," Leanne said.

Everyone looked at her expectantly, though she seemed almost embarrassed to suggest what she was thinking.

"It might be a Golem," she said. "But I haven't seen one of those in ages."

No wonder she'd been hesitant. "Gollum? You mean like in Lord of the Rings?"

"No, that's Gol-lum. I said Go-lem," she said, enunciating. "It's a simulacrum, made of clay.

Yeah, like that cleared things up for me.

Josh came to the rescue. "An artificial man. Huge, and powerful, and really hard to kill."

Sabrina huddled in closer to Leanne for warmth. "And if I recall correctly, they can only be created by a holy man, a rabbi."

"What, the goblins are Jewish now?" I asked.

Leanne squinted at me, not certain if I was serious or not. "Not that I know of," she said, then frowned. "Although they could be, I suppose."

"Well, Golem or not, dem goblins took da kids tru here," Drat said. "If we'se gonna follow dem we gotta go now before da trail gets cold."

"Charlie's going to be pissed we left him behind," I said.

Josh adjusted the strap on his shotgun so that the grip rested at arms length down the right side of his body for easy access. "It can't be helped," he said. "We don't have time to go back for him, and besides, he needs the rest."

I glanced sideways at Josh. "Sure, you tell him that when he wakes up. Let me know how that works out for you."

"Here goes nutt'n," Drat said, and pressed his hands against the garage wall. Greenish light radiated out from his scaly palms and created a shimmering oval that covered the expanse for about six feet in diameter. Drat closed his eyes, concentrating, and the oval became opaque. "Dat should do it," the troll said, stepping back from his handiwork. "I jus has ta warn ya, da goblin Ways ain't exactly like da troll Ways."

"How so?" Sabrina asked, and thumbed the safety to off on the Berretta she carried at the ready.

"D'ere dark," Drat said. "Easier ta get lost. So stay wit da group and don't let go a da rope."

"I'll go first," I said, stepping up to the portal. "Cause I can't...you know...die."

"And we can all watch your cute ass," Leanne said, and fluttered her eyelashes at me.

"In that case you go first," I told her, but she shoved me into the portal ahead of her.

Drat was right; it was dark. The nebulous sky I'd grown accustomed to in the Ways was absent. It was like stepping into a void with a barely discernable handy-dandy pathway winding through it. Leanne stepped through after me, followed by Sabrina, then Drat, and finally Josh.

"Kind of minimalist, isn't it?" Josh said.

I peered into the darkness. "In the Beginning there was nothing, and God said 'Let there be light'—and there was still nothing, except you could see it."

"Pretty much," Josh said.

"You sure this is the trail the goblins took the kids on?" Sabrina asked Drat once we had our bearings.

"Positive," Drat answered.

I gave the hand signal for 'forward.' "Then let's move out. Diamond formation, with Sabrina in the middle."

Leanne loosened her *katana* in the *saya* she carried in her left hand. "Someone's been playing too much *Battlefield* again."

Actually it was *Plantetside 2*, but I wasn't about to tell her that. "I don't suppose you have any idea where this actually leads?" I asked Drat once we were all moving.

The troll twirled the battle axe he carried over his shoulder. "Not really. Maybe da Goblin Lair."

I rezzed my sword, then phased it out again, just for practice. "Lair? That doesn't sound very inviting. These goblins need a PR guy. Maybe change the name to the Goblin Warren, or Goblin Haven."

"Goblins are wanderers," Josh said. "Homeless. They don't stay in one place long. They hole up for a while, and move on. Lair is as good a term as any."

Drat spat off the path. "No matter what you calls it, it'd still be infested by scurvy goblins."

I looked down at the troll, bemused. "What? They're pirate goblins now?"

Drat scowled. "Shaddup, youse."

"Jewish Pirate Goblins," I said. "We're screwed."

"Could be worse," Josh said. "They could be Jewish Ninja-Pirate Goblins."

Josh tried to be light-hearted, but the worry lines around his eyes betrayed how he really felt.

I smirked. "Yeah, right. Now you're just being silly."

"So, once we get the kids back, what then?" Sabrina asked. She sounded confident, no doubt in her mind that we would get them back, just a matter of when.

I took Leanne's hand, entwining her fingers in mine. They were warm now. "Fixing the Veil was a bust," I said. "Someone or something saw to that, and I'd like to know what. Or who. Whatever."

"Do you think they were working with Aine, or maybe the goblins?" Josh asked.

I looked to Leanne for the answer to that one, but she shrugged almost imperceptibly. "No idea," she said. "But I suspect that the goblins, at least, plan on keeping the kids together. They definitely have a vested interest in keeping the Veil in place."

"Which means keeping the kids alive no matter what they may have threatened," Josh said and scratched at his five o'clock shadow. It had been a couple of days since he'd last shaved. The light brown fuzz on his face was barely noticeable, and looked almost intentional.

For a were-whatever, Josh wasn't very hairy. And yes, this is the kind of thing one thinks about when wandering aimlessly about on a path to nowhere in the dark, searching for family that's been kidnapped by goblins.

"You think the goblins purposely kidnapped them to keep them together?" Sabrina asked hopefully.

"It would solve their problem," I said. Whatever troubles the faltering Veil had caused us, the goblins had it worse; it was randomly wiping them from existence itself.

"Ours too, actually," Leanne said.

Sabrina threw a dirty look her way and Leanne smiled a sickly grin by way of apology. "Neither Aine nor Liam can hold us responsible now," Leanne said. "Either could have claimed that we had orchestrated the kids' escape attempt, but no one would intentionally allow their loved ones to be taken by goblins."

"We're here," Drat announced, interrupting our theorizing.

I squinted, and peered into the gloom. The path wound off into the darkness for an eternity. Personally, I couldn't see a difference. A few more steps remedied that, though. A cavern wall sprung up in front of my face, with an opaque portal leading out. Apparently someone had set my render distance to…like…three.

"Everyone ready?" I asked. I didn't have to turn to look. The sound of swords being drawn and weapons cocked was answer enough. "Open it up," I told the troll.

Drat waved a hand in front of the stone wall and the portal shimmered.

I was the first to step through.

Josh followed close on my heels, almost bumping into me. "What the fu…"

"My thoughts exactly," I said.

I heard a girlish shriek from behind me. Drat's battle axe spun past my head, cleaving the air between Josh and I. It sank up to the haft into the shape in front of us. "T-Rexasaurus!" the troll screamed and tried to shove the rest of us back through the portal.

I grabbed the agitated troll by the shoulders to steady him. "Calm down, Drat. It's not real. It's fake, just plastic," I said.

Sabrina peered out from the portal, shading her eyes after the gloom of the Goblin Ways. "Is this—"

"—Canada's Wonderland," I finished for her. We'd come out near the front entrance, by the photo both and just in front of the life-sized Tyrannosaurus Rex that advertised the *Dinosaurs Alive!* exhibit. The view of Wonder Mountain and Victoria Falls was a dead giveaway.

"Canada's Number One Amusement Park." Or so the ads said. "You sure this is the place?" I asked Drat.

"Why does everbody keep axing me dat?" he said, looking slightly offended. He pointed to the footprints in the thin covering of snow that lead to the mountain.

Goblin prints. Lots of them. And a set a prints that could have been made by a Sasquatch, but were probably a golem. And two sets of booted prints.

Sabrina buried her face in Josh's shoulder at the sight of those last prints. Josh closed his eyes and stroked her hair.

The kids were alive. Sure, the goblins had them, but they were alive. That's all that mattered. For all Sabrina's earlier bravado, there had always been that doubt that had infested her sanity and nagged at all of us. *What if the goblins had killed them?* Eaten them. Torn them to shreds. That's what goblins do. They were little more than animals. Rats at best.

Except one had spoken to me. So maybe it wasn't an animal after all. It had shown me its pain and suffering, not just for itself, but for its people.

And, let's face it, it had outsmarted us. So far.

"Get your axe and let's go," I told Drat.

The troll looked sheepish as he pried on the axe handle, working it to pull it from the plastic skin. "How wuz I to know it weren't a real T-Rexasaurus?

"Really?" Sabrina said. "When's the last time you saw a live dinosaur?"

Drat inspected the blade. "I dunno, gotta be at least a 'hunerd years now I guess."

Sabrina raised an eyebrow, but said nothing. Score one for Drat.

The park was abandoned. Canada's Wonderland closes down for the winter sometime around October. Everything was shut up tight and covered in blue tarp. Victoria Falls and the pool at the mountain's base were dry. Water stains coloured the artificial rock on the cliff face where the high divers stood for the summer shows. It had snowed recently, blanketing the park and topping the mountain peaks like the Alps they were meant to imitate. The lights from the surrounding city, Vaughn nearby and Toronto in the distance, lit the cloud-filled night sky and washed the colour from the mountain and surrounding buildings.

"The tracks lead over there," Josh said, pointing toward the bridge that spanned the fountain at the base of the mountain. It didn't take a Sherpa to follow the path left in the snow. I moved out with the rest trailing close behind.

"So this is where goblins hole up for the winter?" Sabrina asked.

"Seems like it," I said.

Drat chomped down on an unlit stogie. "I'm bett'n it don't mention dat in none a da brochures."

We followed the cobblestone street east, crossing the bridge on International Street, "Isn't there a rest room or something in the left side of the mountain?"

"I think so," I said. If I remembered correctly you accessed the restrooms through a kind of tunnel. No doubt you could access other parts of the mountain through there, too, like service tunnels. A roller coaster ran through the mountain after all. There had to be an entrance to the tracks and support structure somewhere. It seemed as likely a candidate as any for the Goblin Lair.

Except the trail led *away* from the mountain. I looked toward the tunnel entrance, and then at the path to the left. "What the hell? Where'd they go?"

Josh squinted and peered off into the distance. "Isn't there an outdoor amphitheatre that way?"

I pointed toward the sign showing the way. *International Showplace.* I shrugged. "Follow me."

We'd all assumed the goblins would be hiding out in the mountain. Out of sight. In the dark, like bats. Why? Because they're evil, right? And evil always hides in dark, dingy places, underground. Of course, we all assumed they were dumb animals, too, which apparently they're not. Maybe we were just racist.

There were two paths that led down to the amphitheatre; one to our right and one to our left. I opted for the one to our left because it was slightly closer, and I'm lazy. That, and the kid's tracks went that way. The prints in the snow aside, we didn't have to go far to confirm we were on the right track. The smell as soon as we began our gradual descent to the amphitheatre was unmistakeable—wet, rancid fur; rotting meat; stagnant swamp water—left no doubt that the goblins were just ahead.

Rows of hard, flat aluminum benches were set into a grey concrete floor that descended in a sort of semi-circle toward the stage. It was an outdoor theatre, the seating area covered by a large, grey tarp that protected the crowds that gathered there for the summer shows. The tarp, held aloft by an engineering feat of support poles and guy wires, looked like a giant, dyslexic spider had spun it. The stage at the foot of the basin was open and set into a square building with faux-temple walls lined with Greek columns on either side, and no doubt housed scenery changes, props, dressing rooms and whatnot.

We followed the short trail in the dim light, through the pine and cedar trees until the amphitheatre came into view. It was just as I remembered it, though covered in a light layer of snow. Well, that—and the goblins.

The benches were festooned with them, seemingly asleep, their gangly limbs wrapped around over-sized stuffed animals: Snoopy; Smurfs; Hello Kitty; a couple of Sumo Penguins; gorillas with pink faces and bellies; long, thick green and blue snakes; and something that looked vaguely like a brown, fuzzy Minotaur. The air buzzed with the unmistakeable sound of goblin snoring. I swear a few of them were sucking their thumbs.

I held my hand up to halt the gang behind me, and shushed them. Maybe we could sneak in and rescue the kids while the goblins slumbered. Besides, if anyone needed their beauty sleep...

Josh touched me on the shoulder and pointed toward the stage. Alex and Cael reclined on a bed of stuffed animals set center dais. Alex snuggled in close to Cael, his arm about her and her head resting on his shoulder. She shifted slightly to get more comfortable and I breathed a sigh of relief. Only asleep, and none the worse for wear.

The golem stood behind them, motionless. At least I assumed it was the golem, and not a statue. A huge, misshapen, clay, faceless lump of a man—if that was a statue, the park had really taken to messing with kids' nightmares.

Something dropped from overhead in the darkness and landed lightly on the path in front of us, scaring the bejeezus out of me. I was rather proud that I refrained from screaming like a little girl and waking the goblins. Josh slapped his hand over my mouth, obviously not as certain of my self-restraint. Drat growled behind me.

The goblin king rose to its hind legs, towering over me, its eyes like flickering candles in the darkness. It raised a blurry finger to its maw and shushed us, then turned and headed for the stage.

I peeled Josh's hand from my mouth. "I think it wants us to follow it."

"You think?" Josh said, and stepped around in front of me to follow the goblin.

It was hard to tell in the dark, but I think he was being sarcastic.

I motioned for the others to follow and rezzed my sword. The schiavona's grip felt comforting in my hand. I noticed Josh's hand at his side, resting on the grip of the shotgun.

The goblin led us up onto the stage. He approached the children quietly. Cael's eyes blinked open, instantly alert, as if he sensed something was wrong. Cael saw the rest of us and breathed a sigh of relief as Alex shifted in his arms. Personally I think the kid was being overly optimistic—he still had Josh to deal with. He might have been better off with the goblins.

The goblin king squatted on its haunches near the foot of the kid's makeshift bed. "*Innocent safe. Shifter safe. Goblins safe. Everyone safe,*" it said in its strained, whispery voice.

I couldn't argue with that logic.

Alex's eyes fluttered open. She stared at us, her mind still apparently fuzzy with sleep. She was obviously not the warrior her boyfriend was. "Mom?"

Sabrina rushed to her daughter's side. Cael rolled to the side to avoid getting pounced on as Sabrina threw her arms around Alex. Mother and daughter hugged in a mess of incoherent babble and tears, with Alex apologizing and Sabrina telling her it was all right and how she was just glad everyone was safe.

Josh stood, taking in the tableau, his face a mix of warring emotions. He wanted to look stern—I know he was angry—but the relief and joy at seeing Alex safe and sound was too much for him. He went down on his knees and soon all three of them were embroiled in a big, messy group hugfest.

Cael stood to the side, watching. He looked over at me, his face impassive, doing his best to hide whatever emotion he felt. "They seem to do this a lot," he said, and the corners of his mouth turned up in a somewhat wistful smile.

"Yep," I said. "You'd better get used to it."

"BEAR PILE!" Leanne shouted, and launched herself at the bed of stuffed animals—very few of which were honest to goodness teddy bears. She got some pretty good air, too. A big, lime green gorilla broke her fall, and she fought for balance in the shifting pile until she was on her knees and hugging with the rest of them.

The goblin stared at Drat. Its flickering eyes seemed to blink in confusion.

"Don't aks me, I don't gets it needer," the troll said. "And not fer nuttin, but where'd you get da Golem?"

The goblin shrugged, a gesture that made it seem almost human. "*Found among dead Fae. Couldn't eat. Brought it with.*"

Goblins could chew through just about anything, but I guess even they drew the line at sand and clay.

I waited until most of the hugging and blubbering was over, then dug around in my pocket. "I think I found something of yours," I told Alex as I approached. I held out my hand with the necklace she had lost in it.

Alex's eyes lit up, even misted with tears as they were.

The goblin king growled—or grunted. It sounded like a cross between an expression of rage and disgust but I could be wrong. I don't speak goblin. It leapt at me and snatched the amulet from my outstretched hand. "*They come now. Track. Find us. Stupid.*"

I looked down at my empty hand and blinked. Of course. The necklace was a gift from Cael's parents. It must have been some kind of homing beacon, one they'd used to keep track of him. The goblins had figured out the trick of it and gotten to the kids first. How else could they have known to find them in the underground garage? That's why the goblin king had taken it from Alex and left it behind.

And I'd brought it back to her.

"Oh, shit," Josh muttered, obviously coming to the same conclusion I just had. "Get that thing out of here, James. As far away as you can."

I would make three mistakes before this night was over.

The first was bringing the necklace with me to Wonderland.

I teleported, back to Victoria, to the underground garage.

That was my second mistake.

I left the necklace on the floor and reappeared on the stage at the *International Showplace*. Too late. I saw the faint outline of a portal coalesce on the back wall of the stage. Someone was coming through the Ways. Maybe, had I realised the thing was a beacon right away, whoever was watching for it might have seen the displacement as a glitch. A blip on the radar, as it were. But we'd spent too much time in Wonderland. I should have gone back to the house. They might have thought we'd brought the kids home then. But I didn't have time to think, and I screwed up.

The goblin king howled. The sound would have made Bear proud. Goblins sprang away, tossing aside stuffed animals. A blur of inky, jagged shapes bounded to the stage and surrounded us. The goblin king barked out orders and suddenly they shifted position, forming a line in front of us, facing the portal. The golem lurched to life and took a heavy step forward. A glyph carved into its forehead glowed brightly in the darkened amphitheatre.

I wasn't sure what to make of this development. I mean, we're they actually helping us? Willing to fight for us?

"The enemy of my enemy is my friend," Leanne said, giving the katana a practice swing.

I smiled at her. "You just make that up now?"

She pulled a *tanto* from her belt, holding it in a back handed grip. "Of course not. I made it up about six-seven thousand years ago."

I swear, I'll never learn.

We pushed the kids behind us. A wall of goblins, the golem, then us, then the kids.

"Watch her," Josh told Cael.

"Yes, sir," Cael said.

Josh nodded. There was nothing more to say, really. If there was one thing he could be certain of, it was that Cael would do his utmost to see that nothing happened to Alex. The boy had earned that much respect at least.

The portal on the wall flashed open and we gripped our weapons more tightly. I half expected a horde of raging were-whatever to rush through, or the Dark Fae in their chitinous armour. I sure as hell didn't expect Day.

She was still dressed in armour, and carried a battle club in each hand. "Whose leg do I have to hump to get a drink aroun' here?" the diminutive blonde troll said in her thick Cuban accent as she stepped through the portal.

The goblins shifted about uneasily. Day smiled, and brushed a lock of hair from her eyes, resting the head of her the club in her right hand on the ground between her feet, like a walking stick.

I lowered my weapon.

That was my third mistake.

CHAPTER SIXTEEN

Something sailed through the portal behind Day. It landed in front of the makeshift bed of stuffed animals with a heavy *thunk* and rolled to a stop. Day covered her ears and crouched down, turning to face the wall.

"Grenade!" Josh yelled. He turned and leapt for the kids and tackled them both off the stage. Alex let out a little scream as she was dropped down the three or four feet to the ground and slammed into the concrete, but Cael took it like a trooper.

Leanne and Sabrina both dove for the sides and tucked into this neat little combat roll manoeuvre, while Drat, who was standing closest to the edge, took a step back and dropped down to safety.

The goblins scattered like smoke, as if they were make of the stuff and someone had just turned on one of those big wind fans. One minute they were there, the next, gone. They took the golem with them.

I, on the other hand, reacted much the way any sane person would.

"Gre-what?"

The explosion blew me off the stage so that I landed in the third row of bleachers. I guess it was a concussion grenade—so not much shrapnel, but a lot of explosive force. It didn't as much tear me apart as it did turn my insides to jelly.

I don't want to imagine what I looked like at that point. Luckily I couldn't see, most likely because I didn't have any eyes. It hurt like hell for a second, then nothing, which meant if I had been alive and not dead, I'd be dead dead by now. Oh, you know what I mean.

I took a few seconds to heal up, then I was back on my feet and bounding for the stage. Well, at least until the tracer fire started buzzing through the open portal—then I cowered behind the drop like everyone else.

Josh popped up and blindly fired three shotgun blasts through the portal. I distinctly heard something scream, and the tracer rounds stopped. It was a magic shotgun after all. Everything went quiet for a moment, except for the ringing in my ears. That's what happens when someone fires a shotgun in close proximity, or maybe it was the residual effects of the grenade.

I stuck a finger in my ear and worked my jaw to try and stop the ringing. "Get the kids to safety," I shouted probably more loudly than I had to. Where safety might actually be at the moment was beyond me, but it was the thought that counted.

Josh looked over his shoulder at the mountain, then at Leanne. "Get them into the tunnel, where the restrooms are," he said. "They'll only be able to attack you from one direction there, and only one or two at a time. James, Drat and I will stay here and try to hold them off."

No one argued. Sabrina grabbed her daughter's hand while Leanne did the same for Cael.

Sabrina took a second to kiss her husband. I'd have kissed Leanne but she was too far away, and the rest of the gang separated us. She caught my eye, though, and I knew how she felt, and I know she knew I felt the same way. I know it's confusing. It would have been a lot easier if I'd just kissed her. Sorry.

"On three," Josh said, and silently counted down. "Three, two, one, NOW!" Josh stood and fired a few more rounds through the portal as the girls and Cael made a mad dash between the bleachers, staying low as they raced for the mountain.

"Serpentine! Serpentine!" I hollered after them. Hey, it works in CALL OF DUTY. I didn't have time to see if they'd taken my advice as I turned back toward the stage to help Josh with the distraction.

I peered over the ledge to reconnoitre. Where had Day gone? I couldn't spot that evil troll anywhere.

Something howled from the other side of the portal. Soon another something joined it, then another, until the racket coming from inside the gateway was almost deafening and not more than a little unnerving. A werewolf bounded through wearing black Kevlar body armour specially designed to fit all his were-wolfy bits. It carried a wicked looking rifle with a folding stock, a big magazine, and a long barrel with a silencer screwed onto the end of it. The werewolf crouched to the right of the portal and peered over the weapon's sights. A red laser dot traced a path along the bleachers wherever it aimed. A second werewolf broke through the portal and took up the same firing position to the left.

A werebear lumbered through next, followed by another, likewise dressed in Kevlar and carrying big, belt-fed machineguns. They moved forward, slightly in front of the two werewolves covering their flanks.

Drat looked at his axe and made a face. "Nuts!"

I know how he felt. The old adage of "Never bring a knife to a gunfight" sprung instantly to mind.

More armed shapeshifters moved through the portal onto the stage until there were about a dozen of them, all armed to the teeth, or fangs.

Most took a knee, sighting over their weapons until the bleachers swarmed with laser dots like little red fireflies. I was glad to see that Gord wasn't among the enemy. I'd taken a liking to the werebear, and he and Josh had been friends once.

I glanced back over my shoulder but couldn't see Leanne and the rest. They must have made it to the tunnel before the first werewolf had come through. The shapeshifters probably thought the kids still cowered with the rest of us at the base of the stage.

Liam stepped through last. The king hadn't bothered to morph and still looked human. He was dressed kind of steampunky, in tan pants tucked into knee high leather boots, and a crisp white shirt with a high, starched collar and black tie. Over it he wore a black, double-breasted vest with silver buttons, and carried a matching black and silver sceptre in his right hand.

He stroked at his black, curly beard with his left hand. It looked like it had been oiled, and I half expected him to twirl his moustache next. If you looked up smug in the dictionary there'd be a picture of him, smugly pointing it out.

"I'm here for my boy," he said, just loudly enough to be heard but not quite shouting. More of a stage voice, which was rather appropriate, considering. I noticed he'd lost the affectation of the Scots accent. "Just hand him over and we'll be on our way. No one needs to get hurt, but if that's the way you want it…"

It sounded to me like he'd be more than happy to oblige those who'd prefer to be hurt. As a matter of fact, I'm pretty sure he'd rather.

"Okay, just a second and I'll ask him," I said, and ducked my head below stage level again.

I heard Liam tap the cane of the sceptre impatiently against the stage, but he waited.

"Hey Cael, do you want to go home with your dad now?" I said loudly enough that those on the stage could hear.

Josh narrowed his eyes at me, puzzled, but didn't question.

"No way," I answered myself in a high falsetto that sounded more like Mr. Bill and nothing like Cael. "Dad's a big douche-waffle. I wanna stay here with you Mister Decker, cause you're so cool and trendy."

Josh shook his head, while Drat banged his forehead against the stage, muttering, "We'se all gonna die. First da torture, an den da death."

I peaked up over the edge of the stage again. "He said no," I said in my normal voice.

"Last chance," Liam offered, deadpan.

"Or what?" I said. "You'll huff and puff and blow my house down?"

I don't think the werewolves found that one funny, cause suddenly there were several laser dots trained on the stage near my head.

Liam slapped the head of the sceptre into the palm of his hand. His complexion paled, so I knew he was pissed, but he kept his face expressionless. He looked sort of like Michael Myers—without the machete, and with curly hair, and a beer belly, and…never mind.

"Get the boy," he said, deadpan. "Kill the rest."

Josh growled, his expression worse, if possible, than Liam's. I knew Josh was capable of killing, physically and mentally. But he didn't relish the thought—well, not counting demons, and the odd vampire. For the most part taking a life haunted him, and on the times that he had done so there had been no real other options. There was a good chance that he knew these men. He'd have grown up with them, trained and fought with them. Under better circumstances he might have been their king. Now they were trying to kill him.

Josh looked determined to return the favour. I'd never seen his eyes so hate-filled, but then he'd just heard his own brother order his execution, not to mention that of his wife and daughter.

I ducked as several rounds tore up the edge of the stage where my head used to be. "On three?" I said.

"Three," Josh said, and chambered the shotgun—which ejected the shell that was already in the chamber. "Damn," he muttered. "It always looks so cool in the movies."

"You comin, ladies?" Drat taunted as he rushed the stage. "KILL DA BASTARDS!" The troll charged the nearest were-bear, his double headed battle-axe held like a shield in front of him. Rounds sparked off the heavy blades as the werewolves to either side of the portal took aim.

Josh and I charged the stage, and suddenly the werewolves were firing at us, giving Drat a little breathing room. The werebear raised the barrel of the machine gun and pointed it at the oncoming troll.

Drat dove into a roll, came up on one knee, and threw the long handled axe at the werebear. The heavy axe-head struck the shapeshifter full in the chest and knocked the beast onto its back. The troll pulled a pair of long knives from his belt and vaulted onto the downed bear's chest, then stabbed down at the breaks in its armour near its collar bones. Both blades bit deep and the bear howled and rolled to its side, shaking the troll off. Apparently it had had enough, because it gave up the fight and bolted back through the open portal.

I know rushing the stage might seem a little fool-hardy on our part—the enemy was armed with high-powered machine guns and whatnot—but it wasn't as reckless as you might think. Josh had his can't-miss-never-run-out-of-ammo shotgun, and we'd both been trained by Skatha, who was kind of like Yoda for the *Lord of the Rings* crowd. And in case anyone's forgotten, I'm a *freaking Eternal*.

And Drat? Well, Drat's just nuts. Whatever works.

Everything slowed. I saw the enemy weapons kick back as star-shaped plumes of fire pushed round after round out of glowing red barrels, all in slow-motion. When you can move as fast as I can the trick is to pretty much be wherever the bullets aren't. Then again, I guess that's the trick no matter how fast you move. It's just a lot easier for me.

I stepped to the right of a stream of heavy machine gun rounds and closed on the werebear. The stink of burnt gunpowder assailed me as I caught an ejected casing in mid-air and shoved it into the weapon's breach just as the bolt clattered back to reload, effectively jamming it. The werebear didn't even have time to realise his weapon had jammed before I punched him in the face, and pretty hard, too. Just how hard do you have to punch a bear to knock it out, anyway? Skatha had skipped that lesson, but apparently my best guess was good enough because the bear fell like an ox—or a bear—whatever.

Josh carried his shotgun at the ready, weapon into his shoulder as he aimed down the barrel. He fired once and turned left, then fired again. Both of the werewolves that flanked the portal howled in pain as their assault rifles were torn from their grips, the 12 Gauge slugs Josh used almost doubling the rifles in half. I guess Josh didn't have it in him to kill his one-time comrades after all, and instead had gone all Lone Ranger on their furry asses. That suited me better than fine.

I turned quickly, throwing my elbow into what I hoped was a second werebear's temple hard enough to stagger him. I shoved hard, a palm-heel strike with both hands, and drove the werebear into a werewolf that was standing too closely behind it, hard enough that it shoved both beasts back through the portal.

Drat brought the heavy head of his axe down onto a werewolf's toes, then punched the beast hard in the solar plexus with the haft. Even through Kevlar that had to smart. The werewolf doubled over and Drat knocked it senseless with a hard overhand right to the back of its head.

Josh spun as rounds tore up the stage at the spot where he'd been standing, and swung the butt of the shotgun in an uppercut that caught another of the werebears in the jaw…er…muzzle? Josh's guess was apparently as good as mine; the bear crumpled into a heap as the machine gun fell from its limp hands.

There were a few remaining shapeshifters left, but Josh left them to Drat and I. He stood facing his brother. Liam pulled on the head of his sceptre and drew forth a long, slim blade from its handle. Josh pointed the shotgun at his head.

Liam stood sideways to present a somewhat smaller target, the size of his belly notwithstanding. "That's hardly sporting now, is it?" he said, and nodded at the shotgun.

The weapon never waivered in Josh's hands. "You just tried to kill me, my friends, and my family. I'm not inclined to be sporting."

Drat and I had finished with the remaining shifters without any real bloodshed. Okay, without fatal blood shed—mostly. We flanked Liam on either side. Even that egomaniac had to know he was screwed.

Liam lowered his blade but didn't drop it. A small bead of sweat trickled from his hairline down the left side of his face, but he still didn't look afraid. As a matter of fact, I'd swear he was excited. "So now what, brother? You going to shoot me?"

"Step-brother," Josh corrected. "And mom always liked me best."

The smug look dropped from Liam's face. I think the jibe had hit a little too close to home. "You're not going to shoot me. Not like this. You're the good son. You haven't got it in you."

Drat raised his hand. "I do!"

I looked over at the troll and shook my head, scowling.

"Well, I do," he insisted. "Why's don't youse two go for a brewski, or check each udder for fleas, or whatever it is youse do when I ain't here. When youse gets back it'll be all done. No muss, no fuss."

Josh glanced over at the troll, the hint of a smile on his face. Shapeshifters and trolls had been enemies for as long as anyone could remember. The fact that Josh and Drat had become friends was unprecedented. Josh understood that Drat's offer to help was earnest. Even Drat could see that Liam was right; Josh couldn't kill his brother, and if there was anyone that needed killing, it was Liam. Drat was just offering to help his friend out, and I could see Josh was touched.

"Thanks, Drat," Josh said, "but I've got this."

"Ju might wanna reconsider," Day said from behind us. She sounded confident, which didn't bode well for us.

I turned toward Day's voice and saw her in the bleachers. She stood at the forefront flanked by four werewolves. Leanne, Sabrina and the kids were on their knees in front of the shapeshifters, their hands bound behind their backs.

Leanne hung her head. I could tell she was ashamed that she had allowed their capture. We all knew better, though. If Leanne had given up it was because there was no way she could prevent their deaths otherwise, even if it meant sacrificing her own near-immortal life.

Sabrina, on the other hand, boiled over with impotent rage. She was the only one of the prisoners that had been gagged. I had no trouble imagining why.

Drat swung his battle-axe and glared at Day "Youse next," he said.

If he'd meant to intimidate his War Chief it hadn't worked. Day flashed a bright smile and twirled the mace in her hand. "Come on, *puta*, if you think you've got the *cojones* for it."

Drat took a step forward but one of the werewolves shoved the barrel of his weapon into the back of Sabrina's head. The troll stopped and ground his teeth in fury, and Drat has a lot of teeth.

Liam sheathed the blade in his sceptre and took a step toward Josh. "Put the gun down or they're dead."

Josh stepped forward, the shotgun pointed at Liam's head but just out of reach. "If I put it down they're all dead anyway. I might as well take you with us."

Liam smiled and shook his head, evidently disappointed. "You've always underestimated me, brother. I know what you're thinking, that I won't really do it. But you're wrong, you know. I'm not you. I do have it in me."

The two stood facing each other, neither giving way.

Liam sighed. "I guess you need proof." He nodded almost casually to one of the shifters in the bleachers. The werewolf hesitated a moment, but Liam fixed him with steely glare.

There was a muffled sound as the silenced weapon fired, the clack of the bolt sliding forward and back, chambering another round. Blood spatter sprayed the bleacher in front of Cael. Liam's son stiffened, his eyes wide in shock before slumping forward, still on his knees.

"Now," Liam said, "Where were we?"

CHAPTER SEVENTEEN

Liam was mad. I'd always known he was an egomaniac. I'd suspected he was a little unhinged, but now I was certain he was some kind of psychopath, or sociopath, or one of those other kinds of paths that no one should ever walk down.

I guess Josh had finally come to the same conclusion. He lowered the shotgun so that it hung by the strap from his shoulder.

Liam stepped closer to his brother. "You never were one for making the hard deci—"

Josh pulled a Ka-bar from the sheath strapped to the small of his back and stepped into Liam. His left hand reached for the back of his brother's head, pulling the king in even closer as he drove the knife up under Liam's chin, through the soft palate of the mouth and up into his brain. The king died instantly, eyes open and words half-formed on his lips. The sceptre fell from his nerveless fingers and clattered on the stage. Josh pulled the blade free and Liam collapsed to the floor.

I rushed the bleachers. The werewolves that held guns to our loved ones' heads had been shocked into inaction by Josh's deed, but shapeshifters are speedy. They have faster reflexes and are faster in motion than any human. I hit the first set of bleachers as the werewolf behind Leanne took a step back. Its eyes widened as it realised what had happened and it slowly tried to bring its assault rifle into play.

Day slammed a fist into a support pole, a look of disgust at our stupidity painting her pretty face. I don't know what her plans were but it was apparent we'd ruined them. Her eyes crept to the right, looking for an escape route.

I hit the fourth set of bleachers as the werewolf's finger slowly tightened on the trigger. I'd never make it in time before he fired into the back of Leanne's pretty head. Had she still been part vampire she might survive even that, but now, pure Fae, lead was more deadly to her kind than ours. The trigger depressed slowly as I hit the tenth row. I screamed. All I could do now was avenge her death.

Something black and smoky, like the sooty exhaust from an old rusty stovepipe, circled about the werewolf's neck. The goblin king appeared behind the shapeshifter, his claws clutched about the werewolf's throat. He yanked back on the beast pulling it off-balance.

I saw the muzzle flash, watched as the round left the barrel and the gasses expanded out through the holes in the silencer, and then I was upon them. I dodged around Leanne and covered her body with mine. The round tore into my back just above the right shoulder blade. The goblin had thrown off the assassin's shot—even had I not arrived in time the bullet would've gone high and right, missing Leanne.

There was a flash in my peripheral vision to the left, and I turned my head slightly to see Josh's Ka-bar slowly closing on the shifter that stood behind Sabrina. The blade pushed its way into the werewolf's throat, just above the collar in his Kevlar vest. The knife's hilt slammed against the shifter's throat and the impact knocked him off his feet into the last row of benches before he even had a chance to fire a shot.

I heard a sharp crack and turned to see the goblin king drop the limp body of the werewolf to the bleachers. He must have snapped its neck. I tried to muster up some sympathy for the werewolf, but found none.

Day turned about to find a row of goblins blocking her escape, just as the portal on the stage collapsed. She turned back to face us. I guess she figured if she were going to die she would rather it be by our hands than at the hands of a bunch of scurvy goblins.

Time had resumed its normal pace. I had my arms about Leanne. I whispered, "Love you," in her ear, and reached down to snap off the flex cuffs that bound her hands.

"I know," she said.

"If you turn out to be my long lost sister this is going to get awkward," I said.

"Shut up, idiot," she said, and threw her arms around me.

Alex looked down at Cael's slumped body. His blood had sprayed her face. Her hands were still bound behind her back and she couldn't wipe it off. Everything had happened so fast, from the moment the werewolf had executed Cael, until now. I don't think the fact that Cael was dead had really registered. She stared at him, unblinking, almost as if comatose.

Drat climbed the bleachers and stopped, facing Day. He still carried his bloodied axe in his right hand. He fixed his gaze upon his War Chief and growled out the word, "Why?"

Day gave her mace a little twirl. She stared back at Drat nonchalantly. "Are ju kidding?" She looked around at the bodies on the stage and at the rest of us standing in the bleachers, inviting Drat to do the same as if the answer should be obvious. "Ju forbid us to eat human meat. Ju consort openly with dis man-mutt, even call heem your fren. Ju broker peace weet da Tor clan and even take me as ju War Chief rather than go to war. Ju are *weak.*"

Drat's mouth curled into a snarl, showing teeth. "Da Clan Chief rules by right of might. If you tink youse can do better, *Daylight*, den take my crown."

Day's eyes narrowed and she pursed her lips at Drat's obtuseness. "What do ju tink I was jus doin?"

Alex screamed. All eyes turned to her, Drat and Day's drama forgotten. It wasn't one of those high pitched girly screams. It wasn't a scream of fear, or shock. It was a cry of pure, unfiltered loss. Of longing and despair so deep and unending that surely no soul could ever bear such misery. Especially an Innocent. Alex stopped. She took a few deep, panting breaths, her face pale and covered in blood and a clammy sheen of sweat.

Josh went to her side, and cut her hands free. That seemed to calm her. She reached out to Cael, his body still slumped forward on his knees, and positioned his head in her lap. She closed her tear-streaked eyes, back straight, head up, and took a few deep breaths. Was she meditating? A look of serenity washed over her.

Alex is the Innocent, the embodiment of hope. Her soul is a beacon of light so bright it would blind the otherworld folk who dared look at her directly with the Sight, like staring into the sun. That light poured from her now, in concentric circles, like a blast wave spreading out from her epicentre. Kind of like when the Death Star exploded. No, not like in the original, but in the digitally re-mastered copy. No, not that one, the second one. Or maybe it was the blue ray edition. Whatever.

The first crest struck, and I felt an overwhelming sense of well-being envelop me. A sense that everything would be all right, that events were unfolding as they should. I could smell apple and peach, and honeysuckle, and even cookie dough, and the air tasted like rain on my tongue. I'd only felt this way twice before, when I'd died and transcended my physical being. But I wasn't dead now. I wasn't even injured, having already healed the bullet wound to my shoulder.

The goblins vanished, disappearing like wisps of smoke. I don't know why they just up and left, but I suspect that—though they had done nothing but aid us lately—there was still something dark and twisted about their souls that couldn't stand the paradise Alex manifested.

I looked about at the others; Leanne, Josh, Sabrina, Day, Drat—the feeling of euphoric bliss written clear upon their faces. The second wave hit and the ecstasy drove us to our knees. The third wave was almost unbearable, and I doubled over. I doubted I'd survive another.

Alex collapsed, slumping forward over Cael so that her long hair spilled over his face, her breathing shallow and rapid. The light about her died.

I climbed to my knees, and offered a hand to Leanne. She looked just as weak and shaky as I felt. "What the hell was that?" I asked.

"Not hell," Leanne said, leaning against me for support. "Just the opposite, in fact."

Cael's eyelids fluttered open. Well, at least the one I could see did; Alex's hair still covered most of his face. The eye rolled about until it focused on me, and the eyebrow raised in question. I don't think he knew what was going on, just that his girlfriend was slumped over him and he wasn't sure he should move her. The fact that his hands were still tied behind his back didn't help make things any less awkward for him.

The werewolf that had tried to kill Leanne pushed its way to its hands and knees, or paws and…whatever. It sat back on its haunches, eyes wide as it ran a hand over its throat and slowly turned its neck from side to side.

The one Josh had killed climbed to its feet. It grasped the dagger in its throat with two hands and pulled it free. The werewolf coughed up a bit of blood and spit it on the floor, but other than that it looked fine. Well, finer than dead. It kept staring at the dagger in its hand, then up at me, and back to the dagger.

"I could put it back for you if you like," I offered, but by the way he scrambled backward over the bleachers I'd say he was more than happy with the way things were.

I looked toward the stage. If Alex had somehow brought these three back to life, then maybe…

Sure enough, Liam pushed himself upright. He sat on the stage, his legs splayed out in front of him like a drunken toddler. He spat blood onto the stage—I'm glad I wasn't the park employee who'd have to clean this mess up come spring—and put a thumb in his mouth and ran it along his upper pallet.

His followers—those we'd incapacitated in one way another—climbed groggily to their feet. At first I worried the party would begin anew, but I guess resurrection had taken all the fight out of them. Most of them looked lost, running their hands over miraculously healed wounds and staring about blankly.

Day joined Liam on the stage. No one was paying much attention to her now. No one much cared. The werewolves that had just tried to kill us gave us a wide berth, moving warily down the aisles to either side until they stood center stage as well. One of them helped Liam to his feet. The Therian King opened his mouth to say something, then ran his tongue against the roof of his mouth and thought better of it.

Day reopened the portal and helped Liam through. His troops followed solemnly behind until they'd all cleared the stage. The portal sealed itself in a bright flash of green light and we were left to ourselves in Wonderland.

Maybe we should have stopped them. We probably should have stopped them, but I couldn't find it in me to care at the moment. Compared to the miracle that had just happened, the power struggle as to who ruled what didn't seem all that important. I guess we were all in shock.

Sabrina gently placed her hands at Alex's forehead and across her shoulders and slowly raised her daughter to a sitting position. "She's still breathing, but she feels so cold."

Cael wriggled to his knees, and finally his feet. Josh motioned for him to turn about and cut the boy's restraints when he did. Cael ran a hand over the back of his head. His hair was still sticky with blood, but the wound had healed.

Sabrina had her arms around Alex, but the girl was still unconscious.

Cael knelt beside them and placed Alex's hand in his own. "She's okay, right?"

Alex was breathing—I marked the slow rise and fall of her chest—but barely. Her normally milk chocolate complexion was pale and waxy. She looked more like zombie Alex than Innocent Alex at the moment. I looked to Leanne, my expression questioning.

"I don't know," Leanne answered. "She just brought a dozen or so people back to life. Maybe she just needs to rest. Maybe this is normal."

Maybe it wasn't.

"We know even less about the Innocents and what they can do than we do about Eternals," Leanne said. "And Alex is still young. She hasn't even come into her own yet."

"Let me guess," I said. "She won't reach her full potential until she turns eighteen, during the odd Tuesday of the month when the moon is full and Jupiter is in Aquarius or something." No doubt the Stupid Rules again.

Leann smiled. "Close enough."

Well that sucked. More so for Josh and Sabrina, I imagine. It's bad enough having to deal with a teenage girl, what with the hormones and their bodies changing and the rebelling against their parents because they know everything now and their parents are just trying to ruin their life. No, Josh and Sabrina had to deal with the Innocent's nature as well, which apparently included raising the dead. I'm guessing there's no support group for that.

Leanne knelt down in front of Alex. She put the back of her hand against the girl's forehead, feeling for temperature. By the expression on her face I don't think she liked what she found.

"There was a boy in Chad once, about 20 years ago," Leanne said as she gently lifted one of Alex's eyelids to check her pupils. "An Innocent—the embodiment of Compassion." No good, Alex's eyes were rolled back in her head. "The rebels would attack his village, killing and maiming the villagers and abducting the young ones as child soldiers. Once the rebels had left, the boy would heal the fallen. As long as they'd been dead less than three hours, he could bring them back."

"Why three hours?" I asked.

Leanne shrugged. "The Stupid Rules, I guess."

Figures. "That's a lovely Afterschool Special, but what's your point?"

Leanne closed Alex's eyes. "Just that this sort of thing isn't exactly unprecedented, I guess."

"So what happened to this kid?" I asked. "I'm betting he didn't grow old and die peacefully in his sleep."

Leanne stood, and wiped her hands on her pant legs.

"After one particularly brutal attack the boy brought one of the rebels back from the dead—he was the embodiment of Compassion after all. The rebel claimed the boy was Satan, that he'd stolen his soul. He beat the boy to death."

Sometimes I hate it when I'm right.

"We should get Alex home," Josh said, ever the practical one. "Or to a hospital."

It sounded to me like being an Innocent was not exactly an easy life, something Josh didn't need to be reminded of at the moment.

My cell phone rang—Joan Jet's "*Bad Reputation*"—and I almost jumped out of my skin. That was Charlie's ringtone—because, you know, Shrek. Anyway, he must be awake, and was probably pissed. I fished around in my pocket and finally found the phone. "Hello?"

"What's happened?" the ogre asked. "Are the kids still together?"

"Um...sort of," I said. "They're both here, but—"

"You had better get back here," Charlie interrupted. "The Veil has fallen. All hell is breaking loose."

I hoped he wasn't speaking literally. Figuratively? No...literal—screw it, I hope it wasn't the real Hell he was talking about, because damn. "We're on our way," I said, and hung up.

Everyone had heard. No need to explain, or come up with a plan. Everyone knew what to do.

Josh removed his long coat and wrapped it around Alex. The wind was picking up and it was getting cold. Colder. Most of us were still dressed for the warmer Victoria weather. Josh gently picked up his daughter and cradled her in his arms, her head against his shoulder. She could have been sleeping. For all we knew, maybe she was. Maybe she was just being really lazy.

Drat opened a portal in the wall beside the stage. The troll was unusually quiet.

"You okay?" I asked him.

"I will be," Drat said, slinging his axe across his back.

"And here all these times I thought Day was trying to kill me just for fun. Who knew she was serious?"

"You do has dat effect on people," Drat said as Josh carried Alex through the portal.

"You guys go on ahead," I said once we were all through. "There's something I need to check on first. I'll meet you at home."

Nobody said much. Just a few nods and mumbled uh-huhs, so I gave Leanne a quick kiss and teleported out.

I didn't want to worry anyone, or worry them more than they already were, but I had to check on Michelle. The last we'd seen her we'd left her with Day. Day was supposed to take her home, but I had this terrible image of the troll becoming peckish along the way and deciding to just make a snack of the witch and have done with it. I teleported to just outside Michelle's house. There were no cop cars and flashing lights, which I took as a good sign, but then would the girl even have been reported missing yet? I looked at my watch. It was past 2 A.M. Christmas day. Well, at least here in Ontario. Christmas would still be another hour off in Victoria.

I tried to convince myself that if something were wrong Michelle's parents would have noticed by now. I moved to the front step, and transformed my index finger into a passable imitation of a key—one good enough to unlock the front door anyway. I crept in as stealthily as I could. Hopefully Michelle's little brother wasn't still up trying to get a glimpse of Santa or he'd be in for a bit of a shock.

Just to be safe, I manifested myself a Santa suit, wig and fake beard. I caught a glimpse of myself in the hall mirror. I did a passable imitation of Santa if I do say so myself. Well, Santa after a six month free pass to *Bali Fitness*.

Everyone in the house seemed to be asleep. I caught Michelle's scent and followed it to a door in a hallway. Her scent was strongest here. It had to be her room. I sighed in relief when I heard breathing inside. I had to be sure though, and carefully turned the door handle, opened the door just a crack, and peered inside.

Michelle lay curled up in her bed, her long black hair fanned out over her pillow. She snored softly, covered in her My Little Pony comforter. There was no way I was going to let her live that one down.

I don't know why Day had followed through on bringing the witch safely home. Maybe the timing hadn't been right for betrayal until after she'd dropped Michelle off, so she'd done as she was told so as not to alert us, but I'm just guessing.

Satisfied that Michelle was safe, I teleported home before someone caught me peeping in on a sleeping teenage girl. Santa or not, that's still a big no no.

I arrived at home, still dressed in my Santa suit. Charlie was pacing back and forth in front of the Christmas tree in the living room, his hands clasped behind his back. He looked up, startled when I appeared. Maybe he thought I was the real Santa, though I don't know what he looked so worried about; I know for a fact that Charlie had been a good boy all year.

The ogre squinted at me from across the room. "James?"

"Yeah, it's me," I said, and changed back into my regular clothes.

He fixed me with those big, expressive eyes of his. Right now they were expressing betrayal. "You shouldn't have left me behind," he said.

"You needed the rest," I told him. "We figured we could handle things without you for a bit."

Charlie held the TV remote in his hand, and pointed it to the wall-mounted flat screen over the fireplace. The TV flicked on, already set to the news channel. Even with the sound turned down it didn't look good. There were buildings burning in downtown Victoria. A banner across the bottom of the screen urged everyone to remain indoors.

Live feed—probably from a hand-held camera on a rooftop—showed bodies digging their way out of the ground in Pioneer Square. Spectral wraiths flitted back and forth between the tombstones, urging the dead to rise. Something big and winged soared past, low over the tree tops. The camera followed as it dove between the buildings along Blanchard Street, then panned down on the line of mounted Dark Sidhe riding in procession past the Public Library. The image jerked suddenly, as if the reporter had suddenly been knocked to the ground. An extreme close-up of something with red, demon slit eyes and a mouth full of jagged teeth filled the screen, then nothing.

Charlie turned the TV off, and turned to face me. "How's that working out for you," he said..

CHAPTER EIGHTEEN

The rest of the gang arrived home just before midnight. Charlie and I decided not to fill them in on what had happened, at least not yet. We figured we'd wait until after we'd taken care of Alex first. It's not like Josh or Sabrina—or any of us, for that matter—would have been any good to anyone otherwise.

Josh carried his daughter upstairs to her bedroom, or the room she used whenever they stayed with us. Cael stayed by her side, his feet curled up under him on the armchair beside her bed. He left only briefly, to take a shower and get the blood out of his hair, and change into clean clothes.

Sabrina cleaned up Alex as best she could, washing the blood from her daughter's face with a warm wash cloth. The girl still looked pale and waxy, but her breathing, while shallow, was regular, and her pulse steady.

I've seen a lot of freaky things since becoming an Eternal. I've run afoul of some incredibly powerful beings, but none of them could hold a candle to Sabrina. She pulled off a feat of magic the likes of which I'd heard about only in stories, and conjured a mythical being even more rare than a unicorn: a doctor who makes house calls. On Christmas Eve no less, and after midnight. Let's see Harry Dresden do that.

Dr. Snowden knocked at our door less than an hour after Sabrina had called. I would have never taken her for a medical practitioner, but then I don't generally assume anyone's a doctor unless they walk about with a stethoscope around their neck. She wasn't wearing a white lab coat or hospital scrubs either, just a pair of jeans, a blue wool pullover, and a black ice jacket with matching earmuffs and gloves. Maybe she was travelling incognito, although she did have what looked to be an honest to goodness doctor's bag in her left hand.

Dr. Snowden was a slight, fair-complexioned blonde with bright blue eyes and one of those pert, upturned noses. She didn't look near old enough to have completed the eleventy-four years of medical school required to be a real doctor. She could have easily passed for one of Alex's friends. Maybe she was one of those Doogie Howser kind of doctors.

"James Decker?" she inquired hesitantly from the front step.

"In person," I said.

She pushed her way past me and into the vestibule, removing her gloves. "Oh. My. God! You have no idea how long I've wanted to meet you," she said in a posh British accent, and stuck out her hand.

"Really?" I said, flattered as I shook her dainty hand. Apparently I had groupies.

"An honest to god Eternal. I'm just beside myself," she went on, removing her jacket and handing it to me. "I was hoping maybe when I'm done here that I could get a tissue swab, and maybe a blood sample?"

They don't make groupies like they used to.

"Let's see how you do with Alex first," I said, hiding my disappointment. I motioned for her to follow me.

"Right, Alex," she replied as she removed her boots and left them at the front door, then trailed behind me up the stairs. "Sabrina told me Alex has been unconscious ever since she reanimated several people. So an hour or so now?"

"That's about right," I said, and led her into Alex's room. The doctor didn't seemed fazed about the whole "reanimated several people" bit, and she knew what I was, so I guess she was in on the whole supernatural thing.

Cael was still in the chair beside the bed, while Sabrina hovered over her daughter, pacing back and forth. I wondered where Josh had got to, then saw that the bathroom door was closed. I guess even badass shapeshifters have to pee sometimes.

Some of the worry seemed to wash out of Sabrina's face at the sight of Dr. Snowden. "Jodie," she said, and rushed around the end of the bed and threw her arms about the woman in a hug.

Dr. Snowden placed her bag at the foot of the bed and returned the embrace. "It's been so long. You look great," the doc said, then glanced at Alex where she lay bundled in blankets up to her chin. "Considering."

"Yes, well I'm sorry we have to get together under these circumstances," Sabrina said, a bit of a British accent slipping into her speech.

Dag nabit! Was Sabrina British? I'd never noticed. She'd certainly covered all trace of her accent until now. Maybe it was the stress that brought it out again, or being around one of her contemporaries. Or maybe she wasn't British at all, but unconsciously affected the accent when British people were around.

I heard the toilet flush, then the tap running, and the door to the bathroom opened.

"Jodie," Josh said, smiling at the sight of the doctor.

"Josh," the doctor replied. Somehow the name sounded better in British Posh. She hugged him, the top of her head barely coming up to the bottom of his chin. Josh even managed to look like he enjoyed it, and wasn't squirmy at all.

"Enough pleasantries," the doc said, disengaging. "Let's get a look at our patient, shall we?"

Jodie moved around to the head of the bed while Josh moved to Sabrina's side. She opened the bag she'd brought with her and took out a stethoscope. I guess she was a real doctor after all.

"And who is this young man," Jodie asked, looking at Cael still curled up in his chair. So far he had contented himself with remaining quiet, bleary eyes fixed on Alex's face.

"That's Cael," Josh answered for him. "Alex's...boyfriend."

I think he was actually getting used to the idea.

"Our little girl really is grown up," Jodie said. She pulled Alex's blankets down a bit and placed the stethoscope on her chest, listening intently as she timed Alex's pulse on the diamond encrusted wrist watch she wore.

"Jodie and I went to college together," Sabrina explained. "She delivered Alex."

Not for the first time I had to wonder how old Sabrina was. She could have passed for twenty five. Maybe thirty at best. Yet Alex was seventeen. Even if Sabrina had gotten pregnant at eighteen that would make her at least thirty-six or thirty-seven. Assuming she'd finished college—and not been pregnant in school—you could tack another three or four years on to that.

Hell, maybe it was magic. Dianecht had given Thomas a potion that kept him young. Maybe Sabrina had partaken as well. Josh was a shapeshifter who would live a few centuries at least. Maybe they'd evened the odds a little. There was no way I was going to ask though. Women are touchy enough about their age. I might as well ask, "So just how much plastic surgery have you had?"

Jodie took out one of those newfangled thermometers and stuck it in Alex's ear. Thank God, cause doing it the other way would have been some awkward, at least for me. The thermometer beeped and Jodie squinted at the readout, then stowed it away in her bag. "Pulse is strong and steady, temp's a little high, but nothing serious."

Maybe I'm right, I thought. *Maybe the kid's just lazy*. But if so, why did the doc look so concerned?

Jodie held a hand out, fingers splayed wide and palm down a few inches over Alex's forehead. She mumbled a few words that I couldn't understand—too guttural to be Latin, and I'm pretty sure it wasn't Arabic. Celtic maybe? Her hand glowed, the light a pale honey-gold, and her eyes darted back and forth beneath closed lids as if she were reading something.

I looked to Sabrina, the question writ clear on my face.

"Jodie's a witch," Sabrina said.

I couldn't help myself. "So you're telling me she's a witch doctor?"

Sabrina nodded, and Jodie grimaced even though her eyes remained closed.

"So she's like Dr. Bombay, only cuter," I said, not willing to let it go yet.

Sabrina ignored me, but then she was used to my antics. Jodie's lips curled up into a slight smile. I don't know if she was smiling at the reference, or the fact that I called her cute. If she got the reference though then it proved my theory that she was way older than she looked, just like Sabrina. Which made sense, I guess, if they'd gone to school together.

Jodie opened her eyes. "She's still in there," she said. "It's not a coma. To be honest I'm not sure exactly what it is, but if I had to guess I'd say she's retreated into herself." She fixed Sabrina with a sympathetic look. "And she's not coming back until she's good and ready."

"But she's okay?" Sabrina said. "She'll be alright."

Jodie bit her lip hesitantly. I could almost see the thoughts spinning in her head. Should she tell them what they *needed* to hear, or what they *wanted* to hear? In the end, I guess she decided on honesty. "Alex has entered the Dreaming." She paused for a moment to let that sink in. "Note I did not say that she *is* dreaming."

Josh growled, then looked embarrassed for doing so. "What's the difference?" he asked.

Jodie lowered her hand as the glow faded. "Dreaming is a construct of the brain. Bits of unfinished business we try to sort out in our sleep, or escapism. The Dreaming is a place. Everyone who was ever born or who will ever be born exists there. It's timeless. It's where we were before, and where we go after. It is the seat of creation. Everything that has or will happen exists in the Dreaming."

"I've been there," I said, and everyone turned to look at me. "Recently."

I'd died three times in the past year, not counting all those times I should have died but managed to heal myself. There was that first time in the parking lot of the Seven-Eleven, when I got shot. Although that time had been different too, in that I hadn't died in the normal sense of the word because I wasn't even aware that I was dead.

The second time was when the vamp blew up my car with me in it. That was the first time that I achieved transcendence. The third time was when Leanne was dying. Bran's Cauldron was sucking the life out of her and she'd reverted to what I'm guessing was her true form. I'd held on to her, throwing my arms around her when even the sight of her was enough to burn me to ash, and again I'd transcended.

If Jodie was right, then the Dreaming is where I'd transcended to. "Everything makes sense there," I said. "It's like the whole plan is laid out in front of you and you can see it from beginning to end."

"Like the akashic records?" Josh asked.

Jodie nodded, rummaging through her medical kit. "Something like that, although the akashic records are more of a glimpse of the magnitude that is the Dreaming. They're the little bit that our minds can hold on to and make sense of when overwhelmed by a concept it can't fathom. As for you, James, well, you *are* an Eternal. You've only one foot in reality to begin with, and the other planted firmly in the Dreaming."

Leanne had once told me that those who transcend rarely return. There was something so comforting about being there, as if you'd finally come home. Why would you want to leave?

I guess that was what Jodie feared for Alex, and what she didn't want to tell Josh and Sabrina.

Personally, I wasn't as worried. Given the choice I didn't believe Alex would leave the people that loved her any more than I had. Alex was way stronger than I was, a lot more responsible, and I'd been there twice and come back.

"Is that why the Veil is failing?" Cael said quietly from his bedside seat. It was the first thing I'd heard him say since arriving. "Because she's not really here?"

Jodie frowned. "Well, as to why the Veil is failing I can't really say."

How could she? She hadn't been clued in on the spell that caused the Veil to fail whenever the kids were separated.

I didn't want to think about what was going on outside at the moment. With the veil down any manner of creepy crawly might be wandering about the island freely. Our only saving grace was that most of them probably didn't realise the veil was down. It's like a locked door you walk past everyday; how are you supposed to know it's suddenly unlocked unless you check it?

"But you're right about Alex," Jodie said. "In a sense, she's not here at all."

"So what can we do?" Sabrina asked.

I'm sure the Veil was the last thing on Sabrina's mind at the moment. All that mattered was getting Alex back. The Veil could probably go rot, for all she cared.

"I'm afraid there's nothing you can do," Jodie said. She rummaged about in her medical bag for a moment, then held up a needle and a cotton swab in a sterile container and looked at me questioningly.

Right, the samples. I nodded, and she rolled up my sleeve. She put on some sterile surgical gloves. "Keep Alex warm and comfortable," Jodie said. She swabbed the area around my elbow with alcohol—as if I were worried about infection—and expertly found the vein. The glass tube filled with dark, red blood.

Hey, I have blood pressure. Who knew?

"If she stays in this state for more than a day we'll have to see about setting up an intravenous feed." Jodie said, and pulled the needle from my skin. She seemed downright disappointed when it didn't bleed. No doubt she had an overabundance of Hello Kitty band aids she was trying to get rid of. Jodie held the Q-tip up and I opened my mouth for her to swab the inside of my cheek. When she was done she placed it in the sterile container and labelled it with a black Sharpie: "James Decker, Eternal."

"I'm sorry I couldn't be more help, dears. I know I said it's not a coma, but for all intents and purposes it may as well be a coma." Jodie expertly removed her gloves, placing one inside the other to contain any contaminates, and sealed them in a Ziploc bag. She stored everything away in her medical kit, zipped it up and fastened the clasp. When she'd finished, she moved in to hug Josh and Sabrina.

Sabrina kissed her friend on the cheek. "Thank you so much for coming. I'm sorry to pull you away from your family like this on Christmas"

Christmas. I'd forgotten. I looked at my watch: ten past midnight. It was Christmas day.

"Anything for you, dear," Jodie said as she gathered her belongings. "Everyone was in bed anyway. I doubt they even missed me."

"Come on, I'll walk you out," I said, sensing the timing was right.

There was something I wanted to ask her, an idea I had, but I waited until we were at the front landing. I didn't want to get everyone's hopes up in case my idea turned out to be moronic, which they often did.

"What if I went in and got her?" I asked Jodie. "I could always off myself and force a transcendence." Of course I had no idea how to find Alex in the Dreaming, although once there the answer might present itself. Like I said, everything made sense there. If only you could remember any of it once you came back.

"I don't know. I suppose it might work," Jodie said doubtfully. She seemed to consider my question, as if it weren't moronic at all. "Alex is there, now. She knows how things are supposed to turn out. If she's meant to come out, then she will."

That wasn't much help. It sounded too much like, "what will be, will be." Right now I was looking for a little more help than the lyrics to a Doris Day song.

"What if I'm meant to go in and get her?"

Jodie laughed. "Maybe you are. To be honest, the whole concept is just a little much for me. It brings up too many questions about the nature of free will."

I retrieved her coat and held it out to help her on with it. "So you think I should wait?"

"For now," she said, sliding her feet into her boots. Jodie put on her gloves as I held the door open for her. She looked me in the eye, for the first time since we'd met, I realised.

There was something there, a depth which belied her apparent age. I felt a sudden sense of unease as I realised that Jodie was a lot older than she looked. Ancient. Timeless.

I wondered if Sabrina knew.

I shivered, and the sense of unease passed.

"Ultimately, the decision is yours," she said, and smiled, nothing more than a youngish twenty-something once more. "See, at least we have the illusion of free will."

Sometimes illusions are all we have, I thought as I said my goodbyes and closed the front door. I hadn't even made it to the stairwell when the doorbell rang. *Maybe the doc forgot something.*

I opened the door to see a homeless guy standing there. Well, not a homeless guy, but *the* homeless guy. The one I'd given the gum to, the gum he'd shared with all his friends. The one I'd bought the hotdogs for. He pulled his coat more tightly about himself, and nodded his head slightly, as if bowing in introduction.

"You're not Jodie," I said.

"No, I'm not," he answered, and removed his toque. "But I hear you're looking for me. I'm Manannán mac Lir, but you can call me Manny."

CHAPTER NINETEEN

"Honey, it's for you!" I called upstairs to Leanne as I held the door open for Manny.

Manannán mac Lir, sea god, necromancer, guardian of the Veil between the worlds, seemingly one of the Powers That Be and no doubt an original founder of the Stupid Rules, stepped inside. I closed the door behind him.

"Would you like some tea…or coffee?" I offered. "Or maybe something a little stronger?"

"Coffee would be nice," he said. "Even nicer with a splash of brandy."

"Coming right up. Um…come in and make yourself comfortable," I said. "Let me take your…toque."

I know what you're thinking, and shaddup you! I suppose you know what the protocol for entertaining a god in your home is? Didn't think so.

Manny handed me his toque, pulled off his boots with his heels, and plunked himself down in the chair beside the fireplace. "Nice tree," he called after me as I wandered into the kitchen in search of coffee and brandy.

"Thanks," I called back. I found a clean mug and poured coffee from the coffee maker—thankfully Josh had brewed a pot—then found the brandy in the liquor cabinet and added a trifle more than a splash. Hey, he's a god. I'm sure he can handle his liquor.

I handed Manny his coffee and he took a sip, peering over the edge of the cup as Leanne sauntered down the stairs. "Now there's a man who knows how to make coffee," he said, then waved at Leanne when she noticed him.

Leanne spotted our guest. A smile turned up the corner of her lips and she joined us, putting her arm around me. "I know you feel guilty about having all this money," she whispered in my ear, "So now we're entertaining homeless people?"

I looked at her and shrugged. *Heck, let her figure it out for herself*, I thought. It'd be more fun that way.

She kissed me on the cheek. "Love you," she murmured, then turned to our guest. "Can I offer you something to eat? Maybe a sandwich, or some homemade soup Mr...?"

"Manny. Manny mac Lir."

Was it just me, or was Manny looking better? It seemed with every sip his face looked less lined, his hair darker, his body more hale.

Leanne squinted at Manny as if the truth would more readily reveal itself through narrowed eyelids. I could almost see the thoughts swirling about in her pretty head. "Chaar-leeee!" she called out, the last syllable much louder and more drawn out than the first as she became more confident that she needed the ogre's presence, and right away.

"I didn't do it," Charlie called out reflexively from the library.

"Soup and sandwich would be lovely," Manny said, and nonchalantly took another sip of his coffee, his eyes brighter, his face less jowly.

Charlie ducked through the archway into the living room and spied Manny sipping coffee by the fireplace. "We have a guest?" the ogre asked warily. It wasn't like us to introduce him to someone like that without fair warning. For all Charlie knew, Manny was a mundane.

Drat peered around Charlie's leg. "Hey, James, I tought youse said youse unblocked all da porn sites on Leanne's compu—hey, who's da mook?"

Manny smiled, and stood. He looked to be in his late twenties or early thirties now. The homeless clothes didn't suit him at all. His hair was dark and wavy with strands that hung artfully from his temples. His eyes were the colour of a stormy sea, his cheekbones high and sharp, his mouth sensual. He was slim, and fit, his back straight and head held high. His image could have easily graced the cover of any romance novel. "I'm Manannán mac Lir," he said, announcing himself formally. "Pleased to meet you."

Charlie nodded in greeting. Somehow he made it look almost a bow of fealty.

Drat was a little less circumspect. "Hey, we was lookin for youse!"

"Ta da!" Manny said, striking out his right foot and raising his hands in a flourish.

"I'll get you that food," Leanne said, and escaped into the kitchen looking even more pale than usual.

I'm not really sure what Manannán mac Lir is. Maybe he's a god. Maybe not. But if Leanne and the rest of the Fae were fallen angels—and I'm not saying they are—then that made Manny something like...I don't know, at least an archangel, or a seraphim or something. Either way he sure as hell made Charlie and Leanne nervous. Drat, not so much.

"Jeeze, people. Quit yer suckin up. It ain't like he's gonna validate yer parkin or sumtin."

Manny laughed and I swear his eyes sparkled. "I love trolls," he said, and finished the last dregs of his coffee. "They're so direct."

"Ya, well how's dis for direct," Drat said, stepping around Charlie to stand in front of a bemused Manny. "Are youse gonna help us er what?"

Leanne had returned from the kitchen just in time to hear Drat's politely phrased request. If it weren't for her lightning fast Fae reflexes I'm betting she'd have dropped the tray she carried.

Josh appeared at the top of the stairs and tapped his ring finger against the wooden banister impatiently. "What's all the commotion down there?"

Sabrina must have sent him out to ask, otherwise neither of them would have left Alex's side.

"We have company," I called up.

That must have made Josh curious—curious enough to leave his daughter's bedside. I heard him barefoot it down the stairs taking them two at a time.

Manny had resumed his seat and was digging into the sandwich Leanne had offered him, following each bite with a spoonful of soup. You'd have thought he hadn't eaten in days. Maybe he'd taken his homeless act to heart.

Josh made his way around Charlie, who still hadn't moved from the archway, and stopped just in front of Manny. "Well, it's about time."

Manny looked up from his soup. "You know who I am?"

"I'll give youse a hint," Drat said. "He ain't Santy Clause."

"Manannán mac Lir," Josh said.

Drat touched the end of his long pointy nose to let Josh know he was on the money.

Josh stood in front of Manny, his face haggard with worry. "Well, can you help her? Can you fix the Veil?"

Manny swallowed the bite of sandwich he was working on. "Which is it? Help the girl, or fix the Veil?"

"Both," I said.

Manny nodded. "No compromise. I like that." He set the tray aside with the finished bowl of soup and picked up the remaining half of the sandwich. "Take me to her."

Josh led the way up the stairs with Manny close behind, followed by Leanne and I. Drat and Charlie brought up the rear. It was going to get awfully crowded in Alex's bedroom.

Manny entered the room almost solemnly. Sabrina shot Josh a questioning look, and he nodded letting her know everything was all right. That didn't stop Sabrina from watching Manny like a hawk, though.

Leanne and I moved in to stand at the foot of the bed, while Charlie and Drat peered through the doorway from the hall. Poor Cael had fallen asleep in his chair. Someone had wrapped him up in a blanket. His head jerked up when we entered the room but he stayed otherwise fast asleep. The kid had been through a lot, what with dying and all. I doubt Spinal Tap playing with their amps turned up to eleven could have woken him at the moment.

Manny knelt beside Alex's bed and placed a hand on the girl's forehead.

A look I can only describe as fondness lit up his face. "I can help, but first there is something I require of you."

He spoke formally, his voice reverberating with power, and I could tell it was the making of a pact. Pacts required formal speech.

"If he asks me to fetch him a shrubbery I'm gonna kick his ass, god or not," I muttered to Josh.

Manny laughed. Maybe he found the thought of me kicking his ass amusing. Maybe he was a Monty Python fan.

Manny stood and faced me. He wore his no nonsense face now. I got the message; this was serious stuff.

"You must perform three tasks," he said. "First, you must find Redemption."

The way he said it I could practically hear the capital "R." I had no idea what he was talking about, either. I mean, what did I need redemption for?

"Second, you must Champion the Scion. And finally, you must make me another cup of that wonderful coffee."

"Is that all?"

Manny shrugged. "Nothing comes free, not even for you, Eternal. You have this lovely home, the cars, these friends, but at what cost? Your old life, your old house, your car, even your love, Alison. All gone. And the bard, Thomas. There is always a price."

Leanne stepped forward, facing the god. She didn't seem as in awe of him all of a sudden. As a matter of fact she looked pissed. "You talk as if he owes you, yet he never asked for any of this. If anything, you owe him. He defeated the demon Aeshma, and saved the Innocent. He ended the Eternal, Azrael, and spared the lives of everyone in the city. He's the one who's fighting to restore the Veil and keep order. No one asked him, but he's here none the less. It's the world that needs him, and not the other way around."

If Manny were piqued at Leanne's insolence, he didn't let on. As a matter of fact he seemed rather unaffected by it. "It's true, there was need of a new Eternal. But that was someone else's bargain, one for which they paid dearly." Manannán fixed his gaze upon me. "Still, tell me true, Eternal; do you feel slighted?"

I couldn't help but wonder who had paid the price that saw me resurrected as an Eternal, and why, but that seemed unimportant at the moment. I looked around the room at the people gathered there, and squeezed Leanne's hand. I shook my head. "No. I do not."

Manannán smiled. "As I suspected. As I had hoped."

Charlie raised his hand.

Manny took a bite of his sandwich. "Yes, you, the ogre in the doorway."

I face-palmed as Charlie actually looked about to make sure he was the ogre the god referred to.

Charlie put down his hand. "I have a question?"

"Shoot."

"Why is it that every major religion in the world preaches that we should be charitable, that we should give freely of ourselves to others with no thought of compensation, yet the universe always demands payment?"

Manny's eyebrows shot up in surprise. Apparently it was something he'd never considered before. "Good question." His face broke into a wide smile. "I'll bring that up at the next meeting."

The answer seemed to satisfy Charlie, but I couldn't be sure the god wasn't just funning with us.

"As for now, however, our deal still stands," Manny said, finishing his sandwich. I don't know how he managed to do that and not get crumbs everywhere like I always do, but then I guess that's why he's a god. "Do you accept?"

I didn't even have to think about it. It's not like we had any other viable options. "I'll get you that coffee," I said.

Manny held out his hand. I guess he required that we shake on it. I grasped his hand firmly and we shook. A bell sounded. A really big bell, deep and resonating like one of those Tibetan temple bells. "Deal," Manny said.

Alex's eyes fluttered open. "Mom?"

Sabrina threw herself on the bed and wrapped her arms about her daughter, blankets and all.

Josh sat down on the edge and smoothed his daughter's hair away from her face, then kissed her forehead. "Welcome back."

The rest of us stood around smiling like idiots. Alex blushed a deep red and pulled the blankets up over her head.

"Someone wake the boy," Josh said.

Drat kicked the chair Cael slept in, rocking it hard.

Cael's head shot up, his eyes barely opened. "What?"

No one needed tell him. He saw Josh and Sabrina on the bed and Alex squirming under the covers, then he was at her side, pulling the blankets back and kissing her face. Not even Josh seemed to mind.

Alex sat up and pushed the covers down to her waist, then threw her arms around Cael. "I thought you were dead," Alex said. "I went looking for you."

"You brought me back," Cael said. "You brought us all back."

Was that it? Had she gone into the afterlife to bring Cael and the others back from the dead, and not had the strength to leave herself?

"Maybe next time you might try just bringing one or two back," Manny said, confirming my suspicions. "Pick a favourite, or someone deserving."

Alex blinked, probably wondering who this stranger was giving her advice. I guess with all of us around her she felt safe enough not to worry much about it, though. "I couldn't do that," she said.

"Oh, right," Manny said, and shrugged. "She's Hope."

Dad and Grandpa appeared, hovering in the corners and out of the way, and Bear popped in, slobbered on everyone in the bed, and popped out again. Josh growled, but his heart wasn't in it, while Sabrina just laughed and wiped the slobber away from everyone with the corner of a blanket. I guess nothing could dampen their spirits now that Alex was back. Not even Bear slobber. I think we all felt the same.

"And where have you been?" I asked the ghosts.

"I think they were with me," Alex said.

"No matter where you go, there's always a Decker watching over you," Grandpa said, pulling on his suspenders. "Even in the afterlife."

Dad nodded, and the two of them vanished.

I pulled Manny out into the hallway, although I practically had to shove Charlie out of the way to do it. He followed me down the stairs and into the kitchen, and I poured him another coffee and topped it off with some more brandy.

"Thanks," I said, and handed him the cup. "For Alex."

"Consider it partial payment, in good faith," Manny said, and took a sip. The bell sounded again, just as loudly as the last time. Manny smiled. "That's one down." He motioned for me to take a seat at the kitchen table. "Perhaps now would be a good time to go over some of the relevant Stupid Rules," he said, and set the cup on a coaster.

I made my startled face.

"Yes, I know that's what you call them. I know everything," he said. "Well, most everything. Usually."

I went to the refrigerator and got myself a diet Pepsi, then sat down at the table. There was no use excusing myself. Besides, I think he was amused by my label. I got the impression he might even agree with it.

He tipped his cup at me and I touched the neck of my plastic bottle to it, and we drank. "First," he said, "the Veil will remain down until after you've fulfilled the last two provisions of our agreement." He shrugged. "I can no more remove a spell without meeting its conditions than I can destroy energy. I can, however, change those conditions. To that end it is no longer linked to the children, but to your quest."

I screwed the cap back onto the bottle. No sense letting it go flat. "Couldn't you have made the conditions something simple, like I have to pat my head and rub my tummy at the same time?"

Manny leaned back in his chair. His fingers traced the symbol of a Celtic knot he wore on a pendant about his neck. "The conditions must be commiserate with the original severity and intent of the spell." He took another sip. "Besides, that would have hardly suited my purpose."

I couldn't help but wonder what that purpose might be. I suddenly had the nagging suspicion I was being played here, that maybe we all were. I also suspected that there was nothing we could do about it. Whatever his plans were, my gut told me they were benevolent, as was he. Of course, it could turn out that we were some of those few he was willing to sacrifice for the greater good, which is awesome if you're one of the many, but sucks when you're one of the few.

"Secondly, the tear in the Veil is restricted to this island. Salt water negates the effect—those witches are powerful, but not that powerful."

That was a relief. At least I only had to worry about defending Vancouver Island and not the entire world. Just a measly 750,000 people or so. Piece of cake.

"Still, the tear provides a foothold in this world, one the Otherworld folk could use to push out from," Manny said, bursting my bubble. He got that thousand yard stare, although I was pretty sure it wasn't merely the distance he was staring off into. "Already there are worlds where the Fae have overrun humanity, where humankind has become extinct."

Damn. I hate it when gods go all *Sliders* on me. "Anything else," I asked.

"No, that about covers it," Manny said, his eyes focused once more.

"Since we're being so upfront and all, what's with the homeless guy act?"

"I think you know," he said.

He was right, I had a pretty good idea, but I wanted to hear him say it.

"We all have our own ways of judging people worthy. I believe a man's true nature is reflected in how he treats those more unfortunate than he, but more importantly, in how he treats those who can do nothing for him. You fed me, always gave freely, were never condescending or judgmental, and you surround yourself with likewise people. Even the Lhiannan Sidhe, who was at one time part vampire, offered me food when she found me here in her home this night, before she knew who I was and thought me simply a vagrant you had been kind to."

"Sure, I get that," I said. "It's pretty much the same way I feel."

"I know."

I got up from the table and put the rest of my drink back in the refrigerator. "Just one more question—why are you talking all formal-like all of a sudden?"

Manny smiled, and I swear I think I made the god blush.

"Sorry, part of me was just in the eighteenth century. I guess I got us kind of mixed up."

"Oh, god stuff."

"God stuff," Manny agreed, and finished his coffee. "Well I should be going, after all you've got your work cut out for you."

I nodded. "I don't suppose you could give me a hint as to how to go about accomplishing these tasks. Let's face it, they're a little cryptic."

Manny shook his head. "Sadly, no.

I looked into his eyes and that irreverent sparkle was gone. What I saw was concern, and sadness, and it suddenly occurred to me that he too was bound by the Stupid Rules, and was just as unhappy about it as I was.

Manny began to fade—kind of like Marty McFly as he was being erased from history. "One last thing," he said. "I wouldn't dally. You only have until sunrise of Christmas Day to complete your tasks, or not even I can raise the Veil again."

I stood alone in the kitchen and glanced at the wall clock. I had a little less than eight hours left to save the world. Piece of cake.

CHAPTER TWENTY

I went upstairs to break the bad news to everyone. They all took it better than I had hoped. As a matter of fact I seemed to be the only one who wasn't expecting it.

I watched Josh in front of the bathroom mirror as he shaved what little stubble he had with an electric razor. Now that Alex was okay, little things like appearance mattered, I guess.

"The Veil's already been down for a couple of hours," Josh said. "I hate to imagine the damage that's been done while we've been…rallying. Just how long did you think we could let this slide?"

Sabrina stepped out from the walk-in closet with fresh clothes for Josh. "Put these on," she said, then wrinkled her nose. "But shower first. Leanne wants us all down in the den in twenty minutes to discuss our battle plan, so you've got time."

"How's the kid doing?" I asked.

Sabrina sighed. "She's asleep—real sleep this time. I sent Cael to bed too, in his own room."

"Damn straight," Josh said, cleaning off his razor in the sink. "I swear that kid would have watched her sleep all night if I'd let him. Who's he think he is, Edward?"

"More like Jacob."

Josh stared at me blankly.

"You know, shapeshifter." And yes, I've read the books *and* seen the movies. Shaddup, you.

Sabrina and I left Josh alone to shower in private. Josh and I are close, but not that close. We all met downstairs in the living room at the appointed time. Josh looked better, but he still looked tired. Sabrina too.

Drat was good to go; trolls are naturally nocturnal. Even Charlie looked refreshed. I guess he'd gotten enough sleep when we'd left him behind. Leanne's Fae constitution had kicked in so she looked downright perky. Of course I was fine.

Nevertheless, Leanne entered the living room with a tray of tall glasses filled with what looked like sambucas—if sambuca were red, like tomato juice, and you could get tomato juice to flame. "Drink up, everyone."

Josh took the glass and looked at the contents dubiously. "What is it?"

"Think of it as sort of a Fae Red Bull," Leanne said. "Trust me, you'll feel much better after a shot of this." She blew the flame out on her own glass and took a sip, which convinced us she wasn't trying to poison us, at least.

I looked down at my glass. Not really tomato juice after all. Maybe if you mixed it with blood. "I don't really need—"

"Shut up and drink," Leanne ordered.

I shut up and did what I was told. "You know, it's not half bad. It tastes kind of like baked pineapple in brown sugar."

"You're just saying that to get us to drink it," Josh said, still eyeing his glass suspiciously.

Sabrina looked to her husband in a show of support. "You first."

"You're just saying that because if I die you get all my stuff," Josh said, but held his breath and took a sip, then a longer one when he realised I wasn't lying. "It's not bad," Josh said as Sabrina and the rest of the gang followed suit. "But I don't really feel any differently. "

Leanne smiled. "Give it a minute or two."

Drat downed his in one gulp. "You got any more a deese?"

"Trust me, Drat. One will do," Leanne said, and collected his glass. She waited until we'd all finished, took the empties back into the kitchen, then returned and sat on the couch beside me.

"So what's the plan?" I asked. The only thing I was certain of is that they weren't relying on me to come up with it, something for which I was immensely grateful. I know my limitations.

Charlie folded his right leg under himself in his giant chair and leaned back to get more comfortable. "I've been watching the news," he said. "Things are bad, but they haven't gotten worse."

"It's Christmas Eve," Leanne said as I put my arm around her and played with her hair. "That's pretty potent magic. Even with the Veil down it will be difficult to cross over. And most people are at home in bed, which is probably the safest place they could be. It's next to impossible for Summerland folk to cross a threshold without an invite, especially now, with all the wreaths and mistletoe on the doors."

"Most of those wreaths and stuff aren't real," I said, twisting a strand of her hair into knots. "They're plastic."

Leanne slapped my hand away and the knots in her hair magically undid themselves. "It doesn't matter. Like I said before, with magic it's the intent that counts. It may not be as potent, but it's still a barrier. So unless the Fae start showing up on people's doorstep knocking on their doors and asking to come in…."

"With the Veil down the glamours are gone, too," Charlie said. "Your average Dark Sidhe won't exactly pass as a door to door salesmen."

"Jehovah's Witness, maybe," I said. "But salesman? Unlikely."

Leanne accidently elbowed me in the ribs. That's my story and I'm sticking to it.

"As fate would have it," she said, "if the Veil did have to fall it couldn't have happened at a better time. But that won't last. A lot of the really nasty stuff hasn't come across yet; things like Red Caps and Kelpies, Fir Darrig, Kobolds, and Spriggans. If we don't get the Veil back up before sunrise and it stays down? Let's just say December 26th will not be pretty."

Josh stood up and started pacing. He almost crackled with nervous energy. Maybe Leanne's concoction had taken effect. "I think we all understand why we need to keep the Veil up," he said. "The question remains: how?"

Everyone looked at everyone else. Drat was the first to speak up.

He sat on the loveseat. His legs were stretched out in front of him and still didn't make it past the end of the cushion. We all had a good view of the bottom of his dirty, scaled feet. "I tink we all knows what da second task is." He looked at Josh when he said it. "We'se got ta take dat rock sucker Liam off'n da trone and crown da true king."

Josh scratched at the back of his head and kept pacing. "You're right," he said. "But you're looking at the wrong guy. Oh, I'll help you depose Liam—as a matter of fact I'll take great pleasure in it, but I won't take his place. I gave up my claim to the throne a long time ago." He stopped his pacing and looked up the stairwell. "It's that boy up there. He's the rightful king now."

Heads nodded all around.

"It seems we're all in agreement on that one," I said, "Which means we're probably wrong, but it's all we have. So, anyone have any ideas as to how I find redemption?"

Leanne took my hand, entwining her fingers with mine. "I can't even imagine what it is you might need redemption for."

I thought it was sweet that she had that kind of faith in me. I didn't tell her that, of course, 'cause I'm a manly man.

Drat had found some stale Doritos in the loveseat's cushions and was happily munching away. "Did youse murderlize someone when youse was young?" Drat asked.

"Not that I can recall," I said. I was a bit of a hellion in my youth, acting out after Dad died, but I don't remember ever wronging anyone. Well, not major league wronging, anyway. Mom and Greg had kept me pretty much in hand and out of trouble. "Look, I'm no saint, but I have no idea what I did that requires redemption. Maybe Manny took exception to some minor or obscure offence that I'll never for the life of me figure out, in which case

I've no idea what to do to atone."

Sabrina rocked back and forth in her chair, her eyes bright and all the haggard lines smoothed from her face. Even her hair seemed to shine with a new lustre. "Maybe you could just go to a priest and confess your sins?"

"I'm not catholic."

"It wouldn't matter anyway," Charlie said. "A priest can only grant you absolution, not redemption."

"Dere's a difference?" Drat asked, licking the nacho cheese powder off his fingers.

Charlie nodded. "Redemption is an act of atonement. You must do something, sacrifice something in order to be redeemed. Absolution is an act of forgiveness. It doesn't necessarily require you to do anything. Someone else grants you freedom from blame."

Everyone took his word for it.

"I say we concentrate on the problem we do have a solution to," Sabrina said. "Maybe the other one will sort itself, or become evident in the process."

I stood up, manifested my sword, and slung it across my back. "It beats sitting around here," I said. "And we're running out of time."

Leanne grabbed my hand and pulled me back down onto the couch beside her. "Not so fast. You think the six of us are going to over-throw Liam all by our lonesome?"

Sabrina stood up and started pacing with her husband, moving in opposite circles. I don't know what was in that Fae Red Bull, and sometimes it's just better not to know. I have an aversion to eye of newt, blind worm's sting, and…snail nipples. I avoid ingesting them whenever possible.

"What did you have in mind?" Sabrina asked.

Leanne grinned. "We call in a favour or two."

I knew exactly who she meant. "Skatha and CuChulainn owe me big time."

"My thoughts exactly," Leanne said, patting my hand. If she'd had a hero cookie I'd have qualified for sure. "I called them while Josh was upstairs in the shower. They'll be here within the hour."

That's why I love her. Well, that and she's hot, and sexy, and…never mind.

"So eight of us then. That's much better," Charlie said.

I'm not sure if he was being sarcastic or not.

Charlie stood and stretched. "I'll go ahead to the Empress so they'll be expecting us, and do a little scouting along the way."

Josh stopped and tilted his head from side to side, cracking the bones in his neck. "Everyone else suit up."

"I'm coming with," Cael said from where he sat on the bottom stairs.

So much for situational awareness.

Josh turned toward the boy. If anything, he looked sympathetic. "How long have you been there?"

Cael stood and moved to the center of the room, stopping just in front of Josh. They were almost the same height and build. Both had that same defiant look about them. They say girls look for men who remind them of their father. I'd say Alex had succeeded.

"Long enough to know that you plan to overthrow my father and set me on the throne," Cael said, speaking directly to Josh. "Did anyone here think it might be a good idea to ask me what I thought about it?"

"I did," Drat said, raising his hand. "But den I got hungry an I kinda forgot about it."

Sabrina moved to stand beside Josh, a united front. "So just how do you feel about it?"

Cael cracked his neck the same way Josh had just done, and shrugged his shoulders to warm up the muscles. "My father had me murdered just to prove a point. Count me in."

I looked to Josh, who nodded.

"Get the boy a weapon," Josh said.

Cael grinned. I think he'd expected more resistance, but Josh had been through this whole ascension nonsense before. And with Liam, come to think of it. If anyone understood how Cael felt, it would be Josh. Besides, no one should have a throne handed to them. Cael would earn his the old-fashioned way.

Sabrina retrieved Josh's duffle bag from where he'd stored it in the hall closet. Cael picked out an AK47, and Josh shrugged as if to say, "To each his own."

Cael eyeballed the magazine in front of Josh before inserting it into the weapon. "You realise if we pull this off you'll have to refer to me as Your Majesty. No more of this "boy" crap."

Josh looked at him askance. "You're not *my* king."

Cael looked up the stairs. There was no one there. "What about Alex?"

"She stays here," Josh and Sabrina said simultaneously.

Josh put a hand on the boy's shoulder. "There's no reason to put her in danger, and we'll be more effective if we don't have to worry about her." He turned to his wife. "You're staying, too." Sabrina started to protest but Josh covered her mouth with the palm of his hand. "Someone has to stay and watch Alex."

I noticed he didn't try shushing her with a finger to her lips. Good thing, too; she probably would have broken it. As it was, I'm surprised she didn't bite his hand. Her eyes said she definitely considered it, but after a couple of seconds the fight went out of them. Josh lowered his hand.

"It sucks when you're right," Sabrina said.

Josh put his arms about her and pulled her in close. "Luckily it doesn't happen often."

There was nothing to do now but wait for Skatha and CuChulainn to show. That turned out to be harder than it seemed. The Fae Red Bull had pumped everyone into overdrive. We were as antsy as a bunch of Ritalin kids off their meds who'd been eating Pixie Sticks, Pop Rocks and drinking Jolt Cola all day.

I looked at the presents under the tree. "Maybe we should open our gifts before we go," I said. Somewhere in the back of my mind there was the nagging thought that we might not all survive to open them later. I pushed it deeper into the recesses.

"Not likely, mister," Leanne said, poking me in the chest with her index finger. "First we defeat the ev-il. Then we open the presents. Got it?"

"Yes, dear."

"Children," she muttered to Sabrina as they rummaged through the hall closet for their coats and stuff.

Everyone was suited up and raring to go. We were all about to play Twister or Red Rover or something to burn off some of our pent up energy, when the doorbell rang. Josh was so wired I thought we were going to have to peel him off the ceiling, just like that cat in the Looney Tunes cartoon every time the puppy snuck up behind him and barked.

"I'll get it," I said, and did.

Skatha stood on the step with CuChulainn just behind her. She stared at me with those Fae-green eyes of hers, unblinking. She'd tied her ginger hair in braids so that they hung strait down and draped over the front of her shoulders. On closer inspection I noted small, razor sharp blades woven into the ends. She dressed in black form-fitting motorcycle leathers—the kind with pockets of protective padding sewn into them in case of a spill. The jacket was zipped to the top of the short military-style collar, and the basket-hilt of her claymore peeked above her right shoulder. She wore a belt slung low on her hips that bristled with knives and darts and throwing stars, and a long-handled knife jutted out of the top of her left boot. And those were just the weapons I could see. Knowing Skatha there were probably a dozen or so more that I couldn't.

She lunged forward suddenly as if to head-butt me and I flinched and took a step back. Her face broke into a wide smile. "Gotcha."

CuChulainn shook his head slowly, behind her back, although I'm sure she saw. His grey-blue eyes fixed me with one of those "What am I going to do with her" looks.

When I first met him I'd thought his hair red; turns out it was just slick with the blood of his enemies. I know…eeewww. Now, cleaned up and without all those nasty wounds, his hair was dark and hung down to his shoulders. A thin war braid wrapped in green leather draped down the left side of his face, and damn but he was pretty. Like, male underwear model pretty. His complexion was dark, too, as if he'd spent all his time outdoors. Of course when I found him he'd been tied to a tree with his own intestines for the last few thousand years. At least he'd gotten a nice tan out of it so it wasn't a total waste.

CuChulainn wore the same leathers Skatha did, just without the accessories. He carried the bone spear, the *Gae Bolga*, in his left hand. It was covered in wicked barbs and hooks, so I'm guessing it wouldn't exactly fit nicely into a sheath or scabbard.

I think what surprised me most about him was his size. He wasn't a big man, only about five-foot eight or nine, with broad shoulders, narrow hips and large, muscular thighs. He looked more like an Olympic sprinter than a fighter.

He couldn't speak, of course. Not since I'd used Bran's Cauldron to resurrect him.

"Hey, Cuckoo. How's it hanging?" I said. It's what I'd taken to calling him, his real name being such a mouthful and all. Actually, Leanne told me his real name was Setanta. Some wise-ass druid named him CuChulainn because he'd taken the place of some guy's dog or something and the name had stuck. His name literally meant *Chulainn's dog*. Anyway, Cuckoo was easier, and if CuChulainn objected he never said anything.

Skatha tapped her booted foot impatiently. "Well, are ya goin ta invite us in or leave us oot standin in tha cold?"

Skatha was Fae; she couldn't come in without an invite. I considered leaving her outside but knew I'd pay for it one way or another. "Come on in," I said, smiling, and stood aside.

Skatha breezed by me, slapping my face affectionately with a gloved hand as she did so. CuChulainn followed, rolling his eyes. I couldn't help but wonder if sometimes he'd rather I'd left him dead and tied to that tree in the ford.

Leanne approached Skatha smiling, but wary—like two cats meeting for the first time. I'm almost certain they'd met before, though. I guess it's a Fae thing. Personally I wouldn't trust most of the Sidhe as far as I can throw them. No wait…I could probably throw one pretty far. Well, you get the picture.

Leanne and Skatha clasped hands at the wrists. It was the most uncomfortable handshake I'd ever seen. Leanne looked like she was checking for weapons, and Skatha like she was getting a good grip to better execute the flying toe hold.

CuChulainn watched much the same way I did, his arms crossed and a bemused smile on his face. He looked at me as if to say, "I bet you my girlfriend can take your girlfriend."

I'm not saying that I'd like to see those two fight—well, not unless it involved a wrestling ring full of pudding—but...where was I again?

Leanne let go first. "It's been ages since I last saw you."

Skatha frowned. "You don't call fer centuries, an when you finally do it's ta invite me ta an apocalypse?" Her eyes got that wicked glint in them I remember from back when she used to beat me up on a daily basis. "I knew I liked you."

Leanne laughed, and hugged the woman. A real hug this time, too.

Skatha had trained me. More importantly she'd arranged for me to kill the Korrigan and free Leanne from the demonic possession that had made a vampire of her. She'd more likely than not done it for her own reasons—to put me in her debt so that I'd use the Cauldron to resurrect CuChulainn—but there was still a part of me that couldn't help but feel she'd done it just because she liked me, in her own way. Of course that's not very Fae-like so she'd never admit it. But I knew, and so did Leanne.

Skatha stepped back and drummed her fingertips along the grip of the old army browning semi-auto in the holster strapped to her left thigh. "So I hear ya want us ta help you take tha pantywaist Liam off tha throne," she said.

"If it's not too much bother," I said.

"Is that the boy there?" she asked, nodding her head in Cael's direction.

"Nah, he's just the pizza delivery guy," I said. "We asked if he'd like to help us with the apocalypse and he said sure, seeing as we're such good tippers and all."

Skatha ignored me, as most of my friends do, and beckoned for Cael to come closer. "Come here, boy. Let me get a gander at you."

Cael sighed but stepped forward nevertheless, probably picturing his coronation should we be successful in overthrowing his father: "*Announcing his Royal Majesty—The Boy!*"

Skatha looked him up and down, assessing him the same way she had Josh and I when we'd first met. I knew from experience just how unnerving that could be, but Cael held up pretty well, meaning he didn't faint, or pee himself.

Skatha completed her assessment and looked towards CuChulainn, who nodded. "When we're done here, if we're successful, come see us for training," she said. "We'll teach ya how ta really fight. Something tells me you are goin ta need it."

Cael tried to swallow, and nodded. I don't know if he realised the honour she'd just bestowed on him. After almost two thousand years Skatha had opened her fighting school again. Everyone who was anyone had flooded to her door, begging for her to teach them. To date, she had accepted none of them.

My phone rang, saving Cael from everyone's scrutiny. It was Charlie.

"The Fae are massing in the street near the Empress," he said. "I think they're trying to blockade it, to stop us from crossing over."

"We'll be right there," I said, and hung up. I turned to the others. "The game's afoot, and it looks like they're not going to make it easy for us."

"The van's outside, warmed up and ready to go," Josh said.

I couldn't help but find it funny that we were going to war in a minivan. Sure, it was a G-Class Mercedes, but still. It would only seat seven of us comfortably, but Drat didn't take up much space and I'd be travelling on my own, as usual.

"I'll meet you there," I said as I held the door open and everyone filed past outside to the waiting van

I waved to them as they drove off before shutting and locking the door. There was still something nagging at me, and I realised what it was just before teleporting to the Empress.

How did the Fae know we were coming?

CHAPTER TWENTY-ONE

Charlie and I watched the line of Fae from an upstairs balcony at the Empress. The contingent was made up of members of both the Seelie and Unseelie court. I guess Light and Dark Fae had finally found something they could agree on. About twenty or so horsemen roamed the streets around the hotel while foot soldiers found what cover they could near the entrances. Archers manned most of the balconies.

The unconscious bodies of the two that had holed up on the balcony we presently occupied were hog-tied and lying on the floor in the room behind us. Fae skulls are rather thick, but when an ogre decides to bounce two of them off one another…

So far most of the Otherworld activity centered on the area around Government Street, from Chinatown to the BC Legislative Assembly buildings and the museum. It's where the ley lines intersected. The Fae had used the Empress to cross over to Darkside for the exact same reason we meant to use it to cross to Summerland: easy access. I'd wondered at how they'd known about our plan to cross there but I guess it wasn't such a mystery after all. I mean, where else would we go?

I could see blue and red flashing lights in the distance as police and fire emergency vehicles tried to cross the bridge from Esquimalt into Victoria. As soon as they hit the spot where the Veil had faltered their vehicles stalled out and went dark. The cops got out of their cars and milled about near the end of the bridge, probably trying to come up with a new plan now that none of their toys worked. I was surprised at how many cops there were. I'd have thought they might be hard to come by this time of night, and on Christmas Eve. The off-duty ones had already had too much to drink to report in. The Victoria cops had likely called for reinforcements.

I wondered how this would go down in the police reports. The Sidhe you could probably write off as some crazy cult or university prank, but the ghosts, and beasties and other nasty things that went bump in the night might be a little harder to explain. Of course if we couldn't get the Veil back up it wouldn't matter. There'd be no need to cover it up; it would be the new reality and everyone would just have to deal as best they could. By morning the entire island would be permanently Amish.

Charlie's pointed ears twitched. "They're here," he said. "I can hear Drat complaining." The ogre grinned, showing off his tusks. "Skatha won't let him smoke. She says it'll give away their position."

I didn't hear anything, but I took his word for it. Charlie's hearing wasn't more acute than mine, he just listened better.

The plan was for Josh and the gang to drop the van off at Josh's place, then make their way to the hotel on foot. Skatha and CuChulainn were good but I doubted even they could sneak a minivan past the Sidhe surrounding the place. At a nod, Charlie followed me down to the Bengal Room. We made our way to the fireplace to await the others just as something poked its head up from the tunnel. It looked female, and mostly human, if humans were greenish and had leaves for hair—kind of like a cross between a Vulcan and a *Ficus*. Its eyes were yellow and vertically slit, and it had sharp, pointed teeth like inward curving thorns in its lipless mouth.

"Pardon me," it said in a crisp, British accent. "Is this the way to Darkside?"

I shoved a hand in my pocket and leaned against the fireplace mantel. "Sorry, no. This is Neverland. Darkside's down the tunnel, hang a left, and four doors on the right."

It blinked, the nictitating membrane drawn across its eyes like shutters from left to right. "Thanks, govn'er," it said, and disappeared back into the tunnel.

"Dryad," Charlie said. "It's a nymph, or as Drat calls them, 'Forrest Whores.'"

I couldn't imagine anyone wanting to sleep with that fang-faced monstrosity, but then I remembered that the glamours were malfunctioning. Normally, I imagine she'd appear quite lovely.

I heard something in the hallway, but just barely. Someone, or a bunch of someone's, approached stealthily, the padded footfalls barely discernable above the muted late night sounds of the hotel. A shadow appeared in the doorway, a silhouette that I'd recognise anywhere, though it was longer and thinner than the one who cast it. Drat was first through, followed shortly by the rest of the gang.

"Any trouble getting by?" I asked once they had all assembled near the mantle.

Leanne pulled the cowl of her leather hoodie back from her face and gave me a quick kiss. "For the most part, no," she said. "We were almost blindsided by a Fluffy Bunny of Doom, but...um...Drat ate it."

Drat coughed a few tufts of grey fluff into a closed fist.

"Fluffy Bunny of Doom?"

"Think killer rabbit a la Monty Python and the Holy Grail," Josh said.

I looked at him wide-eyed, and he nodded, confirming I'd heard him correctly. The Other Realm never ceased to amaze me. I mean, there are Fluffy Bunnies of Doom, but no Hobbits? Seriously.

I nodded to Skatha and CuChulainn. "Are we all ready to—"

Something roared outside. Something really big, like T-Rexasaurus big. I felt the tremor through the floor, like an earthquake as the bottles and glasses behind the bar clinked against one another, chandeliers clattered overhead, and the windows rattled in their frames.

I peered out of the window into the darkness outside. The lights that normally illuminated the gardens had gone out. "What the—"

"Jabberwocky?" Charlie suggested.

"Nae, tis too wee fer that," Skatha said.

Too wee? I never, ever want to come within a thousand miles of a Jabberwocky. The Jabberwocky? Are there more than one?

Gunfire popped off outside, first a few sporadic shots, then some sustained, automatic fire.

Cael gripped the stock of his AK-47 a little tighter. "Whatever it is, it's found another way through," he said. "It obviously didn't come up through the tunnels."

"It must have got here the same way the Migs appeared over Midian," Josh said, "through some sort of overlap between the worlds."

Midian? I guess that was the name of the Therian city. Who knew?

I looked around at the others. "So, what?" I said. "Do we go or do we stay?"

"It dinna matter what's happen'n here," Skatha said. "You want ta fix it? You have ta take on Liam."

CuChulainn nodded, but then he agreed with everything Skatha said. Still, I couldn't fault the logic.

Whatever was outside roared again, followed by more gunfire and the sound of metal rending. I heard howling, first one voice, shortly followed by a chorus of others. Not dogs, or wolves either. It was a deeper timbre with a growling undertone.

Josh and Cael looked knowingly at one another.

"Werewolves," Cael said. "Well that changes everything."

"How so?"

"No sense going now," Josh answered. "They're here."

So Liam had brought the fight to us.

I reached back behind the fireplace mantle for the lever and pushed it up. The fireplace rotated, grinding stone on stone as the portal closed. ""That suits me just fine. We have the home team advantage now."

A brief, bright orange flash lit up the night sky through the window facing the harbour. A contrail traced a path from across the bay to a large, dark shape in the water near the docks beside *Milestone's* Restaurant. The shape roared as fire blossomed against its side. The concussion rattled the hotel windows and plaster fell from the ceiling as black and grey smoke billowed about the impact site, obstructing further view. Someone must have found a rocket launcher. The contrail had come from the general vicinity of the base, so more likely the military had gotten involved.

"It's getting all *Cloverfield* out there," I said. "Let's do this."

No one said anything. They all stood staring at me.

"Oh, right," I said. "Follow me."

They did.

A bunch of regular folk had gathered about the hotel lobby, looking frightened. Someone had found candles—even the emergency lights weren't working. Some of the guests were still in their pajamas. At least none of them were dumb enough to venture outside. One of them screamed when they saw Drat, then fainted when they saw Charlie. The rest huddled into the farthest corner from us and stared wide-eyed in the flickering candle light as we made our way to the exit. Charlie smiled at a little girl in a fluffy pink onesie. Her eyes went wide and she held her teddy bear out in front of her for protection. Drat chuckled, but poor Charlie looked rather stricken.

I stepped out onto the first set of terraced steps. Blue and red flashing lights from across the harbour illuminated the night like a psychedelic strobe. Fires added to the effect, an orange glow against the black soot cloud spewed by a burning Mercedes off to the left, a rooftop fire lighting the skyline to the right.

The Fae arrayed before us, a line of mixed Dark and Light Sidhe foot soldiers fronting the Empress Hotel. Their columns reached back to the harbour wall where the High Sidhe sat astride their nightmare steeds, their mounts' eyes aflame as they pawed agitatedly, steel shod hooves striking sparks from the pavement. Shadows, the inky silhouettes of werewolf and werebear, formed a line atop the retaining wall that separated the upper harbour from the lower. The wolves threw their heads back and howled at the moon that shone fitfully through the cloud cover. A dragon broke through the ceiling of low lying smoke and set fire to one of the naval vessels before tracer rounds from an anti-aircraft battery chased it back into cover.

The front line of Fae parted forming a corridor as a horseman broke ranks and slowly made its way toward the steps where we awaited.

Queen Aine.

Liam walked along beside her and held her mount's reins. That must have been a swift kick to the ego for the shapeshifter, but Josh had told me once you'd be hard pressed to find any of the werefolk mounted. Not even the Fae horses would carry them; you'd be as likely to find a horse carry a wolf, or bear.

Personally, I liked to think any sane mount would balk at carrying Liam's fat ass around, but that's just me.

"Nice night for a party, isn't it?" I said, channelling Frankie Venom and *Teenage Head*. Hey, it's the only demon voice I know, and I tried not to break into a coughing fit and ruin the effect.

Aine and Liam halted a few paces in front of where I still stood on the steps to the Fairmount. My vantage point put me a good head taller than Aine, even mounted, which I'm betting really got her goat.

Josh, Drat, and Leanne stood on the step behind me, with Cael, Skatha and CuChulainn on the step above that. Charlie covered our backs, propping a makeshift club that looked like the broken end of a telephone pole on his shoulder.

The Queen wore a mix of Light and Dark Fae armour, the combination frankly a little unnerving. The Seelie armour shone brightly, reflecting the light, amplifying it, while the Unseelie armour was a black void that devoured light and gave nothing back. Aine smiled, the sprites flitting about a circlet of gold barbed-wire she wore as a crown upon her head. "Give up yet? You're rather out-numbered." She raised her hand and her army took one step forward in unison, first the left foot, then raising the right and stomping it to the ground with a resounding, singular *whumph*.

I showed her my unimpressed face. "What, you expect us to run screaming just because you can Riverdance now? You should have taught them to twerk—now *that's* scary."

Liam's red and gold lacquered plate armor clanked as he stepped forward. He too, wore his crown, forgoing the helm that would have been more useful in battle. He ignored me and spoke directly to Josh. "You should have given up the boy when you had the chance. This is all on your head now."

For Liam, this wasn't about Darkside. It wasn't about keeping the Veil down. It wasn't about Cael; he'd already proven he didn't give a damn about the boy when he'd had him executed. No, for Liam it was all about one-upping Josh.

Josh's voice came from behind me, cold and flat. "You should have stayed dead."

Liam's stroked the underside of his jaw with his thumb, feeling for the spot where Josh had driven home his K-Bar. His eyes narrowed. "And you should have stayed away." He raised his hand and several werewolves bounded over the crowd, alighting to either side of their king. The others along the break wall howled again, and a few of the werebears shuffled right and left to the flanks.

Josh sneered, an honest to goodness Tim Curry patented sneer. "Where's your guard, Liam? I don't see Gord, or Mick. You've barely any of your army with you."

Liam changed. The air went cold around us as he drew in energy for the transformation. Frost formed on the armour of the soldiers within a twenty foot radius, and nearby puddles iced over.

I'd never felt more than a slight chill in the air whenever Josh changed, but then Liam was bigger than Josh. Much bigger.

Liam was a werebear, not a hybrid—a monster grizzly, fifteen feet tall from head to toe and at least eighteen hundred pounds. His armour must have been enchanted, because it grew with him.

"I've more than enough to take care of the likes of you," Liam growled.

"About dat," Drat said from behind me. He placed the tips of his scaly fingers to the corners of his mouth and whistled—a loud, shrill sound more like an incoming artillery round. I had to fight the urge not to duck and cover as the sound repeated off in the distance to my left and right. At first I thought it was an echo. Then I spotted the trolls; one near *Milestones* and the other on the steps to the museum. The stone retaining wall above us just to the left of the stairs shimmered, and a circular portal opened. I heard the clank of armour and the rhythmic stomp of feet as a hoard of trolls marched out and, row after row, lined the steps at our backs. The act repeated at the museum to the left, and at the docks near Milestones to the right. There had to be several hundred trolls all told.

"What?" Drat said. "I'm da Chief of da Tor clan. Youse didn't tink I'd come to a good fight an not bring my boyz wit me, did ya?" Drat waited until his troops were all in position, and whistled again.

As one, the trolls stomped to attention, the resounding *whump* echoing around the harbour. "KILL DA BASTARDS!"

"Ha," I said, gloating down at Aine and Liam. "Now *that's* Riverdancing."

It was nice to have backup. Still, I couldn't help but think how messy this was all going to get. Case in point: a line of police in riot gear had formed up to the right on Government Street. Everyone else turned to see what had captured my attention.

At a command the riot squad moved forward, shields at the ready as more cops with rifles and shotguns filed in behind them. They made it to the intersection of Government and Wharf Street when the front line halted abruptly. It was as if they'd marched headlong into an invisible wall, which, I'm guessing, is exactly what happened. The cops lowered their shields and pressed their hands up against the nothingness that impeded their progress. Those behind milled about in confusion. One cop threw his shield down and sat on the ground cross-legged. It didn't take an expert in psychology to read the "screw this" expression on his face. One of the cops put his hand to his brow and tried to peer through the shield. It must have been more opaque on his side, which was a good thing. The less they saw, the better.

I thought maybe Aine had put up the barrier, but she looked as confused about what had happened as the cops did.

"It must be mac Lir," Charlie said. "He's the only one I can think of with that kind of power."

Aine wrinkled her nose. "Always sticking his nose in where it doesn't belong."

Talk about your daddy issues.

"One could say the same thing about you," someone said from behind me.

This was getting embarrassing. I considered moving up the steps a ways so I wouldn't have to continually be looking over my shoulder at who might appear there next, but was afraid Aine and Liam might see it as a retreat.

Dianchecht stepped out of the portal that Drat had opened, followed by a dozen or so of the Fae. A few I even recognised: Badb, Goibnu, and Luchtaine.

I'd never seen Dianchecht in armour before. He was, after all, the Fae healer. Still, for a scrawny, malnourished guy he looked pretty impressive in scintillating white and gold plate mail, a winged helm tucked beneath his arm, and a gleaming hand and a half sword in his right hand. He was paler than most Fae, who weren't exactly a swarthy race to begin with, and I'd always found his pale blue eyes and silver hair a little unnerving.

Not that I was about to let that stop me. "What did you do, mug a paladin?" I asked.

"Yes," Dianchecht answered, and stepped down beside me to face Aine and Liam.

Aine's face paled, her lips pressed tightly so that the colour had gone out of them. Even the sprites that flit about her head had halted in their tracks. "How dare you! I am your queen."

I put my arm about Dianchecht's shoulder as a show of support. "That's kind of harsh," I said, "I'm sure he'll give the armour back when he's done with it."

Dianchecht scowled at me, even more perturbed if possible than Aine. Served him right for making Thomas eat those tarts.

The healer glanced back to Aine, the annoyance on his face replaced with one that more resembled fatherly concern. "Are you?" he asked. "Our queen? The Dark Sidhe armour you wear belies your claim."

Aine's hand went to her chest, as if to remind herself of the oily sheen of the armour she wore. She looked confused for a moment, but an air of contempt quickly masked her nagging conscience. Aine drew her sword, the blade glinting in the moonlight, and glared at the Fae assemble with us. "I am your queen, by birthright and this sword."

"Listen," I said, "strange women lying about in ponds distributing swords is no basis for a system of—"

Leanne elbowed me hard in the ribs before I could finish. "Now is *not* the time."

"There's always time for Monty Python," I muttered.

Dianchecht ignored Leanne and I, and addressed Aine. "Then why, my queen, have you forsaken us for this...folly?" He looked about, taking in the view of the city. His nose wrinkled as if he smelled something repugnant. "This land is an amusement. Nothing more. Look about you. It is not for nothing we call it Darkside. It is vile, foul, polluted. And you want to bring its corruption to *our* home?"

Aine looked about, unsure of herself, as if seeing the army she had assembled, the city, and the havoc she had wrought for the first time. As if a glamour had faded, and the Veil lifted so that she saw truly.

"I—" she began, but Dianchecht cut her off.

"Since when do we consort with the Unseelie?"

Aine's sword arm dropped to her side, as if the blade were suddenly too heavy to lift. She looked Dianchecht in the eyes, the contempt on her face washed away by shame.

Skatha stepped down to stand beside Dianchecht. "T'is a geis, is it not? Ya have sworn an oath, and now tha boon has come back ta haunt ye."

A geis? Leanne had told me about those once. They were more than an oath, much more than a promise. They were sort of like a prophecy, or a set of conditions that must be fulfilled. You break one, you die. CuChulainn's death had come about as a result of a geis. Well, two, actually. He was forbidden to eat dog meat, or to ever refuse a meal from a woman. Yeah, it's not hard to figure out how they screwed him on that one.

Aine nodded, her eyes downcast. "An oath, sworn to the last Therian king. That I would be an ally should his son ever require aid to secure the kingdom during his reign." She looked up now, to where Josh stood. Her jaw clenched and eyes smouldered with anger. "But that son was supposed to be you, not this—"

Liam growled. It was amazing how fast he could move for a big, fat, hairy guy. Or bear. Whatever. That one final insult must have pushed him over the edge. A massive, armoured shoulder struck me in the gut and drove me to the side. The others scrambled out of the way to avoid getting bowled over as the rampaging grizzly that was the Therian king made a bee line for Josh.

Aine's face paled as the rest of the shapeshifters charged the steps. She raised her arm, sword held high, though it seemed to physically pain her to do so. "TO BATTLE!"

It wasn't quite as catchy as "KILL DA BASTARDS," but it did the trick.

I picked myself up in time to see Josh dance aside from a massive overhand strike. Liam's battle axe struck the steps where Josh had stood, cracking the stone and sending rock chips flying.

Dratz Boyz rushed the harbour from all sides as Sidhe archers let loose a volley that arched high and came down upon the trolls' upraised shields. The cops milled about helplessly behind the force field that held them at bay as the Sidhe horsemen couched their lances and charged the trolls massed near the museum.

I rushed the stairs to Josh's defence, all the while wondering what any of this had to do with satisfying my own geis. What if this battle was a waste of time? The Veil might very well stay down whether we were victorious here or not. We had all assumed that deposing Liam and placing Cael on the throne would satisfy mac Lir's second task, but what if it didn't? Time was running out, and I had yet to find redemption, or even a clue as to what it was I had to atone for.

The sun would be up in a few hours. I hit the step beside Josh just as another portal opened at the top of the rise. Day pushed through, dressed in battle armour and leading a horde of at least a hundred trolls. And here I thought that Christmas I had the measles was a bad one.

CHAPTER TWENTY-TWO

Josh had changed into wereform. As big as he was, Liam was much bigger. Luckily for Josh, bigger doesn't always mean better. Well, it does, sometimes. But in this instance, better was…better. Even as a wolf-bear-whatever, Josh was pretty lean and muscular. It was kind of like watching a Sumo wrestler and an MMA fighter face off…if they were both bears, I guess.

Everyone else on the stairs moved out of the way and ringed about the two combatants like a schoolyard fight, except with bears, and trolls, and Fae and stuff battling it out around us. Oh, and dragons, and the fate of the world resting on the outcome. But other than that—

Josh danced aside as Liam's battle axe whistled by in a left to right arc. Liam over-extended, giving Josh the opportunity to close in and hammer an overhand right into his half-brother's snout. The blow staggered Liam, and Josh followed it up with a left hook, and then another right that stunned the larger shapeshifter. Josh wrested the battle axe from Liam's weakened grasp and stepped back for the coup de grace as Liam wobbled unsteady on his feet, only barely conscious.

Josh bunched his shoulders, loading the muscles for the swing that would decapitate his brother, but Cael's hand on Josh's wrist halted the axe before it could build momentum.

Cael stood beside Josh in wereform, looking more like a slightly smaller version of his girlfriend's dad than he did his own father. He locked eyes with Josh. "My fight. My kingdom. Remember?"

Josh hesitated, then handed the boy the axe and stepped aside.

Cael shifted his hands nervously along the grip of the battle axe. It was one thing to take a kingdom; another to behead your father to do so. It was obvious the boy didn't have it in him, and to be honest I'm glad he didn't. Cael hesitated. That was all the time Liam needed to recover. He charged his son head down and tackled the boy about the waist. Liam's bulk gave him momentum, and he used it to slam Cael into the retaining wall.

I caught an arrow only inches from my face, suddenly reminded that a larger battle raged around us. I heard a jubilant *woohoo!* as Drat sailed on overhead to land amidst a pile of Fae. The troll laid into them with the axe I had gifted him as a wedding present. Drat was somewhat of a virtuoso when it came to axe fighting. He hefted it as if it weighed nothing, the axe a whirring blur of motion that blocked sword, lance, and arrow, and hacked into his foes with the precision of a surgeon's scalpel. Trolls are a lot stronger and faster than they look, and Drat hadn't been their War Chief for nothing.

Day battled through the crowd toward her rival, a mace in either hand. I'd wondered where she'd gotten to. She wasn't exactly a slouch when it came to combat either. Drat had chosen her as his War Chief. That in itself was telling. The two halted for a second, and faced each other. Day bowed slightly, a mere nod of her head and wicked glint in her eyes. She grinned, showing teeth, and Drat followed suit. I had to give that one to Drat; he had more teeth.

In a blur of motion they were at one another. Remember that scene where we first saw Yoda fight? Yeah, it was like that, but with double the Yodas.

Skatha and CuChulainn made a beeline for Aine, who had retreated back amongst the Fae. The two seemed to dance through the throng—turning, spinning, gliding forward—oblivious to the warriors around them. Wherever they moved, soldiers died. The Fae panicked in their haste to escape. They trampled each other until the street in front of the Fairmont had cleared and only Aine and her elite guard remained.

Aine dismounted and pushed her way through her guards to the forefront to meet Skatha and CuChulainn. She raised her head and stared down her nose with the disdain only a Fae could muster. "You would dare cross swords with me?"

I'd never seen Aine fight before, but she held her sword like she knew what she was doing, and she was Queen of the Fae, so who knows?

Skatha inclined her head, a subtle bow. "Nae, I wouldna. I'm bound by oath to ya, and I'll not break it." She grinned. Trolls have more teeth; double rows of teeth, all jagged and filed. Skatha's smile was scarier. "But I can see to it that you'll not join in the fight'n."

Aine looked like she was about to object, but Skatha laid a hand on CuChulainn's shoulder and Aine hesitated. The intent was clear: Skatha may be bound to Aine, but CuChulainn wasn't.

Charlie wadded into the trolls that attacked the stairs from the right, clubbing through swaths of them with the broken bit of telephone pole. Leanne had his back. She'd drawn her long fighting knives and cut down anyone who got in close. She was Charlie's own little Legolas—if Legolas were a hot chick, and not just a dude who looked like a hot chick.

I saw an archer draw on Leanne from his vantage point on the balcony. I moved to intercept but a shadow streaked across the lawn almost too fast to see. It leapt over the balcony and hit the archer high about the shoulders. I heard a sub-harmonic growl as the shadow dragged the archer screaming back through the doorway.

Bear. Leanne had Charlie's back; Bear had Leanne's. Dogs were supposed to hate the Fae, but Bear loved Leanne. Once, when he was alive, I'd caught the dopy mutt playing with several rabbits on the front lawn. I guess no one tells Bear who to hate.

A dragon dove at us from over the harbour, swooping in low and clutching up trolls in its talons, then climbing high and dropping them. I didn't recognise it; I'm sure it wasn't Heckler or Koch. At least it hadn't fire bombed us, although there's no way it could have without scorching its own allies. Our archers fired a volley after it but dragon scales are tough. The arrows careened harmlessly off its hide.

Black wisps of smoke swirled about like acrid dust devils as the goblins apported in. Some dug their way up from underground and dragged the dead below to finish off the remains. The goblins did not engage in combat; they were only here to clean up. The golem shambled about, dragging off the dead that were too large for the goblins to carry. It dumped the corpses near a goblin burrow and went off in search of more food. Spindly arms thrust up through the earth and clutched on to the carcass to drag it underground.

The dragon circled for another pass, strafing low about fifty feet overhead.

Enough of this, I decided, and took a running leap. "Go go gadget legs!" I figured I could make fifty feet, being an Eternal and all. Worse case scenario: I missed and fell fifty feet to the ground, splayed out onto the pavement like Wile E. Coyote.

I shot like a missile toward the dragon. I'd judged well, and should have hit him at the height of my arc, too, but the bastard spied me and zigged left suddenly. I forgot about how good Dragon eyesight is, but then I guess it would have to be to spot a sheep or a virgin from a few hundred feet up.

I missed the dragon by about six feet, but instead of falling I kept climbing skyward. Even I knew something wasn't right. After about another ten seconds I started to worry. Was I ever going to stop? I guess the worrying did the trick, because I stopped. I didn't fall. I just...stopped. I hovered a couple of hundred feet above the battle for another few seconds when it dawned on me. I was flying!

"Son of a bitch! I did it!" I don't know how I did it, but I did it. Tammy had told me the only reason I couldn't fly was because I didn't believe I could. I guess I'd finally reconciled myself to the leap in logic—pun intended—that if I could jump fifty freaking feet, then I could bloody well fly too. Or maybe it was that with the Veil down magic was just that much more potent.

From my vantage point I could see Josh. He was staring right at me. He held a spear in his hand, so I'm guessing he had planned on lobbing it at the dragon, and saw everything. I waved.

Josh shook his head. I didn't so much hear him as read his lips as he muttered, *"There'll be no living with him now."*

I laughed. I was laughing when the dragon hit me, angling down from high and to my right. I don't know what a dragon weighs; a couple of tons at least. I can tell you from experience when one comes barrelling at you out of the sky and catches you up in its talons, the impact hurts like hell. The bones in my back and neck cracked, and a rib thrust its way out through the front of my shirt. I took a second to heal.

I'd just finished fixing myself up when the dragon let go. At first I was like, *Hey dummy, you can't drop me. I can fly!* But the dragon knew something I didn't. The momentum kept me moving along at a nice clip and I had to be doing about seventy or eighty miles an hour when I slammed into one of the totem poles out on the lawn in Thunderbird Park. If you think that's fun, you should try sliding down a totem pole, arms and legs wrapped around it in a half-comatose bear hug. Totem poles have bits that stick out here and there, and…well, I leave the rest to your imagination. To add insult to injury, I'm sure I heard the dragon chuckle.

"How humiliat'n" I muttered. I lay on the ground flat on my back for a moment, healing and hoping that no one had seen me get intimate with the totem pole. No such luck, of course. Josh must have seen, and he was about as good at keeping secrets as Ed Snowden.

A troll appeared at my side and held out a scaly hand to help me to my feet. He was panting, exerted from battle, the head of the mace he carried stained red with blood. "If only I had me camera wit me," it said. "I'd a made a fortune putt'n dat on YouTube."

I tracked the dragon as it climbed and banked left over the hotel, then dove in another strafing run. "Yeah, well watch this," I said.

I flexed at the knees and…well, it wasn't so much a jump this time as it was a lift off. I was still lacking that neat light stream effect that had trailed Azrael when he'd flown, but flying is flying. The dragon saw me and zagged this time, but I circled quickly and hit it between the shoulders. I wrapped my arms about its long, sinewy neck from behind and pulled up, raising its head. Apparently a dragon flies in the direction its head is pointed, because it started to climb. Its wings beat a downward draft and I extended my left arm like Stretch Armstrong, lengthening it until I could grab the horn, or what would be the "thumb" on a bat's wing. I yanked on it, holding the wing in place, and forced the dragon to bank left. I jumped off just as it slammed face first into the Netherlands Centennial Carillon—the big concrete bell tower—in front of the museum. The impact set half the bells to ringing, and the dragon flopped to the ground, unconscious.

"Ha, see how you like it," I gloated.

I looked down from my vantage point and saw Cael. Liam had his son bent backward over a small retaining wall as Cael tried to hold his father's snapping jaws from his throat.

I angled myself towards them, not sure what to do with my hands. I mean, do I hold them out in front of me like Superman, or along my sides like Iron Man. Or maybe I could just sort of sit like I was flying in an invisible plane like Wonder Woman. And if I flew head first, at what point to I do the spin about thing and point my feet at the ground to land. Twenty feet? Ten? This flying was a lot more complicated than it seemed. In the end I kept my hands at my side, deciding that it looked slightly less dorky, and rotated at about twenty feet up, touching down lightly behind the two combatants.

Liam's slavering jaws were only inches from his Cael's throat. I moved to intervene but Josh shook his head. I knew this was Cael's fight, but were we seriously just supposed to stand by and watch him die if that's how it turned out?

I breathed a sigh of relief as Cael's furry knee suddenly caught Liam right between the legs. Liam stopped growling and let out a muted *woof* as Cael shoved his father over and onto the cold, hard stone of the stairs. Cael morphed, a teenage boy once again. He reached down to his right boot and drew a long dagger he'd concealed there, and pressed the point to the underside of Liam's jaw, at the spot where Josh had driven his own blade home just hours before.

Liam's eyes went wide in fear. His form shimmered and collapsed in on itself until he was in human form again, a fat, hairy man, on his back, in plate armour.

Cael pressed the point of the dagger until it drew blood. "Renounce the crown now, and I'll let you live. Resist, and die."

Liam looked into his son's eyes. "You don't have it in you." His voice lacked the bravado it once had, as if he weren't so certain now. Of course he'd said the same thing to Josh, just before Josh had driven his own knife home.

Cael looked coldly back at his father. "Alex isn't here this time to bring you back if you're wrong."

Liam's eyes shifted quickly from side to side, to his men that ringed about, but there was no help forthcoming. It was fair combat, after all. Cael pressed the knife deeper and Liam stiffened.

"I secede," he whispered.

"Louder," Cael insisted, pressing the knife closer.

"I SECEDE. I RENOUNCE MY THRONE IN FAVOR OF MY SON."

A loud gong sounded. It reverberated in palpable waves, spiralling out from where Cael now stood over the prostrate body of his father.

"That's two down," I said, mostly to myself, but Josh and Cael heard, and nodded.

Several of the shapeshifters approached Cael. One by one they took a knee before him and bowed their heads.

Cael looked them over for a moment, then looked toward Josh.

Josh crossed his arms and leaned nonchalantly back against the bole of a tree. "They're yours. What would you have them do?"

Josh was nowhere near as relaxed as he seemed, for the same reason I myself was apprehensive. What would Cael do now? His next words would give us a hint of the leader he'd become. Would he be merciful? Vengeful? Just? Cruel? What kind of man had we set upon the Therian throne?

Cael looked down at his father, who lay with his eyes closed, expecting the worst. "I give you your life, as promised. But I won't have you stinking up my dungeons, or my kingdom." He straightened, and raised his head, speaking loudly. "Liam Moon Hunter, you are henceforth banished from the Kingdom and the kingdom of Meridian, upon pain of death should you ever show yourself there again."

The ground trembled and lightning flared, crackling across the night sky as thunder echoed out across the strait. At first I thought it was an earthquake, maybe the Big One, the one where Vancouver Island sinks along with most of California and everyone goes surfing on the shores of Carson City. Turns out it was just Aine, demanding attention. It did the trick. The fighting stopped. All eyes were on Aine.

Skatha and CuChulainn stepped aside as she approached, and halted in front of Cael. Aine ignored the boy, and stared haughtily down at Liam still prostrate on the ground at the new king's feet.

I'd always seen Aine as a beautiful woman. A somewhat flirtatious, extremely dangerous sociopath of a woman, but still a woman. There was a cold power about her now—as if she was carved of marble and ice—a stark reminder that she was, in fact, Fae, ancient, and not at all human. Aine only played at being human when it suited her. Right now, it did not.

"My oath has been fulfilled," she said. "That I would be an ally should you ever require aid to secure the kingdom during your reign." Aine fingered the hilt of her sword, as if contemplating beheading Liam, as she might contemplate changing the colour of her lipstick.

"Your reign has ended."

She looked to Cael, seemed to study him a moment. "Personally, I'd have killed him." Some of her colour returned, and with it the semblance of humanity, the mask in place again. She offered Cael only the briefest of smiles. "I'm done here, and I'm taking my Fae with me. If the rest of you want to stay and bicker it's up to you." She inclined her head to Cael. It was as close to a bow as she would allow herself. "Long live the king."

One of the shapeshifters lifted Liam to his feet as Aine turned and mounted her horse in one quick motion. She rode off into a portal, moonlight glinting off her armour as the sprites flitted about her and roses littered her path, without so much as backward glance. The rest of the Fae funnelled in behind her and the portal collapsed in on itself. I bet she looks cool walking away from explosions, too.

The trolls looked dejected. "Damn Fae is always spoil'n da good fights," Drat muttered as he climbed the steps pushing Day in front of him, her hands bound behind her back.

Drat looked like he'd been run over by a combine. He had myriad cuts and bruises on anything that wasn't covered by armour—which looked like it had been pelted by a fist-sized hailstorm, by the way—a piece of his left ear was missing, and I'm not sure, but I think he was missing a few teeth. Day looked—winded.

I raised a brow—oh, alright, both—at Drat by way of inquiry.

"It's like wrestling a crocogater, it was."

Day smiled. She, at least, still had all her teeth. I don't know what she had to be so happy about though. I'm not up on troll etiquette but I doubt betraying your Clan Chief leads to a life of pastries and cabana boys.

"What do you plan on doing with her?" I asked.

Drat opened his mouth to answer but was interrupted by a troll who stepped forward. "She did this to you?"

Drat scowled at the interloper. "Ya, what's it to ya, Pester?"

Pester was a tad bigger than Drat, and seemed to be missing more teeth. His left leg from the knee down was prosthetic, carved from the thighbone of some wild animal, and a big one at that. His red armour marked him as one of the Mesa Clan. The fact that he spoke for them marked him as their Chief.

Pester looked Drat up and down, gave Day a quick once over, then looked back at Drat. "If you'se don't want her, we'll takes her."

Drat picked at his broken tooth with a claw. "Victory feast?" Trolls had a habit of eating the losers. For a troll, it was an honourable death. Better to be eaten by a troll then to be left for a scurvy goblin. Or left out in the sun.

Pester threw his head back and laughed. "Hell no, if she can do this ta you, I wuz think'n I'd make her me War Chief."

The trolls seemed to think that was hilarious, Drats Boyz included. Even Drat got a good chuckle out of it. But once the laughter had died down—

"And why woulds I gives her ta you fer your War Chief?" Drat asked. "What's in it fer me?"

Pester winked slyly with his good eye—the right one was cloudy and white. "Cuz wit her as our War Chief, just tink of all da good fights da Mesa and Tor clans would have."

"Ha!" Drat barked, and slapped his knee. "Done!"

And there was much rejoicing. Seriously. The trolls laughed and slapped each other on the back good-naturedly as Drat handed Day over to Pester.

"Do ya swear da oath?" Pester asked Day.

Day tossed her head, whipping the blonde war braid she done her hair into over her left shoulder. She glared into Pesters eyes, her deep green stare more than a match for his one good eye. No one had asked her how she felt about the trade, but being War Chief had to beat being dessert any day.

"I do," she answered as she stood bound before the Clan Chief.

"Done," Pester said, and untied her.

Day rubbed the circulation back into her hands, then turned to Drat and bowed, a full on bow this time. She righted herself, then drew her finger across her throat, smiling. "Next time," she said.

The trolls thought that was hilarious. They were still laughing as they disappeared through the portals they'd opened earlier, all save for Drat.

I looked my friend up and down. He seemed none the worse for wear despite the cuts and dents. "Isn't that the same oath she swore to you?" I asked.

Drat grinned. "It is. I tink Pester's gonna have his hands full wit dat one. I wouldn't be surprised if da Mesa Clan has a new Clan Chief soon." His grin widened. "Da fights'll be awesome!"

Leanne joined us, looking unscathed with not a hair out of place, and put her arm about me. "Trolls, what can you do?"

I had to agree with her as I looked out across the harbour front. The goblins had done their work. Even the behemoth in the water was gone. The dragon by the bell tower climbed to its wobbly feet and shook its head roughly to clear it, then flew off towards Mount Baker. There were a few fires still burning, but nothing that would spread. The only people left were the gang and I, and the several shapeshifters that ringed about Liam, and even they were in human form now.

The force field was still up. The dragon had flown off, not gone back to Summerland. Even from the front lawn of the Empress I could see the shimmer of ghosts that haunted Government Street. I looked into the trees surrounding the park and saw red, glowing eyes staring back. Hundreds of them, most of them in pairs, but some were grouped in fives and eights. What the hell had five eyes?

The fight here was over, but the Veil was still down. I could see a tinge of orange on the eastern horizon. The sun would be up soon.

There was nothing to fight. No enemy to engage. Soon it would be morning, and the Veil would stay down, forever.

And I had no idea how to stop that from happening.

CHAPTER TWENTY-THREE

We stood on the front lawn of the Empress Hotel, facing it as the night sky behind it grew brighter with the approaching dawn. About thirty shapeshifters ringed about Liam on the stairs, keeping him prisoner. Were these the sycophants Gord had spoken of? They'd been awfully quick to abandon Liam when the tables turned, which I suppose is what one would expect from a sycophant.

No one knew quite what to do with the former king. Sure, Cael had banished him, but there were arrangements to be made. Would the queen—Cael's mother—leave with her husband? Would others? Would Cael allow Liam to take any of his belongings with him into exile? Where exactly in exile would Liam go? The Therians had estates here in Victoria and in other human cities in Darkside. Maybe Cael would allow his father to keep possession of one of those. All I'm saying is there's a lot more to exiling someone than just telling them to begone.

And why the hell was I worried about Liam when the freaking sun was coming up? I needed redemption, and I needed it *now*.

"Anyone got anything?" I asked. Everyone stared at me blankly. As hard as I tried, I couldn't think of anything I'd done that required redemption. All over Victoria and across the island kids were waking up for Christmas morning. They were dragging their parents out of bed and clustering around the tree, opening presents and drinking hot chocolate. At least that's what I'd done as a kid. I suppose some of them were getting dressed and going to church. Maybe if I'd been one of those kids I wouldn't need redemption.

I shook my head. *What crap.* I was a good man. Not a great man, but I never went out of my way to hurt anyone. Well, not anyone who didn't deserve it. I tried my best to help whenever I could, whomever I could. I hated to see people hurting. And now the world was going to hell because *I* needed redemption? What kind of *Nightmare on Elm Street* Christmas had I doomed everyone to? Why put that on me? Why should everyone have to suffer because of something one asshole did or didn't do? It didn't make sense.

Leanne put her arm around me. She knew it was hopeless; everyone did.

We stood, staring at the skyline over the Empress, waiting for the inevitable.

I turned to look out over the harbour. Something moved in the water, something decidedly Loch Ness-y, its serpentine coils breaking the surface and submerging. I was watching it when it happened.

Someone shouted, "NOW!" drawing my attention back to the others. One of the shapeshifters tossed Liam his rifle. Two more stepped out of the former king's way, leaving him an unobstructed line of sight to his son. I started to move as Liam took a knee and sighted down the weapon. The laser dot danced over Cael's forehead.

Liam's accomplices took a knee to either side of the werebear and trained their weapons on Josh. The rifles barked, bolts slid back, and shell casings ejected as the rounds sped towards Cael and Josh.

Even as I moved I knew I wouldn't be fast enough. Not to save them both. It was one or the other.

If I saved Cael, Josh would die. My best friend; Sabrina's husband; Alex's dad.

If I saved Josh, the new Therian king was dead. He was just a kid, and Alex's boyfriend. Cael had already been murdered once in the last 24 hours. Maybe Alex could bring him back again, or Josh.

Last time we'd almost lost her. It had taken Manny, a god, to rescue Alex from the Dreamtime. She wasn't strong enough yet; she might not come back this time.

I raced the bullets towards Josh and Cael, certain that no matter what I did we were going lose someone today. I watched Josh's face, frozen in mid smile at something Cael had said, unaware of the doom speeding towards him. I pictured that smile, knew how his expression would change to shock as the bullet struck home, imagined his eyes glossing over as life fled, his body crumpling to the ground in slow motion.

And Cael? The trajectory of the first round would hit him in the left temple. The spray of bone and brains as the bullet punched through his skull would erase the grin that teased his lips, if it didn't obliterate his head completely.

I was almost there. I had to choose.

Josh's face went dark. A shadow blanketed his features, portending his death. The shadow deepened, and suddenly I knew what I had to do.

I covered Cael with my body as the rounds struck home, and prayed that I was right. The first round hit me in the back of the head, the second at the base of the neck, with two more into my left shoulder and one near my kidney. *Lousy grouping,* I thought as the hot lead bounced harmlessly off the Kevlar plates I'd morphed along my back.

I turned and raced towards the Therian traitors. I hit them at full speed and tossed them aside like pins after a hard thrown bowling ball. There wasn't a one of them left standing. The ones that weren't unconscious or dead rolled about on the ground, screaming and clutching at broken bones.

Liam sat, one leg out in front of him and bent at ninety degree's to the right. His chest plate had been badly indented and his ribs crushed. He had trouble breathing, and blood frothed at his mouth. I can't say as I felt any sympathy for him whatsoever.

I heard keening, the wail of a people mourning their dead. I turned towards my friends and prayed that I'd been right. Not about the fact that we were going to lose someone today, although I'd been right about that, too. It just wasn't the someone I'd expected.

Josh knelt, alive and unharmed, cradling the bullet-ridden body of the goblin king.

The darkness that had overshadowed Josh had not been death, at least not his. It had been the goblin king, teleporting in to serve as a human shield much as I had for Cael. I was immortal however; the goblin king was not.

Goblins have never been known to be heroic, or cowardly either for that matter. At best, they'd been non-players, little more than Otherworld garbage disposals, one step below sharks.

Josh stared down into flickering image of the goblin that bled out its life for him.

"Why?" Josh asked the goblin.

The goblin king shrugged, and struggled to speak. "*Felt good*," it whispered.

"That's two lives we owe you," I said. "One for when you saved Leanne at Wonderland, and now."

He would never get the chance to collect on our debt. I'm not even sure if he heard me. The keening intensified as the red glare of the goblin king's eyes faded to flat back. Even dead, the goblin king shimmered between realities, hard to look at.

The bell sounded. Long and loud, echoing off the harbour's break wall on one side and the Empress Hotel on the other. I felt the spider web sensation crawl across my face as the Veil snapped into place. "What the—"

"I said you had to find redemption," Manny said, appearing at my side. "I never said it was *your* redemption."

"Son of a bi—" I started, but cut myself off. It probably wasn't a good idea to piss of a god, even if he did look like he just stepped off the cover of a romance novel.

Manny wore black leathers with green trim that made the ones Skatha had given me look like they were made from diseased cows. His hair glistened—I think it was oiled—and there was this aura about his body, a glowing bit of otherwhere, as if his image were cut and pasted into this reality from a much nicer place and some of the background had bled through. This wasn't Manny; this was the god, Manannán mac Lir

The goblins ringed about their king. The keening had stopped once Manannán appeared. He knelt down beside the fallen king, a melancholy smile on his face. "Took you long enough," he whispered, and touched the goblin's forehead with the palm of his hand.

The shimmering stopped, as if someone suddenly replaced the shaky cam with a steady cam. A man in his mid-thirties, dark-haired and dark skinned and dressed in green and gold Fae silks, lay in place of the misshapen body of the goblin king.

"The Fomori were the original people of *Inisfail*," Manannán said.

"Ireland," Leanne whispered in my ear.

"When settlers arrived on its shores, the Fomori were disinclined to share their homeland. Finding they could not defeat their foe in battle, the Fomori kings cursed their enemy to die of plague."

Talk about your cheat code, I thought.

Apparently Manannán agreed. "Later, when Nemed's people came, the Fomori defeated and enslaved them, demanding heavy tribute of grain and cattle, and their very children. When Nemed's people rose up against them, the Fomori called upon their magic and had the sea drown their enemies.

"So Formori is Celtic for douche bag?" I whispered in an aside to Leanne.

"Pretty much."

The history lesson wasn't for my benefit. It was an intonement, and smacked of ritual. The goblins listened, attentive and unmoving.

"As punishment for their evil and cowardice I cursed the Fomori. They would be wanderers without a home, banned from the sea, living on the dead. Goblins. By the time the Fir Bolg arrived in *Inisfail* the Fomori people were no more."

"Thus they have remained throughout the centuries, until this day, when their king sacrificed his life so that another might live. This selfless act was his redemption, and the redemption of his people."

All about us the goblins blazed suddenly bright, engulfed in pillars of light that flared, then slowly faded. Humans stood where the goblins once had, young men and woman, all dark haired and dark complexioned. They blinked under the light of the rising sun, and as one fell to their knees and pressed their faces to the ground, weeping.

Manannán stood over the body of the fallen Fomori king. "Elatha, before me," he commanded.

A young man rose to his feet, rushed to mac Lir's side, and quickly prostrated himself. "Stand," Manannán commanded as a portal appeared behind him, a glowing, golden oval that opened onto a magnificent castle by the sea. "You are king now. Take your people and bury Morc there, in Summerland, in this home I have prepared for you."

"Yes, lord." Elatha motioned to his people, his eyes still brimming with tears. Two of the young men stepped forward and gently raised Morc, taking him from Josh's arms, and carried him reverently through the portal. It closed without fanfare after the last of the Fomori had passed through.

"COPS!" someone shouted.

I looked across the lawn of the Empress to the intersection of Government and Wharf Street. Apparently when the Veil reasserted itself the shield that had kept the police at bay vanished too. Sure the glamour was up, but glamour or no, the weapons the gang and I carried would simply look like weapons. Same goes for the wounded shapeshifters in Kevlar, I suppose. We could skedaddle, but there was no way to move the rest before the cops arrived.

"We can't just leave them here," I said, pointing to Liam and his wounded posse. Most of them still lay where they'd fallen.

"Not a problem," Manannán said. He approached Liam, looking down upon the bloodied shapeshifter. "You," he said, "are what the kids today refer to as a waste of skin."

Liam spat blood at Manannán's feet, then glared up at the god. "Actually, asshole, what I am is a king."

Manny disagreed, shaking his head. "The Therians have a new king," he said. "But as it happens, a position has recently become available."

Liam screamed as his body began to shake uncontrollably. It started as a bad case of the shivers, escalating until he thrashed about on the ground as if in the throes of an epileptic seizure. The vibrations increased in intensity until his shape blurred and it was difficult to look at him directly.

The new goblin king climbed to his feet, indistinguishable from the old one. His broken body healed, he rested his knuckles against the ground, raised his head back, and howled, a pitiful, keening sound of horror. All about him his followers echoed their king, transformed as he had been.

The sun peaked over the horizon, its light spreading out across the lawn of the Empress Hotel. The first rays touched the goblin king and his form started to smoulder. The thing that had once been Liam screamed in pain and vanished in a wisp of black smoke, his minions following suit.

"Couldn't have happened to a nicer guy," I said. No one disagreed.

"Dat's my cue," Drat said, still protected by the shadow of the Empress Hotel, and opened a portal.

"Make sure you and Tirade drop by the house today," Leanne told him as he stepped through. "It's Christmas after all, and we've got presents."

Drat waved her off in acknowledgment as he stepped through the portal. The last I saw of him he was lighting a cigar he'd pulled from his pocket and sighing in contentment. That's one of the draw backs of fighting evil on a regular basis, I guess; there's not a lot of time for smoke breaks. Especially not with Leanne and Sabrina around.

"So," I said, shoving my hands in my pockets, "That's it? The world is safe again. Nothing to see here, move along?" I looked about at the still smoking buildings, at the firefighters aboard the navy vessel putting out the last of the flames from the dragon's firebombing, and at the golem standing abandoned and immobile on the steps in front of the Royal Museum. "Um…any idea how we're going to explain all this?"

Manannán crossed his arms and leaned up against the stair rail. "Explain all what?" He waved his hand and a strong wind buffeted us, almost throwing us off our feet. It was short duration though, and once I'd gained my equilibrium I noted that all the fires had gone out. He cocked an eyebrow as if to say, "Anything else?"

"What about the TV footage and the eye witness accounts? Those cops marching toward us must have seen something."

Manny shrugged—he looked a lot more like Manny now, still cover model hot, but without all the godly after glow. "The shield kept anyone from seeing much of anything." He pursed his lips for a moment as a thought dawned on him. "As a matter of fact the shield itself is harder to explain than anything they might have seen had I not put it up." He shrugged again, apparently dismissing it as trivial. "As for the news, what did it show, really? A bunch of shaky footage and blurry images, mostly by amateurs whose veracity isn't exactly reliable. Eventually some kid who works at the news station will come forward. He'll be one of us, or someone we pay off. He'll claim it was a hoax, a film school project that got out of hand or something."

I couldn't believe what I was hearing. "The navy fired a missile! A dragon set one of their ships on fire."

Manny rolled his eyes in mock exasperation. "Sailors. What can you do?"

Leanne took my hand to calm me down, which brought me to the realisation that I was, in fact, agitated. "I keep telling you, you're an Eternal," she said, "not the World Police."

That didn't help much, especially since I suddenly imagined us all as marionettes.

Charlie rested his big, calloused hand lightly on my shoulder. "It's not up to you to try and explain this, or cover it up. It's really not necessary anyway." He nodded toward the cops that were slowly, nervously approaching. "They don't want to believe this. They'll come up with excuses and explanations all on their own. Sure, there's a few that'll swear to what they saw—for a while anyway, until they get tired of people telling them how insane they are. The more stubborn ones will probably become conspiracy theorists; the lucky ones will form some kind of support group. The odd one might even develop the Sight."

Josh brushed at the blood that stained the front of his shirt, tried to wipe it away, and only succeeded in staining his hands. They trembled, unnerved as he was at the reminder that the goblin king had sacrificed himself so that he might live. No matter that the sacrifice had saved the world, it had to be a bitter pill to swallow, the realization that he was alive at the expense of another.

"This event was actually relatively painless compared to some of the stuff that's happened," Josh said, though the sorrow lining his face hinted otherwise. "Do you honestly think the Chicago Fire was just a fire, or the San Francisco Earthquake just an earthquake?"

"Um, guys?" Leanne interrupted. "Those cops are getting awfully close. What do you say we continue this discussion somewhere else?"

Apparently even Leanne wasn't worried. Why should I be?

I sighed in defeat. "Well, as Leanne said, there's presents at our place." I turned to face Manny. "Care to join us for Christmas?"

The god looked genuinely surprised. "I…well…yes." His face broke into a wide grin. "Yes I would."

I probably should have asked Leanne first. She looked a little green when the god accepted, but come on, how often do you have a god over for dinner? Shapeshifters, ogres, trolls, faeries, witches, and even the odd Eternal? All the time, but a god? I just hope he wouldn't get all mopey when he realised there weren't any presents for him.

In hindsight it was a good thing I did invite him, because Manny graciously opened a portal to get everyone home. He's a god, apparently he can do that. Otherwise Leanne, Charlie, Josh and Sabrina might have found it awkward trying to avoid the cops. I had a sudden mental image of us all running around on the lawn of the Empress while the police gave chase with the Benny Hill theme song playing in the background. Come to think of it, though, the police were no doubt jittery. They'd probably just shoot us.

Skatha and CuChulainn must have bailed after the fighting was done because they were nowhere to be found. Or maybe they were just practicing "How Not To Be Seen." I had half a mind to blow up the odd shrubbery just to make sure they weren't hiding behind one.

Oh, and we took the golem with, too.

Christmas was nice, considering.

Cael spent the day with us, which made Alex happy. Trust me, you've never seen happy until you've seen the embodiment of Hope happy. As for Cael, it was a good thing he had Alex in his corner; his life was about to get a lot more complicated. He had a coronation to plan. Sure, he had to explain everything that had happened to his mother, and Crom only knew how well she'd take it. Personally I doubted she'd even care. It's not like I'd ever seen her show Liam any love, or even affection. And if she did kick up a stink, well, Cael had some pretty powerful friends backing him, even if you didn't count Manny.

Speaking of Manny, he'd been right, of course. The debacle at the harbour barely made the news. Oh, there was a big headline about how the Navy had accidently fired a missile into the city and the investigation into that, but apparently it's not the first time that's happened in Esquimalt. Seriously. There were another couple of headlines about how a bunch of 2012 End of the World cultists had set fire to a few cars and buildings, and that was about it. Oh, and one about how the Navy, in cooperation with the local police, had joined forces in a joint training disaster relief exercise.

No muss, no fuss.

As for me, well, I couldn't help but feel like I'd been played. Again.

The first time, Tammy had manipulated me, using me to distract the demon Aeshma so that she could take him down. Azrael had done the same thing, manoeuvring me so that in the end I would take *him* down. This time, Manny had played us all, positioning us to ensure that Cael would usurp his father and become the Therian king, and that the goblin king would finally earn his redemption and end the Fomori curse.

"Don't feel bad," Leanne said, trying to comfort me after I'd confided in her. We sat on the sofa in front of the fireplace, watching Bear sleep. "You're still a rookie. Tam-Lien, Azrael and Manny all have thousands of years of experience on you."

Manny entered, brandy in hand and wearing the garish green sweater with the red Christmas Tree pattern I'd re-gifted him with pride. He even managed to make it look good. "Don't sell yourself short," he said, eavesdropping on our conversation. "You were *the* catalyst in all of these machinations. They all hinged on a belief, a confidence, that you would surmount almost impossible odds to achieve a goal. For my part, I put my trust in you, that you and your friends would set the example, so to speak. I had faith that you would kindle the noble spirit I believed Morc, the goblin king, still possessed, and allow him to save his people."

"So you knew how this would turn out all along?"

"Hell no," Manny said. "I saw the *possibility* for success. But those odds—seriously." He took a long sip of his brandy to punctuate how bad the odds had been.

I have to admit, I did feel better after that. The sex later helped, too.

With Leanne, not Manny! Seriously, you people.

"Well," Leanne said, snuggling in closer, "I don't know about you boys, but I for one am seriously looking forward to a bit of dull monotony. No demons, rogue Eternals, or fate of the world scenarios."

Manny looked down at his feet. "About that."

I swear, if I wasn't an Eternal I'd have an ulcer by now. "Damnit,

Manny, can it at least wait until after Christmas?"

Manny hemmed and hawed, then nodded. "Yeah, sure. It's just that when I brought Alex back from the Dreamtime? I'm afraid something might have...um...hitched a ride."

I facepalmed. "Oh, please tell me it's Mother Theresa, or Elvis?"

Manny winced. "Not *quite*."

The End

ABOUT THE AUTHOR

S.K.S. Perry is a Sgt currently serving in his 33rd year in the Canadian Armed Forces. He has a lovely wife, two great kids, and a house full of teddy bears that totally put lie to his tough guy image. When no one is looking he's also a drummer in a rock band, and holds black belts in seven different martial arts.

His plan is to one day be independently wealthy, or even dependently wealthy—he doesn't really care whose money it is as long as they let him spend it. He has written five books to date and plans to write more—unless someone pays him enough to stop.